The Car Share

Lucy Mitchell

BLOODHOUND
— BOOKS —

Print ISBN: 978-1-916978-69-0

For Catherine and Sue

Chapter 1

Lia

'I'm sorry, Lia, I've got bad news...' Bill the mechanic paused to rub his grease-coated hands on his blue overalls. He averted his eyes to the floor, and I braced myself.

'Maria has a faulty head gasket,' he explained, still staring at the grubby floor of his garage. 'She's also got a nasty problem with her oil tank. It's going to cost you a lot to save her and judging by the amount of rust I think it might be time to...' There was a lengthy pause. My heart ground to a halt as he lifted his face and uttered the words, 'to let Maria go.'

Maria, my beloved Mini, was dying. The plume of white smoke, the foul burning smell and the gradual loss of power were Maria's final cries for help. Blinking away tears and trembling I tried to keep hold of Daisy, my eighteen-month-old daughter, who was desperate to wriggle her way out of my arms. His words, 'to let Maria go,' echoed inside my head. A sinking feeling took hold of my stomach. If I had wanted Bill to try and save Maria, I couldn't have, as I didn't have much money in my savings account.

Bill waited for me to say something, but I couldn't find the words. Maria was more than a car to me, and Bill knew that. Maria was my link to another life.

Three years ago, my fiancé Joe and I pooled our savings and started hunting for an old Mini to buy. Joe was a mechanic, and he knew about my lifelong dream of owning an old classic Mini. When I was little my father bought me a toy car, a tiny blue Mini. Back then I wasn't girly like my little sister, Angel. I hated dolls and dressing up. From the moment I'd laid eyes on this tiny car I was in love. At the age of six, I told my father one day I would own a Mini. Joe had heard this memory many times and when he saw a photo of Maria in his used car magazine, he knew she was the car for me. In secret, he met the bloke who was selling her and made him an offer. A week later, on our fifth anniversary, Joe turned up at our house with Maria. He appeared at the downstairs window with a huge grin on his face. I will always remember flinging open the front door and rushing towards him. The sight of him dangling the keys with Maria, a 1998 Mini Cooper in royal blue parked behind him, looking like the toy Dad had bought me all those years ago, made me cry with happiness.

That evening after we'd sorted out my insurance, I drove us around town in Maria to celebrate her arrival. After I parked up in the local park, Joe and I lay on the grass on a travel rug beside Maria and ate a takeaway pizza. It was one of the best evenings of my life. At that time Joe and I didn't have any pets or children, so we put all our love into Maria, buying her blue fluffy dice to hang from her mirror, making sure she had the best floral car air freshener and fitting new creamy white leather car seats. I named her Maria because I'd been a *Sound of Music* fan all my life. We even planned for her to take part in our future wedding.

Every celebration in our life from that day onwards resulted in a drive around town in Maria; when Joe got promoted to senior mechanic, when I got a promotion to marketing manager, when Joe ran his first London marathon, when I got made captain of our local women's football team the Tigresses, when I scored the winning goal in a local tournament, when Joe proposed by sticking the ring box on Maria's steering wheel and when four pregnancy tests all said the same thing – Joe and I were having a baby.

Maria was also there for us during the bad times. She gave us comfort when Joe's dad Frank collapsed and died suddenly on the golf course, when Joe's best mate Alex left to live on the other side of the world in New Zealand, when I was stretchered off with a badly twisted ankle during a vital football match, when Joe became ill, and when the hospital told us he had leukaemia. We wouldn't drive anywhere on those bleak days. Instead, we'd sit inside Maria, hugging mugs of steaming tea, and stare out of her windows in silence.

'Do you want me to get you a cup of tea?' Bill said, jolting me out of the past. He wiped his forehead, leaving a trail of black grease before casting me a look of concern. Years ago, he had worked with Joe in this very garage. They'd kept in touch after Joe had left. Bill knew how precious Maria was to us both. 'There's a tea and coffee machine in reception. The tea is...'

'Like treacle,' interjected one of the mechanics over Bill's shoulder. I sensed they were trying to get me to smile. Bill nodded. 'Yes, I admit the tea has a treacle consistency to it, but it has cheered a few of my customers up... after an unexpected MOT fail or a bump to the rear end.'

I shook my head. Bill's treacle tea was not going to repair my broken heart.

'I'm going to have to let her go,' I croaked, trying my hardest not to cry in front of Bill. He allowed me to say goodbye to Maria. He watched me, with Daisy on my hip, lean over and lay my hand on Maria's bonnet. Bless Maria – she was still warm.

Silently, I told her she would always have a place in my heart, and I thanked her for being there for me in my darkest of hours. In the background, the garage radio began playing Joe's favourite song by Coldplay and I dissolved into tears. Luckily for me, Daisy wasn't at all perturbed by my distress. She squealed with delight, kicking her tiny legs.

'Are you sure you don't want that cup of tea, Lia?'

Politely declining Bill's tea offer again, Daisy and I left the garage. Outside, the mid-March sun tried to cheer me up by creeping out from behind a dark cloud and caressing my damp face with its spring rays, but I was too wrapped up in my grief.

For a few minutes, we sat on the wall outside Bill's garage. Daisy pointed at the white tow truck Bill had used to rescue us at lunchtime. She began to babble away to me, which made me force out a smile. My phone vibrated in my pocket. It was a text from my sister, Angel.

> Not coming to visit this weekend. Too much going on. Give my love to Dad.

I hadn't seen my sister for months, so another cancelled weekend visit wasn't going to matter.

Dad's face flashed up inside my head. Checking the time on my phone I saw it was nearly three o'clock. I needed to pack away my sadness from losing Maria and get across town to his nursing home.

Without Maria, we had no option but to get the bus to visit Dad. With my work laptop case and handbag slung over my shoulder, one hand holding Daisy and my other hand carrying her car seat and a plastic bag full of Maria's car accessories, we shuffled across the road to the bus stop. Daisy wanted to run around the bus shelter, but I wouldn't let her, so she did what any other *spirited* eighteen-month-old would do and threw a huge tantrum. I was sandwiched between a woman who kept rolling her eyes at Daisy wailing on my lap and an old man with a nasty cough. Two teenage boys were standing at the entrance to the bus stop. Both were smoking whilst waiting for the bus. They tried to direct their smoke outside of the shelter, but the wind had other ideas and sent it back inside, which caused the old man to erupt into a huge coughing fit. Spittle and phlegm flew out of his mouth as he coughed, spraying the side of my face. He apologised and offered me an old tissue. I declined and used my own. By the time Daisy and I had got on the bus, I felt mentally and physically drained.

It was packed with a noisy group of college girls who were shouting and playing loud TikTok videos. Daisy rested her head against my chest. I dug out her dolly from my handbag and made her do a silly dance for Daisy on my lap. She giggled, grabbing her dolly and I tried to hold back my grief.

By the time we got to Dad's nursing home *Escape to the Country* was ending on the day room's large TV. Residents sat in straight-backed chairs lining the walls. Some were watching for what was coming next on the TV, some were asleep, some were reading the newspaper and others were either talking to the person next to them or to themselves. The air inside the day room was stuffy and warm. All sorts of aromas filled the air: antiseptic creams, lavender soap, the aroma of cooked food and the faint smell of wee.

Daisy rubbed her eyes and yawned. Without Maria, we wouldn't be home till later as we'd need to get a bus back. Everything already felt so much harder without a car. My arms ached and I felt a wave of exhaustion, mingled with emotion, crash over me. I couldn't see Dad sitting in his usual royal blue high-backed chair by the window.

Sharon, one of the nursing home assistants, smiled before pulling a silly face at Daisy, who was on my hip clutching her dolly. 'He's in the back room, listening to the piano.'

'What?' I took a little step back with surprise. Dad had spent the last three years almost glued to his chair in the day room. Sharon nodded. 'One of our new residents here has a son who plays the piano for anyone who wants to listen. This afternoon was his first performance. Your dad and several others were interested in listening to him.'

'That sounds great,' I said, placing down the car seat, the plastic bag, my handbag and my laptop case to switch Daisy from my right hip to my left.

Sharon pointed out of the door. 'It's the room where we had your dad's birthday celebrations. Remember? Turn right and follow the corridor until you hear the piano.' She checked her watch. 'He will be on his last song now, so you'd better be quick.'

I put Daisy down to walk with her dolly and we made our way along the corridor whilst I carried my laptop case, handbag, plastic bag and car seat. Halfway down, the plastic bag dropped to the floor, spewing its contents. I bent to pick up the blue fluffy car dice, my summer berries car air freshener and Joe's collection of Coldplay CDs. Daisy came to help me put things back in the bag. The urge to sit on the floor and cry was strong. My back ached and my legs were like two heavy lead poles. I knew I had to carry on for Daisy and Dad's sake.

The back room was normally reserved for residents' birthday parties, wedding anniversaries or daytime activities. Last year we had celebrated Dad's seventy-fifth birthday in this room. I'd organised a cake and blew up some balloons. Angel was supposed to attend, but she had cancelled at the last minute. His party ended up consisting of me, Daisy, Sharon, Frances – the lady who lived next door to him for years – and Derek, one of his old friends. Dad complained throughout and said he would have rather listened to Radio Four by himself. It was nice though to speak to Frances. To pay for Dad's nursing home costs, we'd been forced to sell his house, so Frances filled me in on her new neighbours and what changes they'd made to my old family home.

It was a bright, airy room, painted a warm sunny yellow colour, with an old piano in the far corner. Several rows of seated residents were swaying to the beautiful sound of the piano. Both Daisy and I were mesmerised by the captivating classical sound. I surveyed the room for Dad and saw him on the far side. He was gazing at the piano. What robbed me of breath was his wonky smile. Dad's stroke a few years ago had frozen half his face so his smiles were now always lopsided. He hated me calling them lopsided, so we agreed on wonky, which always made us both chuckle. I couldn't remember the last time I'd seen him so happy. The sight touched me deep inside and the room went blurry.

My exhaustion and grief for Maria subsided as I let the melodic tinkle of the keys caress my ears. It was a beautiful sound that loosened my stiff neck and shoulders. When the song came to an end the pianist stood up and took a small bow. He was met by a round of applause, cheers from the three old men lining the wall, and a deafening whistle from a tiny grey-haired woman who was sitting in the corner. Surveying his audience of appreciative residents, he nodded to the grey-haired man in the wheelchair by the piano. The pianist was tall, with broad shoulders and toned arms. His hair was almost black and full of unruly curls. As Daisy tugged on my arm to get my attention, the man's eyes travelled across the room until they found me. They were dark and intense, and filled me with an odd sensation. My body didn't know what to do with the strange feeling, so it flooded me with panic. In a hurry, I decided it would be better to wait for Dad in the day room, so I picked up Daisy and all our stuff and hobbled back down the corridor.

'Ah, Lia, did you hear that wonderful music?' Dad gushed

as a male nursing assistant wheeled him into the day room and helped him into his chair. Daisy and I had been sitting waiting for him. The piano music had eased my car grief, but when my phone pinged to inform me that an email regarding my motor insurance renewal had arrived, it came rushing back with force. My mind became overrun with memories of Joe sitting in the passenger seat of Maria as I drove us to the seaside with the window wound down, a breeze ruffling his blond hair and his laughter about my driving skills echoing in my ears.

Wiping my eyes, I turned to see Dad and forced out a smile. Once in his spot by the window, he stared at me. His pale blue eyes narrowed. 'Why are you upset? Is everything all right?' The stroke had left his speech slurry. Over time I'd become an expert at deciphering what he was saying.

The last thing I wanted to do was to make Dad worry about me. He thought I was coping remarkably and that's the way I wanted it to remain. To Dad, my sister, Angel, and the outside world, I was doing fine. I let out a nervous laugh. 'I'm fine. The music made me cry.'

Taking a deep breath, I held back my tears and watched Daisy thrust her dolly at Dad. If Dad didn't go anywhere near a car-related conversation, I would be able to hold back my tears until Daisy and I got home. Dad relaxed. He stared at my wrist. 'I see you still haven't found the bracelet I bought you.' Dad always asked about my lost bracelet. The gold one, which had my initials, 'J C E', hung like tiny charms from it. My name is Julia Claire Edwards. I've never liked the name Julia, so I got everyone to call me Lia. My response was always the same. 'Dad, if I found it, I would tell you.' It was unlikely I would see my bracelet again, but I didn't want to admit that to Dad. A few years ago, the clasp on my bracelet broke so Joe took it to the jewellers to be fixed. Somewhere between collecting my repaired bracelet and coming home, he lost it.

'Why have you come with so much stuff?' Dad asked, surveying all my bags and Daisy's car seat. 'Are you moving in with me?'

I tried to force a smile but failed. Ruffling Daisy's golden curls with his good hand, Dad made her giggle. 'I was telling Sharon earlier about how you still drive around in your old Mini... She's thinking of buying one.' His voice faded as I shot out of my seat. As soon as the words, 'old Mini' left Dad's lips, the image of Joe sitting in Maria appeared in my mind. His face went blurry. *I had to go. This was all too much for me.*

'I need to get Daisy home, Dad. I'll see you on Friday.' With a trembling hand, I collected all our things and gave Dad a peck on the cheek. With Daisy toddling behind me I hurried to the day room door. Without watching where I was going, I walked smack-bang into someone who was solid and had a warm hand to steady my arm. I saw the pianist's dark eyes staring down at me. In a panic I grabbed Daisy's hand, swung the laptop case and handbag over my shoulder, picked up the car seat and plastic bag, and hurried away.

Chapter 2

Lia

Burrito the cat escorted us up our garden path. The bus back from Dad's nursing home had broken down and we'd been forced to wait an hour for a replacement. Burrito cast me his stern feline face, which always lifted my mood, before letting out his signature low rumbling meow.

Before I got pregnant Joe and I adopted Burrito, a giant ginger-striped cat (his real name was Dave, but Joe insisted on changing it), from a woman who ran a local cat rescue charity. From the moment Joe brought him home in a huge crate, Burrito had assumed the role of house manager. In Burrito's brain, we all reported to him. He liked to get his way and was a big fan of forcing his way onto your lap, pinning you down with his orange striped paws, rubbing his massive head against your face and using his solid body to keep you seated. According to the vet, Burrito was one of the biggest domestic cats he'd ever seen.

After feeding Daisy and playing with her, I gave her a bedtime bath, dressed her in fresh pyjamas, and let her watch her favourite children's bedtime TV programme. Burrito climbed onto the coffee table and watched over us both.

Wrapping myself in a blanket, I lay on the sofa. All I could think about was Maria. Pain radiated out of my chest and stinging tears filled up my eyes. I'd been storing up my grief for hours and I could not keep it in any longer. *She was gone and so was Joe.*

Joe passed away a month before Daisy was born. He had put up a brave six-month fight against an aggressive form of leukaemia. He died leaving me to raise our unborn daughter alone. We were planning to get married after Daisy had arrived, but his cancer put an end to that dream. In those early days after he'd gone, when I was in my final few weeks of pregnancy, it was Maria who kept me together. I was too big to drive her, but I could somehow squeeze myself into the passenger seat. I'd sit for hours parked outside our house, rubbing my giant belly and praying it was all a bad dream. If I closed my eyes, I could hear Joe's van pull up alongside Maria. If I inhaled deeply enough, I could still smell the aroma of his wood pine aftershave.

When Daisy was tiny, and I was still reeling from the crater-sized hole Joe had left in our lives, I would place her in her baby car seat, and we'd drive around in Maria. Daisy would sleep whilst I talked to an imaginary Joe. I would point to Daisy asleep in her car seat, tell him how beautiful she was, and that her first smile would have melted his heart. Some days I would moan about how our daughter had a good pair of lungs on her, and on other days I would say Daisy would have had him wrapped around her little finger.

Wiping my eyes, I stared at what I called my "Joe wall". In the depths of grief, and with a few weeks to go until Daisy was due, I'd dug out every photo I could find of Joe and bought loads of cheap frames. One afternoon I tearfully hammered them all to the wall. Joe's laughing face was everywhere and so too were photos of us hugging each other on faraway beaches, standing outside our first house, me hugging Joe in my orange and black football kit and us waving from Maria. *It was all too much to process. Tears streamed down my face.*

My phone buzzed with notifications, which I ignored. Daisy turned around to see me crying. She climbed onto my lap. Snuggling into the crook of my arm she distracted me from my sad thoughts. Her hair smelt of sugary strawberries. She gazed up at me with her beautiful brilliant blue eyes and I saw Joe staring back at me. Burying my face in her soft, golden curls, I held her close. It wasn't long before Burrito decided he was joining the unofficial sofa snuggle party and curled up by my feet.

We all fell asleep. I dreamt of watching Joe outside on our drive with his head underneath Maria's bonnet fixing something. He lifted himself out several times to glance up and wave at me. 'Come see what I've done to Maria,' he shouted. Excitement pulsated inside of me. *Joe was alive and he'd given Maria a new lease of life.* To my dismay, I woke up in my darkened lounge. The warm, fuzzy feeling inside my chest was replaced with a sweeping wave of disappointment. *It was a dream. Joe was not outside.*

After closing my eyes for a few seconds, a knock at my front door made me sit up and my heart thump. *Who the hell was at my front door at this time of night?* A sleeping Daisy was curled beside me, so I checked she hadn't stirred and carefully rose from the sofa. A familiar croaky voice came through the letterbox. 'Lia, it's Dee.'

On the doorstep was my best friend Dee, who was so drunk she was swaying. Her electrified, dyed black hair gave the impression she had been hooked up to the National Grid, one false eyelash was clinging onto her eye for dear life, and the other was wonky. She was dressed in her leather jacket, a black miniskirt, a glittery gold vest, tights and stilettoes. Under one arm was a football.

'Ah, Lia,' she said, before hiccupping, 'all the football ladies have been out on the town tonight and everyone agrees with me that you should come back to training. Please come back, and we've bought you this as a present.' She tried to offer me the ball, but was so drunk she wobbled on her heels, letting the ball fall from her grasp and bounce away.

There was a giggle from the garden gate. I looked up to see an array of familiar faces staggering down my path towards me. Before I could yell at Dee, who still insisted on pulling stunts like this, everyone started cheering and waving at me. In a few seconds, they'd all rushed to envelop me in a team hug.

This drunken rabble was the Tigresses, the local women's football team I used to play for until life sent me several curve-balls. During the week we worked in offices, call centres, theatres, and hospitals. On a Thursday evening and at week-ends we played for the Tigresses. We didn't have a fancy foot-ball pitch or a stadium to play in. Our matches took place on the old training pitch the school sometimes used.

Once I'd been released from the team hug, Flo (aka Florence Hill) grinned. 'Lia, we miss you so much – isn't that right, Tigresses?'

Their drunken cheer was deafening. Hope linked her arm through mine. 'Hey, Lia.' She looked incredible in her dazzling gold satin dress as she pulled me into a drunken embrace. Hope was always glamorous. Even after a wild night on the tiles, her make-up remained perfect, and her mane of ice blonde hair had that *just stepped out of the salon* vibe. Hope never left a club with sweaty hair stuck to her face or make-up running down her face like the rest of us. She was the team striker, and she had scored an incredible number of goals. On the pitch when she got the ball she lived up to her nickname and gave The Tigresses hope. She dazzled everyone with her intricate footwork, her goals turned games around and she always exploded into the penalty area in what we all claimed was a flash of bright white light. 'How are you doing?'

'Hope, you look amazing,' I gasped.

'She's a Libra, like me,' Flo shouted before giving a chef's kiss. 'Libra women set the standard when it comes to beauty and fashion.'

Hope planted a sloppy kiss on my cheek and pressed her head against mine. 'You don't come out anymore, Lia. We still miss you at training.'

Mitzi (aka Mia Muswell) was holding up a groaning Gee (aka Gillian Peet). The other girls behind them began laughing at Gee. A few began chanting, 'The Tigresses!'

Gee, Dee, Hope, Mitzi, and I all grew up on the same housing estate. Back in those days, there was nothing for kids to do so we'd sit on pavements and watch a group of annoying boys playing football in the street. The boys were in our year at school and were never nice to us. One day we got tired of their taunts and decided to nick their ball. I gave it back to them once they agreed to a football match. Girls versus boys. We lost that game, but it sparked something inside us. Football took away our boredom, and what excited our rebellious ten-year-old minds was that everyone back then frowned upon us playing it. *Girls were not footballers.* This just made us want to do it more. We told ourselves when practising that one day we would beat those boys. Our passion for football intensified, when at the age of thirteen, we finally beat the boys. The victory sent us football crazy. Years later we would discover the boys let us win because three of them, including Ben, fancied Hope.

In our twenties Gee, Dee, Hope, Mitzi, and I joined the Tigresses, the local women's football team, as we were all bored with going to the gym. Joe's best mate Alex used to be our coach, and he was amazing at improving our skills and fitness. We all marvelled at our thigh muscles, went on boozy football tours, persuaded our local pub The Nag's Head to sponsor us, and buy new orange and black striped kit. We even tried our hardest to not party the night before a match.

Despite our weekly hangovers, and at times our questionable levels of fitness, we somehow scored goals and we defended well too, although we put that down to having a loud and angry goalkeeper. It was such a laugh, and it wasn't all about winning matches. The Tigresses even had a group of proud supporters who cheered us on. Somewhere in my loft was a box full of dust-coated medals and trophies, won at local tournaments.

Sadly, Alex moved to the other side of the world. He was replaced by a new coach, a woman called Petra. She wanted younger, fitter, and faster girls and we all found ourselves in Petra's newly created second team. When I got pregnant, I stopped taking part in second team matches, but Joe and I still used to go for training. He would hang out on the sidelines and in the old clubhouse. On match days he would talk to the boyfriends, girlfriends, husbands or wives of the players, whilst my attention would be firmly fixed on the game. Football was something we both enjoyed. He would always watch the matches I played in and on occasions when I scored a goal, he would be jumping up and down on the sidelines.

When Joe became ill, I stopped going as all my time was spent nursing him. When he died, football was the last thing I wanted to do as it reminded me so much of him.

Jazzy (aka Jasmine Roach) stepped forward and surveyed my creased work shirt and my crumpled grey trousers. She'd taken up the role of team captain once I'd left football. Her signature braids were impressively coiled up on top of her head in a high bun and adorned with golden beads. Her electric pink dress was amazing. Midfielder Jazzy saw everything on and off the pitch. She knew everyone inside out. Nothing escaped her sharp hazel eyes. 'Are you having a late one, Lia?'

'Erm... I fell asleep on the sofa with Daisy.'

Jazzy studied my dishevelled state and cast me a look of concern. 'Are you okay?'

Gee saved me from answering, by staggering towards us. She sat herself down on my doorstep. 'I should not have had that kebab, ladies.'

'You shouldn't have drunk all those vodka chasers you mean.' Dee rolled her eyes at goalkeeper Gee, before snatching the cigarette hanging out of the corner of her mouth. She stamped it out. 'Gee, you promised us you'd given up.'

Jazzy nudged Dee and whispered something I couldn't hear as Gee had started coughing. They both glanced at me. 'Right,' said Dee, authoritatively clapping her hands and making me think they were all going home. 'Everyone inside Lia's. Those who need a taxi or an Uber can call one from here.'

'WHAT?' I glared at Dee.

She ignored me and before I could say anything the entire team staggered past me into my house.

Chapter 3

Mateo

'I want to toast you two wonderful people.' Holding aloft my pint I watched Harry and Claire, opposite me at our usual pub table, raise their beers. 'The last twelve months for me have been the worst ever. If it weren't for you two constantly checking in on me, being there at the end of a phone or a text message, letting me sleep on your sofa when I wasn't well and forcing me to come out with you every week, regardless of the state I was in... well, I don't know where I'd be.'

Harry leaned over and pulled me into a hug. 'Anytime, Mateo buddy. This is what best friends do. My bill for all my support is in the post.' My best mate Harry is a friendly giant. At six foot three he towers over us all. His arms are like tree trunks and his hands are so big he can lift several of his children off the floor without breaking a sweat. He let me go and I gasped for air.

Claire smiled and squeezed my arm. 'We accept all major credit cards.' She turned to her husband. 'Harry, I knew letting all of our seven kids jump on top of Mateo at the same time whilst he was asleep on our sofa would sort him out one way or another.' We all laughed and Harry high-fived Claire.

I've known Claire for as long as I've known Harry. They were my two best friends growing up. We formed a band as teenagers, played mini concerts in my dad's garage and argued a lot. Dad used to say he could always hear us squabbling over song lyrics, me and Claire telling Harry his drumming skills were awful and Claire shouting about the cringey way I danced with my electric guitar. (She always said it was best I remained behind a keyboard.) They fell in love. Our band didn't survive but they have been happily married for years.

'Well, I have some news.' Their smiles began to fade as soon as the words had left my lips. This reaction was understandable given what they'd endured with me over the last year. 'Earlier today I returned to the piano.'

Claire gasped and her eyes widened in shock. 'Really?' Harry's mouth fell ajar. I had rendered him speechless.

When my life imploded last year I stopped playing the piano. To this day I don't know why I cut myself off from it – the only true love of my life. I should have spent my time losing myself in sheet music and pouring my sadness onto the keys as opposed to drinking myself stupid, sleeping for hours and turning up drunk to visit Dad. Guilt wrapped itself around me and squeezed until my chest hurt. I shook away my dark thoughts. 'Dad's new nursing home has an old piano in a back room. One of the nurses was complaining about how it never gets played. I found myself asking whether I could have a go.'

'And?' Harry said, before swigging a mouthful of beer.

I took in a deep breath and thought back to how magical it had felt earlier to be sitting at the beautiful old piano in Dad's nursing home. 'It was like a firework display going off inside my chest. There were all these fizzing sensations shooting up and down my arms and fingers. My whole body came to life as I started playing. When I lifted my eyes from the music the world seemed a lot brighter.'

'Did anyone come to listen?' Claire asked, studying my face.

Before answering I took a sip of my pint. 'I got the nurses to wheel Dad down and I asked if any other residents wanted to listen.'

A huge smile spread across Harry's face. 'That's amazing. This is the start of your new life, Mateo.'

His words coincided with my mind bringing back a memory from earlier. The face of the woman standing in the doorway of the back room. It had been her huge brown doe eyes that had initially drawn me to her. She'd peered out from behind a curtain of ruby-red hair. Clinging onto her shoulder was a golden-haired little girl holding a doll. The woman's eyes had the same sadness to them as mine did when I stared at my reflection in the mirror.

I noticed Harry was observing someone behind me. He instinctively placed a hand on my shoulder. 'Don't turn around.' Claire hadn't heard what Harry had said and was busy tearing open a packet of crisps before placing them on the table. 'Dive in,' she said, before wedging a giant crisp into her mouth. I tried to stay focused on the crisps in front of us, but the look of disapproval on Harry's face was something I couldn't ignore. My heart began to thump. Nausea engulfed me as I watched my best mate mutter something under his breath. Claire lifted her face towards the bar over my shoulder. I heard her gasp and glance at her husband who had a stony expression on his rugged face. I knew exactly who had come into the pub.

Harry and Claire rarely had a cross word to say about anyone. They never complained about their grumpy neighbours who regularly stuck handwritten notes through their letter box about the noise coming through the walls from their seven children. Harry and Claire didn't get angry when Claire's mother accidentally reversed into the side of their house, when teachers at school kept repeatedly sticking their eldest boy in detention for poor behaviour, and neither of them flew into a rage when they got delayed for twenty-four hours in a Greek airport and their seven children all had a nasty stomach bug.

Harry and Claire were smiley people, happy with their life, their cluttered house, Harry's plumbing business, Claire's gang of cats from her fostering days who never found their forever home, so Claire adopted them all, and their army of spirited children. They were the most easy-going people I'd ever known. Everyone was met with a warm smile, a huge hug, and an invite to their next house party or one of their legendary summer barbecues. Well, I say everyone, but that's a lie. There was one person who had managed the unthinkable. Judging by Harry and Claire's reaction, Natalie my ex-fiancée was in the pub.

Harry mumbled under his breath as his green eyes narrowed. He sat up straighter at our little table, which made his chair give out an angry screech. It was too late. My nostrils had already detected Natalie's Chanel perfume and I could hear the click-clack of her heels across the stone floor. She was close. Harry fiddled with his beard and Claire folded her arms across her chest.

'Mateo,' Natalie's squeaky voice filled the air. The hairs on the back of my neck rose in defence. 'I'm back from America...'

Before I could open my mouth, Claire spoke for me. 'We can see that, Natalie.'

I didn't want to turn around. Seeing her face would unlock all the painful memories from last year. An uncomfortable silence descended upon our table.

'How's your dad, Mateo?'

Her mention of Dad made every muscle inside me clench.

'Natalie, please turn around and go back to wherever it is you came from.' Harry's frosty tone made the couple at the opposite table pause their conversation and glance in our direction.

She wasn't finished. 'Mateo?'

'Please leave me alone, Natalie,' I muttered before draining my pint. 'There's nothing to say.'

Another silence followed before we could hear her heels click clacking away. Harry scratched his chin through the mesh of his beard. 'She's got a bloody cheek, coming in here.'

I lifted my head. 'Has she gone?'

In unison, they both nodded. 'She's left the pub,' Claire said. A wave of relief flooded through me. 'Thanks, both.'

Harry reached over and squeezed my shoulder. 'Good job.'

Claire took a sip of her pint and smiled at me. 'Let's get back to talking about you. Did your dad enjoy your performance?'

I recalled the moment that day when Dad's face had lit up as I began the first song. 'I played Frank Sinatra's "Fly Me to The Moon". The song I played repeatedly when I was a kid.'

Harry nodded. 'I remember you playing that at birthday parties and impressing all the girls.'

'Dad told the nurse it was one of his favourites and that he used to listen to it all the time when his son was young. He might not recognise me anymore, but he can recall my piano music. I also played some classical stuff.'

'That's so lovely, Mateo,' gushed Claire, flicking her hair to one side.

Harry nodded in agreement. 'How's the new house?'

'Still full of boxes. I haven't had a chance to unpack,' I explained. 'The main thing is that it's a bus ride away from Dad's nursing home.'

Claire laughed. 'Don't worry, our house is still full of boxes, and we moved in twelve years ago.'

Harry leaned forward and folded his hands together. 'Mateo, your new house is more than that. It's a new start and it's away from... you know who.'

Claire nodded. 'We were so worried about your old living

arrangements. It can't have been easy living in that house after everything that happened. Thank goodness she ran off to America and you started living on our sofa before buying somewhere new.'

'It's a great little house,' added Harry. 'Again, my invoice for all the plumbing work I did on it is in the post as well. I removed the mates' rates discount as you have had enough of my time over the past year.' He chuckled. Claire playfully swatted her husband. 'Ignore him, Mateo. I love your new pad. It will be great once you start to feel at home there.'

I tried to muster some enthusiasm for my two-bedroomed house, which felt cold and strange. It was situated on the outskirts of the city, in a small suburb where I knew no one. It was miles away from a train station and had been cursed with an unreliable bus service. Getting to work in the city every day was going to be a daily trek.

Claire sipped on her pint. 'How will you get to work?'

I shrugged and they both laughed. 'Think I might have to hitchhike.'

Harry frowned. 'Why don't you get yourself a car? You can then pick me up and we can go watch the football together.'

'I would rather stick pins in my eyes than go watch football, Harry.'

Harry rolled his eyes. 'Why did I get a best friend who doesn't like football?'

Claire tapped her beer mat on the table to get our attention. 'Mateo, answer Harry's question. Why don't you buy a car?'

I shook my head. 'I've got Dad's old car in my garage. Plus, driving in the city will be a pain and I would need a small mort-gage for the cost of parking.'

Taking out her phone Claire held up her hand. 'Well, I might have a solution to that problem, and it will get you out and meeting new people.'

I felt myself recoil at the words, *new people*. My chest still felt like there were too many open wounds inside it for me to interact with new people. If anyone asked me about my dad or what happened last year, I would become an emotional mess. *No one needs that.*

'Someone on Facebook was raving about this Happy Car Sharers app,' explained Claire. 'It matches you with a local car sharer who gives you a daily space in their car. They work and park in the city. You, along with other car sharers, all contribute towards petrol. It means fewer cars on the road and it's a good way to get to know others.'

I shook my head at her suggestion. It was far too soon for me to be meeting new people. 'Thanks, Claire, but the thought of travelling to work with a load of ridiculously happy people on a morning is not my cup of tea. You both know I am not a morning person and the people who travel together in my office never make it sound enjoyable.' I recalled Linda from work who announced in a team meeting that the people she was driving into work with had been delighted to listen to her initial attempts at opera singing. Her husband had recorded her singing and she'd played it to them while she drove. I couldn't think of anything worse.

Harry nodded in agreement with me. 'He's got a point, Claire. This man is a grumpy arse on a morning. Remember the lengths we had to go to, to pull him out of his foul mood on a morning; setting the kids on him whilst he was sleeping and hiding cat biscuits under his cushions so Wiggles went batshit crazy on top of him as well?'

Harry and I started laughing at the memory of me being trampled on by seven little kids and a snarling black cat every time I stayed over.

Claire shrugged. 'It was just an idea. Mateo, you do need to start meeting new people.' Maybe even one day get back to dating again.'

I flinched at the thought of romance after what happened with Natalie. 'Claire, I will never love anyone again after what she did to me..'

Chapter 4

Lia

Daisy's shrieks of delight at seeing the football girls enter the living room made me groan. I could hear them all making a fuss of her. It was half twelve and it would take me ages to put her back to sleep. When I entered, Hope, Mitzi, and Flo were sitting on the sofa whilst Gee was lying across their knees moaning about how ill she was feeling. Gee was known for her acting skills both on and off the pitch. The rest of the team was on the floor inspecting Daisy's toys. Daisy was climbing all over Dee in my chair and Jazzy was tidying up my old mugs and plates.

Dee put Daisy down so she could be lifted by Hope onto the sofa. Gee let out a dramatic wail as Daisy clambered all over, her which made everyone laugh. Dee reached over and took hold of my hand. 'Where's Maria? She wasn't in the drive.'

I could feel my face heating up. Blinking away tears I looked at the wall. My trembling body gave me away, signalling to the girls something was wrong.

'Where's Maria?' Dee said softly, getting up from her chair and coming to my side.

Tears streamed down my face as I let out a huge sob. 'She's gone. She broke down and the garage couldn't fix her.'

The room went silent until Gee let out a yelp. She'd been pushed off the sofa by Flo, Hope and Mitzi, with Daisy clinging to her hip. Together with Dee, they came to stand around me. Once my tears stopped, they all worked as a team to get a smile out of me. I was forced to sit on the sofa and watch Gee's drunken dancing in a bar recorded by Mitzi on her phone. It did make me smile. Mitzi had also recorded the moment Flo kissed the woman she'd been in love with for months. Hope showed me the hilarious video of Gee losing her goalkeeper rag in a match and bellowing at the opposition's striker with such force the striker was seen scurrying away in fright. Jazzy and Flo brought in a tray of steaming cups of tea, whilst Gee was stretched out on a pile of coats by the window with a cold flannel on her head. Daisy was given a biscuit to nibble on. Dee, who had smoothed down her hair, removed her false lashes and was almost sober by this point, handed me my mug. 'We've all decided you've been leading a hermit life for too long.'

'I'm not a hermit.'

Gee lifted her head from the pile of coats. 'Yes, you are, Lia. When was the last time you came out with us?'

'I don't have a babysitter.'

Hope raised her hand. 'Lia, I sent you the name of that girl I use when Ben and I are out. She's amazing... if she doesn't sneak her boyfriend in while you're out partying and post pics of her kissing him on your sofa on social media.'

Mitzi turned to Hope. 'Please tell me you're not still using that babysitter?'

Hope shrugged. 'It's fine. She's promised not to do it again. Anyway, I used to do it all the time with Ben when I was babysitting, but we didn't have social media back then.'

I shook my head. 'Sorry, Hope, but I couldn't cope with that.'

Dee took over. 'Lia, you get up on a morning. Drop Daisy at nursery. Go to work on your own, come home alone, pick up Daisy and come back here for the evening. A few times a week, you visit your dad. You don't come out socialising with your friends, you don't go for drinks after work, and you don't play football anymore.'

Her words set off an angry sensation inside of me. 'I'm not a hermit. I can't go out or play football anymore because I still... miss Joe... terribly.' A sob burst out of me. 'He used to come with me and watch every match. Now I've lost Maria too.'

Dee squeezed my hand. 'The Tigresses are going to get you through this.'

Everyone apart from me cheered. Daisy squealed with delight and began to dance.

'Have you heard from Alex?" Mitzi asked. 'Is he still with Georgina?' This got her a few raised eyebrows. She flicked back her shiny black tresses and grinned. Mitzi started crushing on Alex when he started coaching us. Alex was single at the time. For the first few months, he and Mitzi spent most training sessions engaging in flirty banter. Mitzi made us all laugh as she tried to impress Alex by doing all his punishing training exercises. She came to training with her wild mane of black hair, her enviable plump lips, and her shapely body. Sadly, Alex got into a whirlwind relationship with a doctor called Georgina and ended up moving to New Zealand with her. Mitzi claimed she would do her best to manifest his return. Alex was a handsome man with his styled brown hair and piercing blue eyes. He also used to be a model in his youth, which Joe frequently took the piss out of him for, asking him to strike a pose on every night out.

I pointed to the fluffy toy football on the coffee table. 'Now and then. He sends me the odd email. That came in the post for Daisy the other day. He said he can imagine Daisy playing football when she's older.'

Mitzi checked her phone. 'I haven't stalked him on the Gram for two days. Let me get an Alex update.'

Jazzy sighed. 'If you put the same effort into training as you do into watching Alex's Insta stories you would be amazing on the pitch.'

Everyone giggled. Mitzi's sparkling blue eyes widened at his profile. She let out a squeal of excitement. 'Tigresses – grab your tea and listen to this.' We all leaned closer. 'Alex has *broken up* with Georgina.'

Everyone went quiet, except Daisy, who was babbling away to herself whilst cooking something on her toy stove.

Dee spoke first. 'Wow – that's big news.'

Gee lifted her head off the coats once again. 'I never liked Georgina. Alex needs a woman who's into football.'

Mitzi clapped. 'Gee, you are still my favourite goalkeeper.'

Flo's mouth fell open as she leaned across and stared at Alex's post. 'Mitzi, all that manifestation work you have been doing has worked!'

Mitzi placed her hands on her temples and closed her eyes. 'Tigresses, I am the queen of manifesting. All I need now is for him to come home.'

I went over to Daisy, who was yawning by her toy stove, as a heated discussion began in my living room. Mitzi, Flo, Dee, and Gee dived straight into the timeline of Alex and Georgina's relationship, the reasons they felt were behind the split, and how they all believed Alex ran away to New Zealand instead of going there to start a new life. Scooping up a weary Daisy, I went and tucked her up in her bed. She was too tired to complain. When I returned, they were all still arguing over the reasons for Alex and Georgina's split. A warm rush shot up my spine as I realised how much I'd missed their company. Agreeing to disagree with Gee, Dee and Flo, Mitzi explained how she'd spent months writing out the phrase, '*Alex has come home for true love,*' in her manifestation journal.

'You should manifest a new car for Lia,' Gee said, 'or a new babysitter so she can come out with us.'

Mitzi nodded and tapped something into her phone. 'On it, Gee.'

Hope tapped me on the shoulder. 'Let me know if you ever need me to pick up Daisy from nursery. Bella would love a play-date. They're in the same toddler group so it's no trouble and they always play so nicely together.' She cast me a mischievous grin. 'Also, it would help me persuade Ben we should have a second.'

I smiled. 'Thank you Hope, I appreciate that.'

She kissed me on the cheek. 'Don't think you have to do all this on your own. You have your old football besties to help you.'

'Not that I am doubting Mitzi the Manifesting Genius over there,' piped up Jazzy, which caused a ripple of laughter to go around the room. 'We do need to look at a plan B for you getting to work, Lia.' She scrolled through her phone. 'I'm checking the bus situation for your commute,' she explained. Jazzy was the practical one on the team. 'There might be one direct from here.'

I let out a groan. 'I have a horrible feeling I will have to catch two buses to get into the city centre. Driving is much easier.'

Jazzy sighed. 'Yes, it will be the number 45 and then the 156.'

Flo got out her phone. 'The train might be good.'

Dee shook her head. 'She'd still have to get a bus to the station.'

Mitzi nodded. 'The train is always packed, Lia. I get on a few stops before the city centre, and I can never get a seat.'

Gee removed her flannel and sat up. Her long red hair was plastered to the sides of her sweaty face and black mascara was smeared across her cheeks. 'You should sign up on the car share app everyone at work is talking about. There's this app that matches you with someone local who has a spare seat in their car and wants company on the way to work. A lot of firms are encouraging their employees to use public transport and to think of the environment but in places like this, where the buses are terrible and the nearest station is miles away, I have heard this car share app is useful. I also heard it can be a laugh.'

I stared at her in horror. 'Commute in a stranger's car?'

Gee nodded. 'My friend Melanie is a huge fan. She says it's like a form of therapy. Her car sharing lady lives two streets away and they work in offices that are opposite each other. It made sense for them to travel together and use one car.'

Jazzy raised an eyebrow at Gee. 'Commuting with others – a form of therapy? I tell you now, catching the 7.56 train every morning and being squashed up against the sweaty city boys who forgot to spray on deodorant and are still wearing yesterday's shirt, is not T-H-E-R-A-P-Y.'

Gee shook her head. 'Jazzy, you might want to use this app too. Melanie has invited her car share lady to her hen party in Croatia.'

Jazzy looked at Gee. 'I will think about it. Send me the link. Is that the hen party you're going on?'

Gee nodded. 'Tonight was the start of my hen party training.'

Dee stood up and stared at my "Joe wall". 'You've been living like a hermit for too long.' She placed her hands on her hips.

I remained silent. Grabbing her tea Dee turned to face me. 'You should join this car-sharing app and come back to football.'

Everyone except me cheered and raised their mugs of tea in my direction.

I scowled. I was not going to join a car share app and I was not going back to football.

Chapter 5

Mateo

'I feel like a right idiot. I tripped and fell in the high street,' I explained to Harry, outside the Accident and Emergency unit. He'd come to help me home with my strapped-up swollen ankle and bandaged hand. Over his shoulder, I could see his two eldest boys pressing their faces against the van passenger window and making loser hand signs at me.

'One minute I was walking along and the next minute I was sailing through the air.'

Harry put his arm over my shoulders. 'Did anyone rush to your aid?'

'A man in an orange jacket ignored the fact I was injured and told me it was going to rain soon. He then informed me he had to leave and pick his kids up. A few concerned passers-by stopped to ask whether I was having a heart attack, but when I told them I thought I'd broken my ankle and cut my hand, they hurried off.' I had to hobble to the taxi rank with no help. Even the taxi driver who dropped me here didn't seem concerned.'

Harry grinned. 'Aww, poor Mateo. At least you have not broken anything. Come on, Claire is making you a bed on the sofa.' My ankle was hurting so much it was making my eyes water. The last thing I needed was a night at Harry's house of chaos. 'It's all right. I'll go home.'

My best mate chuckled. 'Have you seen the state of you?'

'No – why?'

Harry pointed to my hand. 'You're in a state; plus you fainted at the sight of blood on your hand when the nurse was cleaning it. I am also under strict instructions to bring you home. Claire is desperate to nurse you.' He laughed. 'You get more attention from my wife than I do. Now – get in the van.'

As he drove me back to his house and his boys giggled beside me, my brain retrieved the two events that I had been thinking about before I took a tumble in the high street. After work I'd gone to visit Dad. His face had lit up at the sight of me walking into the day room. For a split second, I thought he was going to say, 'Hello, Mateo.' He stopped recognizing me a few years ago due to his dementia, but I still longed for him to just remember me one last time. All I wanted was ten, maybe twenty, seconds of recognition. Dad thought I was the man who had come to fix his chair.

The woman with the sad doe eyes and the little girl came to listen to me play again. Lifting my face from my sheet music I spotted the woman leaning against the doorway. The sight of her made me feel on edge and tense. As I continued to play, anxiety crawled over me. I was obviously still reeling from everything that had happened with Natalie.

When we got to the house Harry and the two boys helped me hobble up to the front door. A pack of pyjamaed little children guided me onto the sofa. My bandaged foot was elevated and placed on a pile of cushions. A blanket was thrown over me. I was also given a cup of extra sweet tea made by Claire. 'You look pale, Mateo,' she said, making Harry roll his eyes and laugh.

As the evening progressed, I lay on the sofa watching Harry

have a play fight with his eldest, ten-year-old Raff, and Claire combing the knots out of her second eldest, Reuben's hair. After his first play fight of the evening, Harry made their youngest and only girl, Ruby, a slice of toast. He also handed out biscuits to two of his sons and helped Reg with some reading homework. Once Reuben's hair was knot free, Claire let the cats into the living room and Harry had two more play fights with his two youngest sons and then Ruby.

The old, threadbare sofa nearest the doorway to the kitchen was always the one I slept on when I stayed over. With all their kids needing beds, and floor space for toys, there was no spare room. The new posh sofa at the other end of the large room had arrived a few weeks ago. Up until then, everyone was given the old sofa. Harry jokingly claimed he would now be directing people he wanted to impress to his cream sofa. Everyone else, including me, would be relegated to the old one.

It wasn't a big house but somehow, they all fitted into it and lived alongside six cats. Most of the walls were adorned with shelves full of photos of Harry and Claire on various holidays, Harry and Claire's wedding, and embarrassing photos of our band from when we were teenagers. Plants hung over ornaments and a lot of the books. One half of the room was full of toys and the other half was kept clutter free. The cats lived on the shelves. Harry had made them little bridges between the shelves, which allowed them to roam above everyone's heads.

Opposite me was a wall dedicated to photos of their seven children, who all had first names starting with 'R'. Harry had said using the same 'R.S.' initials had saved them a lot on personalised clothing, which could be handed down. In each photo, there was always a red-faced screaming baby, two tired parents and a row of naughty little boys. My favourite was the one where Raff was picking his nose, Reuben was sulking, Robin was crying, Reg was pulling a silly face, Ronnie was clinging onto his mother, Ricky was sitting on Harry's shoulders and baby Ruby was having a meltdown.

Lying back on the sofa and zoning out of the family evening chaos I recalled sleeping on this sofa all those months ago, in my wedding suit, hours after my world had been ripped apart. Natalie had left me standing at the altar in front of a packed church. She'd told her father a few streets away from the church she wouldn't be marrying me as she'd been having a secret affair with one of the men from her gym. Before he could say anything, she'd opened the door and climbed into a waiting car.

Harry, my best man, had bundled me into his van as soon as people started whispering and pointing. He'd driven me back to his house whilst Claire and the frantic wedding planner took control of the wedding guests. That was when my world went dark.

A familiar large grey cat jumped onto my tummy and settled itself down with an engine-like purr. As I stroked its back, I realised it was the same cat who had slept by my head on what should have been my wedding night. The cat hadn't been put off by my tears, and had wrapped itself around me, which I'll never forget.

'Do you need any painkillers?' Claire asked, casting me a concerned look.

I shook my head. 'I had some in hospital.'

Claire smiled at the cat sitting on me. 'Ghost still loves you. Maybe a pet cat might be in order, Mateo? You could adopt Ghost? Harry keeps moaning about me having six cats.'

Ghost stretched out her silvery paws and gazed up at me. The thought of adopting Ghost wasn't a bad one. *She'd make good company in my little house.*

'I have been meaning to ask, how are you finding getting to work from your new place?' Harry asked, before inspecting his beard in the mirror. Ruby wrapped herself around her father's legs whilst Rubin climbed on a chair to check his imaginary beard in the mirror.

Claire came to perch on the arm of the sofa. 'How *is* the commute going, Mateo?'

I grimaced, which made her smile. 'It's awful. This week alone I have been late twice, and I am down to my last umbrella due to the wind. My painful ankle is going to make things a hundred times worse.'

She took out her phone. 'Remember that conversation we had last week.'

Harry looked over at me and laughed. 'You should know my wife is always right.'

I let out a groan. 'Not that happy car share thing.'

Her phone screen was thrust in front of my face. I could see the bold blue words HAPPY CAR SHARERS emblazoned across the screen. 'This will solve your ankle crisis and make your commute easier.'

'I don't want to meet a gang of happy commuters who spend their journeys taking selfies and oversharing,' I moaned. 'There's a reason why I don't go on Facebook. I'll get dragged into conversations I don't want to be in, and I'll spend the entire time hating them all.'

Claire popped a cushion behind my head to make me more comfortable. 'Look, Mateo, I'm going to be honest with you now.'

Harry let out a groan. 'Leave the poor man alone.'

She shook her head and stared at me. 'Mateo, it's time for you to get back into the world.'

'I am back in the world. I get up, get to work, do my job, and come home again.'

Harry and I watched Claire begin to pace their living room. 'Yes, but that's just going through the motions.' She stopped.

'You only socialise with me and Harry. As much as I love your company, it's time for you to make new friends.'

The thought made me flinch. 'I've lost all trust in people.'

'Mateo, I get sad when I hear you talk like this.' Claire turned to face me. 'Before Natalie, you were so full of life and outgoing. You were following your dream of songwriting. You had your song-writing career, you networked with bands, and you used to play in that fancy hotel bar in London. Natalie came along and you changed. We need to find the old Mateo because he's in there somewhere.' I watched her grab my mobile from the arm of the sofa.

'What are you doing, Claire? Give me that back!'

She grinned. 'I know your password so don't worry.'

Harry patted me on the shoulder. 'She has a point. Go find yourself and piss off so I can get rid of this old sofa and get my wife back.'

'Claire, please don't do this to me!' I whined. 'This car share thing is my idea of hell. They'll all want to ask me stuff and if I get matched with someone who wants to know all about my disastrous love life, I'll end up losing my shit on the way to work.'

Harry winked at me. 'Poor baby.'

As I threw a cushion at Harry, Claire downloaded the app.

'I'm going to watch the footie,' Harry said, grabbing the TV controller.

Covering my face with my hands I let out a frustrated wail. Football was my least favourite sport. Over the years, Harry had tried to make me love his beloved game, but I still couldn't understand why he enjoyed watching it so much. 'Can we watch something else?'

Harry stared at me. 'You are injured, I collected you from the hospital, brought you home and we have given you a bed for the night...'

'An old sofa, you mean?'

'My wife has sorted out your transport issue, my kids have been nice to you and now you complain about watching a little bit of football with me. Ungrateful git!'

In a few seconds, I was surrounded by small children all armed with cushions and giggling at me. 'Kids, be gentle with him.'

Eight hours later as sunlight poked through the living room curtains, I woke to the upstairs sounds of children shouting, screaming, laughing, crying, slamming doors and murdering a school violin. Cats hissed above my head as my phone decided to join in with the fun and buzzed with a notification. I'd been matched with a car sharer. I sat up and threw my feet to the floor. *For goodness' sake, it was just a sprained ankle.* I did not need to share a car full of happy corporate commuters who talked non-stop about life and walked into the office every morning with an annoying smile. They were the very people I avoided at work.

The second I put weight on my ankle a ball of angry pain shot up my calf. It made me tumble back onto the sofa in shock. Letting out a groan I closed my eyes. There was no way I could walk twenty minutes to the nearest station. I hated to admit it, but I needed to join in with that Happy Car Sharers nonsense.

Chapter 6

Lia

Dee placed a mug of tea on my bedside table before lifting the duvet so Daisy could scurry in beside me. 'Morning, Lia. I thought you could do with this before your new commuter life begins.' The orange and black striped mug she'd used made me groan. It was a Tigresses Football Team Tour 2017 mug. Dee had been rooting through my cupboards for old football merch. My best mate was the most persistent person I knew. Daisy giggled as she burrowed under the duvet. Dee got into bed as well and started tickling Daisy with her feet. 'I'm sorry I can't drive you to work all the time.'

Leaning against Dee I smiled. 'Thank you for last week. You didn't have to spend your week off work carting me and Daisy about. You also didn't have to stay over last night.'

After the Tigresses had left in a series of Ubers Dee had slept on the sofa. In the morning she announced that after going home to get changed she would be returning and staying with me for a week. She drove me to work, collected Daisy, batch-cooked a load of nice meals and cleaned the house. In the evenings we binge-watched a Netflix series, drank wine, and talked for hours.

Dee wrestled with a squealing Daisy who was still under the covers. 'Yes I did, because I knew how much Maria meant to you and... Jazzy told me off for not seeing the state you are in.'

I shot up in bed. 'I am not in a state.' It was a lie and Dee knew it.

She pointed to my collarbone jutting out of my pyjama top and then took in a load of the pyjama top material with her hand. 'I bought you these PJs last year and they're now two sizes too big.'

I cast my attention away from her and towards the window.

Dee continued. 'Last night when I cooked tea you hardly ate anything. Are you eating properly?'

'It's so much effort when I get in from work. Daisy is my priority when it comes to food.'

Her almond-shaped eyes narrowed. 'Lia, Daisy needs a healthy mother.'

'I've just got car grief. Is that a thing?' My phone vibrated. It was a text from Angel.

> Thinking of coming down – maybe next weekend. That okay?

Dee squeezed my shoulder. 'Lia, Joe's not coming back. It's time to start rebuilding your life.' She stared at my phone screen. 'Please tell me that's not Angel once again promising to come down and give you some support?'

'It's a regular thing for Angel. To make me and Dad think she's going to be visiting sometime soon.'

Shaking her head, Dee folded her arms. 'I know Angel struggles to see your dad now, but leaving everything to you whilst she covers her Instagram with pics of her staying with her rich boyfriend in the suite of some swanky hotel does make me bite my tongue. You never used to let Angel walk all over you.'

I fiddled with a strand of hair. Daisy emerged from the

duvet. With a giggle she let Dee lift her gently down onto the floor.

'Angel is not walking all over me.'

Dee stared at me. 'Angel hasn't been to visit your father since Joe's funeral, and I couldn't say whether she's ever met Daisy.'

'Angel met her once when she was a tiny baby.'

Dee shook her head. 'Lia, I used to hear you arguing with Angel on the phone and you didn't take any of her bullshit.'

'Things are different now.'

We both went silent until I thought of a change of subject. 'Jazzy is good as captain – isn't she?'

Dee nodded. 'That's why she's captain. She sees through everyone's bullshit. Jazzy is an Aries; she was born to lead. Before you get stroppy Lia, you were a fantastic captain too.'

She carried on. 'You should come back and train with us.'

I let out a wail of exasperation. 'Dee, I've not done any exercise since having Daisy, and football reminds me of Joe. Football was our thing. I would keep seeing him standing on the side of the pitch...' I stopped as Dee was holding up her hand.

'Football started a long time before Joe came on the scene, Lia.'

'What?'

Dee stared at me. 'Lia, Joe was not around when we all used to play with the lads from the estate. Your lack of exercise excuse is rubbish, too. We are all in our thirties now, and not as fit as we once were, but we all still train and play. Hope had a kid too, remember. Gee went travelling for a year and Mitzi has given up countless times; I've lost count, but she can't keep away. Flo has given up on her diet, Jazzy has had problems with her dodgy foot, and I've piled on the pounds, so you see none of us are like we were years ago.' She clasped her hands together in a prayer-like pose. 'Pleeeaaasssse come back to training. The Tigresses need you.'

I batted her hands away. 'Don't be silly. The Tigresses are fine.'

Daisy knew how to distract me. I turned my attention to her peering inside my shoe cupboard and bringing out the old football I'd hidden from her last night.

'She can't stay away from that bloody ball,' I murmured.

Shaking her head Dee glanced out of my window. Her partner Shona was picking her up. 'I'll keep trying to get you back to training. You know I am a Sagittarius, and we don't give up.' She flashed me her annoying cheesy smile and flicked her eyes towards Daisy who was trying to kick the ball. 'Hey, Daisy, do you like football?'

My daughter squealed before throwing herself on top of the ball. Dee draped her arm over my shoulders. 'As Jazzy says, no one ever leaves the Tigresses. Right, I better go as Shona hates me being late. Good luck on the buses, and if things get too much, join that car-sharing app.'

Once I dropped Daisy off at nursery that morning, I would need to catch two buses to get to work and two buses home again. The memory from the day before came back to me. I went to see Dad while Dee took Daisy to the park. I sat on the 156 with the rowdy college kids and everyone squashed inside the hot and sweaty bus. The journey home on the 45 with the scary teenage girl with pierced eyebrows, a violet bruised eye, and giant pink lips who kept staring at me wasn't much better.

Normally, I dropped Daisy at nursery and drove Maria into the city centre. On the way, I'd listen to Joe's Coldplay CD collection, drink coffee from the car mug he bought me, and talk to him. This is how I had survived going back to work after maternity leave without him. On the way to work, when I wasn't listening to the songs we used to play, I would tell him about Daisy and all my stories about some of the funny stuff she'd done – like running through the house laughing, carrying my old football from under my bed, or walking around the living room with one of my handbags under her little arm. On the way home I'd always tell him I was missing him, but I would reassure him I was okay. I didn't want him to worry if he could see me from heaven.

Things were different now. Once I'd dropped Daisy off at nursery, I waited in the queue for the first bus. Above my head, grey swollen clouds threatened rain. I prayed the bus would arrive before it started to pour as I'd forgotten to bring my umbrella. The bus was ten minutes late, which wasn't great, but I managed to get a seat to myself. Plugging in my earbuds I played my eighties and nineties playlist and wondered what Dad was doing. Probably sat in his chair listening to Radio Four on his headphones.

Dad and I both cried, the day Joe and I moved him into the nursing home three years ago. I promised I would visit him twice in the week and once at weekends, which I have done religiously, even since Joe passed away. Once in the nursing home, Dad stopped being himself after a few weeks. He no longer greeted me with a smile, his silly jokes became a thing of the past, and he turned into the quiet old man in the corner who rarely spoke to anyone and sat listening to Radio Four on his headphones.

As the bus passed the parade of shops on the high street, I caught sight of the musical instrument shop with the piano in the window. The memory of the pianist came rushing back. I'd seen him play again last night. He'd been doing another of his performances. I recalled the little burst of excitement I'd experienced as I waited for his hypnotic eyes to locate me. It gave me a weird giddy feeling when he stared at me.

I groaned as the bus pulled into the stop where a load of

rowdy school kids who went to the local secondary school were waiting to get on board. My palms became sweaty and my shoulders tensed as they barged onto the bus, shouting, screaming, and wrestling each other for seats. The air inside the bus became filled with sugary perfume, LYNX aftershave and the aroma from a hot meat pasty in a girl's hand. A hooded older teenager battled his friends to sit next to me. He was at least six foot and had to almost fold his giant legs into the seat. Turning up my music I tried to ignore him, but he kept peeping at me from behind his hood. There was a smattering of teenage acne around his mouth, and he had the start of a moustache on his top lip. I shuffled up nearer the window and tried to ignore his hand, covered in blue biro drawings, which kept rubbing his thigh. It was the longest bus ride ever.

When I reached my stop, I had to ask him to move so I could get out. As I accidentally brushed past him all his mates shrieked with laughter. With jellied legs, I stepped off the bus and watched him blow me a kiss out of the window as the bus drove away. I prayed I would never have to sit next to him again.

Chapter 7

Mateo

Stella was the name of the lady whose car I would be travelling back and forth to work in. The Happy Car Sharers admin provided me with all the information I needed to know about Stella. She had a black Ford Fiesta and could take up to four car sharers, one in the front alongside her and three in the back. There was only one space remaining so I knew there would be others with me in her car.

Her profile photo did scare me. She had a mass of red hair, gigantic purple glasses with thick frames, and a face covered in freckles. Her circular glasses were far too big for her tiny face, and they reminded me of an old schoolteacher who used to get overexcited when taking the morning register. The teacher would sweep her eyes over the classroom full of tired, grumpy schoolchildren and start singing out our names in a bid to wake us all up.

The freckles reminded me of Linda from work. She sits opposite me and is always in a good mood. I have often questioned what Linda has for breakfast because I never see her arrive in the office with a thunderous expression on her face, slump over her laptop like I do, or snap at anyone during the day. She has a permanent smile on her face and possesses a lot of freckles. Linda chats and giggles to anyone who passes her desk. She also covers a multitude of conversation subjects; stuff she's read on Facebook, her ex-husband's latest girlfriend who is into body paint, her brother's worrying obsession with nude fishing, and the trials and tribulations of her singing lessons. At fifty-seven Linda is following her life dream of one day becoming an opera singer. All these noisy people with larger-than-life personalities have one thing in common – an excessive number of freckles.

I did message Claire a pic of Stella and said that she didn't strike me as the sort of person I would want to drive me to work every day. Claire replied:

> Stop moaning and start meeting new people.
> Stella looks like a lot of fun.

Stella had agreed to meet me on the high street where she claimed she could easily pull in and pick me up. I grumbled away to myself as I slowly limped up towards the high street. With no ankle injury I could walk to the high street in ten minutes. I'd set off twenty minutes early as I knew my injury would slow me down. Thinking about Stella, and how I knew she was going to be the most annoying person ever to share a car with, distracted me from the pain that was radiating from my ankle. *If Stella expected me to talk about myself, she could think again.*

My ankle was throbbing, it was drizzling, and my mood was souring. I'd been drinking wine and playing my piano until the early hours. My eyes were puffy due to lack of sleep, and the urge to hobble back home, phone in sick and forget all about the car share was strong. I tried to force out a smile but failed. *This commute was going to be hell.* I wished I'd grabbed my phone from Claire when she'd signed me up for this last week.

With the high street in sight, I checked my phone. I was five minutes late. Cursing my stupid ankle, I looked out for a black Ford Fiesta but couldn't see one. There was an annoying bright pink four-door Mini with a white roof parked by the express supermarket. Stella would not be able to pull in safely. Irritation bubbled inside of me. The pink Mini would force me to hobble out into the road so that I could get into Stella's car. Once I reached the other side of the road to wait for Stella, a woman got out of the Mini with purple glasses and massive red hair. I let out a silent groan at the sight of her. 'Mateo?' she asked. 'I can see you're not a morning person either.' She pointed to herself. 'I'm Stella. You'll fit in.'

A young woman with black hair was peering at me from the front passenger seat. I couldn't take my eyes off Stella's pink monstrosity of a car. I cast her a puzzled look. 'I thought you had a black Ford Fiesta.'

She nodded. 'Sold it and bought this little beauty. Don't you think she's fabulous?'

I stared at the small pink Mini. It looked like a piece of candyfloss on wheels. There would be limited space in the back for my legs and no escape from cheery car sharers. *This was not going to work.*

'Mateo,' shouted Stella, making me jolt. 'We don't have all day. Get in.'

Climbing into the back seat made me wince. I found myself beside a young man who was asleep. His head was against the window and his mouth was gaping open. His chin was coated in stubble, his face was pale, his brown hair flopped over his face and his blue shirt was untucked.

Stella climbed into the driver's seat and nudged the woman

in the passenger seat. 'Say hello.' The dark-haired woman stared at me and scowled. After putting on her seatbelt, Stella looked at me via her rear-view mirror. 'Mateo, that's Ed asleep next to you. We call him "the Sleeping Man". He works in the city somewhere. Every morning, he gets in my car and falls asleep. We think he has started a new graduate job, but is still living the life of a student. Burning the candle at both ends. This is Alice.' She pointed to the dark-haired woman. 'We were worried that you, Mateo, would be a morning person.'

'I hate mornings,' I muttered. Stella and Alice nodded in unison.

'What have you done to your hand?' Stella asked, pointing at my bandaged hand.

'Tripped in the high street. Twisted my ankle and cut my hand.'

I waited for some sympathy, but both looked away. 'There are some rules to my car sharing,' said Stella. 'You might have read them on my profile.'

I'd glanced at her profile but hadn't bothered to read her rule list.

She continued. 'We always have fifteen minutes in the morning where we listen to music, and no one talks. This starts when we pick up the last person. As you live nearest the motorway, I am making you the last person. Both Alice and "the Sleeping Man" live near me so it's easier if I pick them up first.'

I was still thinking about the fifteen minutes' no talking whilst Stella explained the order of car sharer pick-ups. The thought of being forced to listen to music and not talk made my face break into a smile. 'Oh... I see.'

Stella tapped the steering wheel with long pink nails. 'Trust me, listening to good music and not talking for fifteen minutes works. It allows us to mentally prepare ourselves for another day at that marvellous place we call *work*. Secondly, the only music I play is eighties and nineties. I like to alternate between my CDs or listen to my favourite radio DJ, Rick Carter on the Memory Lane radio station.'

Alice nodded. 'We also love to text in to see if DJ Rick Carter reads out our texts on air.'

Stella continued. 'Zoning out to nostalgic hits is a form of what I call commuting therapy. If you want anything else to listen to go find another car sharer. Thirdly...' she paused and took a deep breath, 'there's no romance allowed between car sharers as it can make an uncomfortable journey for everyone.'

'Thank God for that,' I blurted out. Stella and Alice turned to stare at me. I could feel my face getting hot. 'I detest romance as well as early mornings,' I snapped.

Stella raised her hand. 'Let's start the fifteen minutes of good music and no talking.' She pressed play on her car CD player and soon the music of Prince filled the car.

Gazing out of the car window I felt my hunched shoulders sink. *This wasn't as bad as I thought it would be.* The fifteen minutes of no talking appealed to me plus having a sleeping person beside me meant I didn't have to make small talk. However, it was a case of squashed sardines in the back with Ed and me. There was no room to stretch my legs. It would have to do whilst my ankle healed. I wished Stella had made it clear on her profile that her car had changed. The queue for the bus on the other side of the road caught my attention as it snaked along the pavement. Everyone looked miserable and some didn't even have umbrellas. I could have been one of those poor commuting souls.

Shops, the petrol garage, the furniture store, and a school all flashed by as Stella headed for the motorway, which would take us into the city centre. My mind drifted and I thought back to playing the piano a few hours before. Natalie and our failed wedding had been on my mind as I played. I wondered whether she ever thought about what she did to me. By 2am, my mind had leaped down the same familiar rabbit hole – *how long had she been having the affair with Zane from the gym?*

Signifying the end of the fifteen minutes of music, Stella turned down Prince. I leaned back in the car seat. Ed started to snore next to me. The sound of his rattling nostrils made me jump. Alice leaned across and shouted, 'Ed – stop snoring.' He moaned and groaned before turning away from me and facing the window.

'When does he wake up?' I asked, pointing to Ed.

Alice shrugged. 'When Stella arrives in the city and turfs him out.' She leaned over and turned on the radio. After a loud and jolly jingle, a male voice informed us that we were listening to Memory Lane Radio Station and DJ Rick Carter. Silently, I prayed for DJ Rick Carter to match my grumpy morning mood, but sadly he sounded upbeat and excitable.

'Here's the latest Breaking Commuter News. Barry has contacted us to say that his blue sandwich box, containing his lunch for today, is now making its way to London as he left it on the train. He doesn't care about the sandwiches, but he is sad about missing out on his daily Scotch egg. Toby got back from a fabulous holiday abroad last night and is now stood in the rain, waiting for his bus to work, which is late, and he can't remember the password for his work laptop or his new boss's first name. We feel your pain, Toby. Brooke is hungover on her train, wishing she'd not drunk cocktails on a school night, and cursing the bright spark in her department who suggested having a team day in the office. Ouch, Brooke. Sarah is having a nightmare on the school run as she's got to school and has noticed one of her four children is in the back of the car in his pyjamas, not his school uniform. Fay has just driven to work in her fluffy pink slippers, and

realised her shoes are at home. More commuter news after Tears for Fears.'

I wanted to smile at the funny commuter stories on the radio, but my grumpiness prevented me. Sinking back into my cramped seat I hoped there would be silence for the rest of the journey.

Alice turned her attention to Stella. 'They won't like me, Stella. I can feel another rejection coming.'

Stella spoke into the driver's mirror. 'Mateo, Alice is an aspiring actress,' she explained. 'When she's not working in a call centre, she's doing auditions. Today we're dropping her at the station as she's got an audition in London.'

'Oh, good luck.'

Alice didn't turn round. Instead, she carried on. 'I don't want to feel like a failure again.' Her voice sounded croaky. 'Everyone in my family is either starring in a BBC period drama, has a key role in a grizzly crime series on ITV, or is busy learning lines for a theatre show. Even my grandmother is auditioning for *Eastenders*. I can't stand another rejection.'

Stella ran her hand through her red hair, which I found bewildering to look at. It was short at the back, but ginormous at the front and sides. 'Alice, I've been doing some thinking.'

The train station was approaching. Up until this point I'd not found any issues with Stella's driving skills. It was the dramatic way she swung her pink Mini into the station carpark, making me grip onto the door handle and question whether she was taking the corner on two wheels or four, which changed everything. Muttering under my breath I was going to lodge a complaint to Stella when I heard Alice sniffing in the front. Stella pulled into the station's drop-off bay and cut the engine. Reaching over, she placed a hand on Alice's shoulder. 'I want you to think about what *you* want to do with *your* life.'

Alice gave her a puzzled look. 'What do you mean?'

Stella spoke slowly and calmly. 'This is *your* life, Alice. Hear me out – okay? I have a hunch deep down... You don't like acting.'

Alice hung her head. There was a moment of silence. 'Is it that obvious?' she mumbled.

Stella shrugged. 'It was something you said a few weeks ago that got me thinking. You said acting didn't light you up inside.'

Alice sniffed. 'You remembered what I said?'

Stella nodded. 'I'm very good at solving other people's issues, but rubbish at sorting out my own life.'

Alice blew her nose on a tissue. 'I don't have the guts to tell my family.'

I found myself pressing my face up against the car window and wanting to escape as Alice began to sob. This car share had now turned into one of those ghastly daytime TV shows where guests come in and air their problems. *Why did I let Claire sign me up for this?*

Stella took her hand and rubbed it. 'Has anyone ever reminded you that it's your life, Alice? You can do what you want. Even if your dreams don't resemble everyone else's.'

Alice lifted her head and turned towards Stella. 'I want to see the world. I've always wanted to travel.' She blew her nose for a second time. 'I'm twenty-six and I am still worried about what my parents will say if I don't pursue an acting career.'

Stella began to clean her glasses. 'I bet you've known this since you were a child – right? About not wanting to act.'

Alice nodded. I was trapped in a car share which was turning into Oprah on wheels.

'Everyone around you told you that acting was what *they* wanted you to do and gave you a million reasons why you couldn't do anything else with your life. You gave in because you thought they knew more than you.'

I heard Alice laugh. 'This is weird – how do you know all this, Stella?'

Placing her glasses back on her nose Stella turned to Alice. 'I know, because as a child I was talked out of a lot of things, and even more so when I was an adult. Every week I still remind my mother that my life is my own and not hers. 'Go to London but use it to think about your life whilst you are on the train. If you don't want to go to your audition, then don't. Instead, go see the sights. Take some time to yourself and decide what you want to do.'

Alice nodded. 'I would love to see New Zealand and Australia. In one savings account I have enough for a few months travelling.'

'Take control of your life, Alice,' said Stella. 'Regret is a terrible thing.'

With a sniff and a sob Alice opened her arms and pulled Stella into a hug. I watched tears stream down Alice's face. 'You're the only person who has seen right through me.'

Stella nodded. 'You know what I am going to say. In life it's who you have beside you that matters. Just know that I am beside you, Alice.'

I grimaced. *Stella even had an Oprah-style life quote.* I promised myself that I would never get emotional in Stella's car.

After what felt like forever, Alice got out and after blowing a lot of kisses to Stella she headed towards the station. Stella sighed. 'I hope she does take control of her life. I was young like Alice once,' She gazed out across the station car park. 'I wish I'd grabbed my life with both hands. Instead, I let others make decisions for me.'

Her words echoed in my mind. A memory of Natalie materialised. I could hear her voice. 'Mateo, I think you need to forget being a songwriter and get a proper job. We're not going to be able to afford one of those new houses I want if you don't have a regular income coming in.'

'Mateo, come and join me,' Stella gestured for me to move into the front. Reluctantly, I did what she asked.

As I put on my seatbelt and prayed this car journey would soon be over, Stella's mobile bleeped from its stand on the dashboard. She pressed "accept call". A teenage girl's voice boomed into the car. 'Mam.'

'Lauren – are you on your way to school?' Stella asked.

I waited for Stella to turn the speaker off on her phone. Neither Ed nor I wanted to hear her conversation with her daughter. Ed was still asleep, but I was sure he would agree with me if he was awake.

'I'm not going to school,' barked Lauren. 'My classes today are boring.'

Stella took a sharp intake of breath. 'Your first year A Levels exams are important, Lauren. You promised me there would be no more skipping school. Still to this day I wonder how you did so well.'

'Mam, where's the packet of fig roll biscuits you bought yesterday?'

'Lauren, don't ignore me. You are not bunking off school to lie on the sofa eating fig roll biscuits and playing on Connor's Xbox. Will you please go to school.'

The phone clicked and went dead. Lauren had hung up. I could hear Stella muttering some words under her breath. Finally, she turned around in her seat to face me. 'Mateo, in this car I persuade people to take control of their life, but I have zero control over my teenagers.'

I gazed out of the car window and prayed my future children would not turn out like Stella's daughter Lauren.

I had never been so relieved to see my office when Stella dropped me off. Her car share had certainly been an experience.

Stella shook Ed until he woke up. As I limped away he staggered out of Stella's car. He shaded his bleary eyes, yawned and walked in the direction of an office block.

As I got into work, my phone bleeped. It was from Claire.

Well – how did your first car share go?

Think I might go back to getting the bus once my ankle is better!

Chapter 8

Lia

Why had I left my umbrella at home again? I was drenched, cold and shivering in a shop doorway waiting for a bus. The bus I'd wanted to catch had been cancelled by the time I got to the stop. I'd left Daisy's nursery and made the long walk up to the high street holding my handbag over my head to shield myself from the rain. This was my third day as a bus commuter, and I could safely say I wasn't loving catching the bus.

Last night on the way home one of my buses had broken down and it had taken ages for the bus company to deploy a new one. I'd been forced to call Hope to see whether she could pick Daisy up from nursery as it would have been closed by the time I could get there. Hope had squealed with delight and said she would love to collect Daisy. By the time I reached Hope's house Daisy and Hope's little girl Bella had both fallen asleep on the sofa. It had been nice briefly seeing Hope again and her husband Ben. They wanted me to stay a bit longer, have a glass of wine with them and go home later, but the sight of them kissing each other in the hallway brought back a load of painful Joe memories. Hurt and anger at losing Joe had mixed inside me. *If he was still alive, he would have fixed Maria for me, and if I was ever late, I know he would have picked up Daisy from nursery.* In my dreams he and Daisy were inseparable. She would have been a daddy's girl and he would have been besotted by her cute blonde curls and bright blue eyes. With a sleepy Daisy in my arms, I'd hurried out of their house, blinking away tears and feeling wretched.

With a shiver, I pulled my damp coat tighter around me. *Where was the next sodding bus?* At this rate I was going to be late. My phone bleeped. I took it out of my coat pocket and saw it was a text from Dee. She'd sent me an old photo of herself, Gee, Hope, Mitzi, and me as ten-year-old girls. We were sitting on the pavement outside Dee's house. Behind us, our bikes were scattered across Dee's front garden. We were all wearing cut off denim shorts and T-shirts. I smiled until I saw what was under my arm – a football. I read Dee's text.

Football was before Joe x

She was right. An uncomfortable feeling passed over me.

I stared at my ten-year-old self and the goofy happy smile across my face. The football was from Mitzi's brother who had gone to uni. *This photo must have been taken shortly after we'd discovered football.* I remembered using our denim jackets as makeshift goalposts at the bottom of our road and making everyone practice scoring.

My heart ached as my mind became awash with football memories. Even though we never reached the dizzying heights of professional football, Dee, Mitzi, Hope, Gee and I had always had a laugh in training. We made new friends from other local teams, we socialised as a team on nights out, and we escaped whatever life threw at us off the pitch.

As I boarded the bus, I told myself to get a grip. It was pointless yearning for football; I couldn't go back knowing Joe would not be cheering me on. It would be torturous. My phone buzzed again. It was Angel.

> Something has come up at work, which I can't get out of, so won't be able to come up at the weekend. Give Dad a big kiss from me.

On the bus, I flicked onto Angel's Instagram. I knew before her grid loaded that I wouldn't like what I was going to see. Sometimes I wondered why I even bothered checking it. It was filled with shots of her wealthy boyfriend's palatial bathroom, Angel sprawled across his corner beige sofa, bunches of expensive flowers and Angel in the driver's seat of his huge black Range Rover. Her first story, which had been up for two hours, showed two plane tickets to Paris. There was a caption that read, "OMG – *he's taking me to Paris for a long weekend TONIGHT.*" Her second story was a short video of her trying on different outfits for what she called her "*AIRPORT LOOK*" My sister's hair looked better than ever and hung in caramel curls just above her shoulders. She had a light dusting of a tan, and her eyes were sparkling blue. In the bus window reflection, I could see my damp red hair had stuck to my forehead and my eyes looked sunken.

Part of me wanted to get cross with Angel for lying about a work commitment when really, she was going away with her boyfriend. That part of me got lost in a wave of exhaustion that crashed over my body. I didn't have the energy to call Angel out on her lies. She'd start shouting about how distressing it was to see her father dribble down one side of his face, how the left side of his body didn't work anymore, how he struggled to talk and how it made her have sleepless nights. It would end with me falling apart on the phone.

Before Dad and Joe had got sick Angel and I had a different

relationship. She came to visit Dad and we all spent Christmas together. We'd have to put up with her moaning about how much effort it was for her to drive down, how her boyfriend didn't like her being away so much and how family time interfered with her busy social life in Manchester, but we put up with her. Whenever I felt Angel was out of line, I told her. When she had a hissy fit about a birthday gift Dad bought her, it was me who told her to be grateful. When she turned her nose up at the Christmas dinner he had cooked one year, I took her aside and got her to apologise to him. When he took us both away to Paris for a weekend and she complained non-stop about the hotel, the décor, the food, and the excursions he'd paid for it was me who had a quiet word with her when he wasn't looking.

I wasn't that person anymore. I opened my handbag and slipped my phone inside.

Chapter 9

Mateo

It was the second morning of Stella's car share. As the pink Mini approached I could see that Alice was not in the car and Ed was asleep in the back. The thought of sinking into my seat in the back with the Sleeping Man next to me whilst Alice and Stella nattered in the front had kept me going as I hobbled up to the high street in the rain. Stella gestured for me to get in the front. 'There's no Alice today. If you sit in the back, I won't have anyone to chat to after our fifteen minutes of no talking,' she said, giving me a friendly smile.

Before getting in I picked up a book lying on her front seat. She smiled. 'Stick it in my glove box.' I stared at the book, titled *One Night with The Duke* by Jodi Ellen Malpas. It was dog-eared and its pages had been earmarked with coloured Post-it notes. 'I like to read the good bits again,' she beamed. 'I don't suppose you are a fan of regency romance, Mateo?'

Shaking my head I climbed into the front, shoved the book inside the glove compartment, and she set off. Stella's hoop earrings jangled as she changed gear. I gripped the door handle for dear life. She turned on Pulp to signal that it was time to listen to music. Pulp was one of my favourite bands from the nineties. I tried to relax, and closed my tired eyes. I'd made the mistake of offering to babysit all seven of Harry and Claire's children, and it had been exhausting. All seven of them had wanted to argue with me, along with three of the cats. There was so much noise as they all shouted, laughed, screeched and screamed. I also couldn't chase them as my foot hurt. When Harry and Claire got home, I'd lost control and was tied up on a chair in the kitchen, surrounded by a load of giggling children. Harry dropped me home and told me I was the worst babysitter they had ever had.

Resting my head against the cool window, I watched the wet, grey world outside rush by. As I listened to Pulp, I silently forgave Stella for yesterday's car share chaos. Once the fifteen minutes had ended, she switched on DJ Rick Carter's show.

'Here's the Breaking Commuter News for today. Ryan got onto the express train thinking it would be quicker, but it still hasn't left the station, and he's seen several local trains come and go. Pam has been listening to an emotional audiobook on her bus to work, and is dabbing away tears. Claire has decided she is working from home. Beth is late for her time management course and Steph, who lives a few streets away from where she works, and yet is always late, has just realised she might be the problem. Keep smiling everyone.'

Stella giggled throughout DJ Rick Carter's slot. Once again, I wanted to giggle at Steph's funny commuter news, but my sour mood prevented me.

'Are you Spanish? I mean with a name like Mateo – you must be?' she asked, once she'd turned down the radio.

I shook my head. 'Not really. I was born in Yorkshire. My dad is English, and I had a Spanish mother, who I don't even remember. She died when I was three. She named me.'

Stella nodded and kept her eyes fixed on the road. 'Do you have any family left in Spain on your mother's side?'

'My mum had a sister. Elena. She sends me a Christmas card every year. I've never met her.'

Dad used to have photographs of Mum and her sister dotted all over the living room. I would spend hours gazing up at the photos wanting to know more about the smiling women with their thick, shiny black hair and olive skin. Every time I asked Dad if we could go to Spain, he said that it would make him sad to return to the place where he once fell in love. He once admitted he'd never recovered from losing my mother in a car accident, and going to Spain would be hard for him. I ended up visiting nearly every other country in Europe, but not setting foot in Spain. The thought of going to visit Elena frequently tugged at my heartstrings, but I told myself I would be betraying Dad.

Stella pulled up at a set of traffic lights. She turned and gasped at the driver of the car next to her. 'Oh, wow – it's Useful Kim.'

I glanced at Stella. 'Useful who?' Stella was waving at a woman with frizzy blue hair who was waving back at her. The lights changed and we watched Stella's friend roar away in her old jeep. Its back doors were open and tied up with blue rope as she had a car full of what looked like boxes and furniture. 'That woman, Useful Kim, can get hold of *anything*,' Stella explained, pointing at her friend's jeep. 'If you ever need something and you can't get it in the shops or online, Useful Kim will sort it. She's not cheap but she's reliable. You just don't ask where she got it from.'

I gasped. 'What do you mean? She sells dodgy stuff?'

Stella let out a sigh. 'Useful Kim gets the job done. She can get her hands on anything, and I mean *anything*. Now, I'm not saying her goods are quality, but when you're desperate...' She fiddled with her earring, and I stifled a yawn. It was warm inside her pink car and my eyelids felt heavy. If Stella stopped talking, I could rest my head against the window and have a little nap.

Stella continued and I let out a silent groan. 'My best mate Sharon and I went on a mermaid-themed hen do in Newcastle, and we left sorting out our costumes until the last minute. A quick text to Useful Kim, and within a few hours she turned up after work with two mermaid costumes.'

I gave Stella a quick smile and turned to stare out of the passenger window, hoping she'd get the hint. I did not want to hear more about her hen weekend in Newcastle.

'The fish tails were so tight we both lost blood supply to our legs,' Stella said with a laugh. 'Sharon's shell-encrusted bra top had a lot of shells missing, and my mermaid hair wig looked like it had been fished out of a canal. Despite all this, we had a grand time in Newcastle.'

Pressing my face against the window, I promised myself to never ask Stella about her friend or resort to asking dodgy Useful Kim for anything. Stella cleared her throat. Her piercing blue eyes studied my face. 'So, why are you here, Mateo? Why did you want to car share?'

'One of my friends suggested the app because getting the bus wouldn't have worked with my ankle injury.'

'Are you able to work from home with your job?'

I nodded. 'I can, but for the next few months my firm's implementing a new finance system so I need to be in the office.'

It was then she uttered the words no person who struggles with early mornings and just wants to be left alone wants to hear. 'Tell me about yourself?'

She must have spotted the panic which flashed across my face. 'It's okay, we don't have to talk about you. I assume everyone is like me – loves a natter.' An awkward silence descended until Ed let out the loudest snore from the back, which made us laugh.

'Does he go to sleep as soon as he gets in your car?' I asked Stella.

She nodded. 'He comes out of his flat half-dressed and sort of falls into the back of my car. By the time I am leaving his street, he's asleep.'

'Has he ever been awake in your car?'

Stella shook her head. 'No. Even on the way home, he's asleep. Yesterday was a one-off as he had a dental appointment and didn't need a lift home.'

I stared at sleeping Ed. This young guy was a genius. He'd found a nice warm car to sleep in, to and from work, and the best thing was that no one disturbed him. He also avoided being told about Useful Kim's underworld connections. 'Well, that's one way of avoiding early mornings.'

She laughed. 'He's so young. You can tell he's a party animal. Judging by the state of his crumpled clothes, and his unshaven look, I think he's living his best life. Didn't you do the same when you were younger? I did?

I thought back to my early twenties when Harry, Claire and I would spend our summers going to all the good music festivals in Claire's father's old campervan. We would jack in our jobs at the start of the summer, pack as much as we could into the campervan, and go to as many festivals as we could. In September, we'd return to the working world with what felt like a three-month hangover and the effects of severe sleep depriva-tion. They were fun years; all that mattered was listening to good music, eating crap food, and drinking ourselves silly. I glanced over my shoulder at Ed. 'Yes, you're right, I was the same.'

Stella pressed play on her CD player, and Erasure filled the car. Her head bobbed from side to side as she drove us past the cinema and the shopping centre. 'Today is going to be a good day, Mateo. I have finally found my favourite shade of red hair dye. Useful Kim is delivering it tonight.'

Even though Stella seemed unable to talk to her teenage daughter on hands-free without shouting, and she had a friend called Useful Kim selling her dodgy goods, I was starting to warm to her. She played good music, and I liked the fact she insisted on fifteen minutes of no talking. The Happy Car Sharers app had been reminding me to review Stella's car share. If I was honest, I would suggest she extended the fifteen minutes of no talking to the entire journey, but had no other complaints.

We were at the traffic lights when I noticed Stella was staring at something in the shopping centre car park to the left of us. In a flash, she indicated, pulled into the lane for the shopping centre and dramatically swung into the car park. I gripped the door handle for dear life and groaned out loud. 'Stella, this is not a racing car.'

Luckily, it was mostly empty apart from a crowd of teenage girls laughing and joking in the middle of it. Stella drove into a space, and slammed on the brakes, sending us all surging forward. Ed sat up in shock. I turned around to see him awake and in a trance.

He asked, 'Roman – is he awake?'

'Huh?'

In a panic, I looked across at Stella, who was frantically winding down her window. I surveyed her dashboard for any red flashing lights. Perhaps she had an engine fault, and this was why we were in an empty shopping centre car park. To my horror Stella leaned out of her window. 'LAUREN!' she screamed, 'SCHOOL IS IN THE OPPOSITE DIRECTION.' I watched a teenage girl with long black hair turn to spot Stella. The girl cast Stella a look of total shock and began to sprint for the shopping centre doors behind her.

'LAUREN – COME HERE!' roared Stella as the girl disappeared into the shopping centre. 'That daughter of mine will be grounded for eternity when she gets home.'

Ed went back to sleep. Stella glanced at me. 'Sorry about that, I take my children's education seriously. Lauren is not going to pass her A levels by spending the day make-up shopping with her mates.'

I nodded and tried to calm my jittery nerves. By the time we got to my office I felt like a shadow of my former self. I spent the day at work soothing my nerves with sugary tea and searching Google for fast and effective cures for a sprained ankle.

Chapter 10

Lia

My commute by bus was getting harder. The hooded teenage boy insisted on sitting next to me each time he got on. He even came to find me upstairs when I tried to sit somewhere else. His mates still thought it was hilarious, and sat behind us, which made it an uncomfortable journey. Earlier that morning, things had got out of hand, as he had touched my thigh. He claimed it was by accident. I stood up in shock and tried to shout at him, but only a squeak came out. His mates screamed with laughter, as I went downstairs to complain to the bus driver. The driver was beyond useless and did nothing. For three stops I stood up near the driver. With trembling hands, I messaged Dee about what had happened.

> I tried to shout at him. My nerves got the better of me. A pathetic sound came out of my mouth.

She rang me straight away. 'Lia, you used to be formidable on the pitch. You'd be shouting at us *and* the opposition. If we ever lost, that changing room would be a scary place, as you would be yelling at us. Why didn't you let Captain Lia Edwards shout at him?'

'Captain Lia Edwards is not here anymore,' I mumbled. I vowed to save harder for a car.

———

Daisy clung to my hip as we stood in the nursing home, once again captivated by the man playing the piano. It had rained all day and even though I'd remembered my brolly, the wind had destroyed it. Luckily, Daisy had a coat with a hood, but I'd stood for buses in the rain with my handbag over my head or cowered under packed bus shelters. On the way to Dad's nursing home, after we'd got off the bus, it had bucketed down. I resembled a bedraggled rat. My clothes were damp, my feet squelched in my shoes, and the stress of the hooded teenager had been replaying in my head. However, it was slowly being drowned out by the beautiful sound of the piano. All the tension slipped away as I listened to the wonderful lullaby being played.

I noticed the piano had been repositioned, which meant the pianist had a full view of the doorway when he lifted his eyes from his music sheet and surveyed the room. Our eyes kept meeting over the silvery heads of some of the residents. His serious stare made heat blossom over my cheeks. Five seconds later, and filled with panic over the warmth of my face, I clattered down the long corridor holding on to Daisy and vowing not to watch him the next time we visited Dad.

Daisy and I watched Dad return from the back room. 'Lia, you look terrible – are you not sleeping?'

I kept all my emotions inside. 'Maria broke down. She's gone, Dad.'

'I'm so sorry,' he said, touching my arm. 'You should have

told me. Have you heard from Angel? She's so busy nowadays I never seem to hear from her.'

I made a promise to myself to text Angel to ask whether she could phone Dad.

Daisy was on my lap, chewing the fluffy football toy Alex had given her. It was half the size of a real football and made of fabric. She adored it despite me encouraging her to play with other toys. We both watched the pianist appear in the day room pushing his father. The pianist was limping and judging by his grimace he was in a lot of pain.

Daisy wriggled and climbed down off my lap. She waved her football at Dad and lay her little blonde curly head on his knee. He smiled and ruffled her hair. 'Are you still Grandpa's Little Princess?'

'Yes,' she cooed, making me smile.

'How's work, Lia?'

I worked as a Marketing Manager for *Companion* – an online clothing firm that specialised in quality fashion for the senior man. We'd just launched a new corduroy trouser range with an elasticated waist, which I was excited about, and I'd given a free sample to Dad.

'I don't like these trousers by the way,' Dad added, pointing to his brown corduroys. 'They are so itchy, and I feel about one hundred and five, not seventy-five.'

'Oh no,' I groaned, hoping this was not the consensus on the new trousers. 'I will feed back to the supplier.'

I searched for Daisy. She was gone from the side of Dad's chair. 'Where's Daisy?'

Dad surveyed the room and pointed over to the far side of the day room. Daisy was standing watching the pianist kneeling beside his father. She was holding out her fluffy football. The pianist was saying things to his father, but the elderly man's face was blank. To my surprise, his father lifted his head. He saw

Daisy and a smile broke out on his face. I watched as the elderly man held out his hand. Daisy strode over to him, and handed him her toy ball. I was on my feet in seconds and raced across the day room to get her. The pianist's mouth had fallen open at his father's reaction. He watched his father turn over the little fluffy black and white ball in his hands. As Daisy rested her head against his arm, I said in a loud voice, 'Daisy, come here, please.'

My daughter ignored me. The pianist's father handed the toy back to Daisy. 'My little boy Mateo will be here any minute. You can show him your ball. I wish he liked football.'

Daisy laughed and ran past me, back to Dad, leaving me staring up at the pianist. 'I'm sorry,' I mumbled as he stood up.

'No, it's fine,' he replied. 'Your daughter got a better reaction from him than me.'

His eyes had a rich depth to them. I found them captivating. As soon as my brain came to its senses, I wondered what he must be thinking about me – a strange, damp-haired woman who couldn't stop staring at him. I mumbled something and ran back across the day room like a frightened animal.

Dee, Hope, and Jazzy were standing on my doorstep when we got home. Burrito was glaring at them all for daring to enter his territory. On the way home there had been a change of bus drivers. Daisy and I sat for ages on the stationary bus. I tried to distract her, but she wasn't patient and kept shouting and screeching, which made a woman behind me exhale loudly and tut under her breath.

'Can you get the key for me?' I gasped, pointing to my coat pocket.

Jazzy stepped forward and retrieved my key. 'We thought we would surprise you.'

Exhaustion and anxiety bubbled up inside of me, and I burst into tears. Hope lifted Daisy off me. 'I'll sort this little princess out for you.'

Dee and Jazzy led me to the sofa whilst Hope fed Daisy, played with her, changed her into her PJs, brushed her teeth and her hair, and read a few pages of a bedtime story.

I went to kiss Daisy goodnight, and she grinned from her bed. 'Do you like Hope?' I asked, and Daisy shouted, 'Yes,' before erupting into giggles. Daisy loved my friends. Hope and I snuck out. Dee had opened a bottle of wine she had brought with her. I was handed a glass and told to stay on the sofa whilst Jazzy cooked up tomato and vegetable pasta. She handed me a plate and said in an authoritative tone, 'EAT.'

Dee and Hope brought out their plates and we tucked in. They all watched me wolf down my food.

'Lia, we're worried about you, and this hooded teenager,' explained Jazzy. 'The team is concerned.'

I let out a nervous laugh. 'He's a teenager and he'll get bored.'

Dee shook her head. 'You've been saying that for about a week now, and today he touched your thigh.'

I nodded and felt anxiety crawl all over my body.

'Why don't you get a later bus?' Hope asked, before shoving a fork laden with pasta in her mouth.

I shook my head. 'My boss wants me in for nine. I'll be fine.'

Taking a sip of wine, I turned away from them all and blinked back tears. Every day my commute got worse, either due to the hooded teenager, the weather or late buses.

'Well, the Tigresses have intervened once again.'

My head snapped towards Dee. 'What?'

She smiled and held up her phone. 'We've joined the car

share app for you, and we've found the perfect car share. I used my email to get you signed up.'

No words came out as I watched her get something up on her phone screen. 'The app matched you with this lady. So, we've sent her a message from you.'

'That's fraudulent,' I muttered. Dee thrust her phone at me. 'No, it's called helping out a stubborn friend.'

I stared at the app, which had been designed to make the commute to work more pleasurable.

'It works like a dating app,' explained Jazzy. 'You find a car sharer organiser who you would like to share a car with by searching here.' She pointed to the top of the app. 'Or you can put in your interests and the app matches you. We've sorted out all that for you. Here's Stella's profile pic.'

'Stella?' I muttered. The car share organiser's photo was at the top of her profile page. Stella had flame-red hair cut short. It had amazing volume and was majestically swept to one side at the front. She had the trendiest purple glasses I had ever seen, and a powerful smile. My eyes darted over her profile description. *'A friendly, sometimes wacky working mum of three, who loves listening to eighties and nineties music and chatting about random stuff.'*

I saw that someone called Alice had written an amazing online review of her car share saying that she'd loved every minute of her daily commute. *"Stella was the best tonic for a weekday morning commute to work!"* According to Alice, Stella's car share came at the right time in her life, and during her time sitting in Stella's car, *"she figured everything out"*. I wondered what Alice meant by that.

At the bottom it read:

The Rules of Stella's Car Share
  We don't talk for fifteen minutes on the way to work. We

just listen to music. None of us are morning people so we all need time to adjust.

The music is 80s and 90s pop hits. There is no discussion on music from another era.

No romance between car sharers. This is forbidden. In my experience, relationships between car sharers can make an uncomfortable journey for everyone else in the car.

Dee took her phone back. 'Well, what do you think?'

The thought of carrying on with the bus commute made me feel anxious. Perhaps a car share with this woman would be better than being sat next to my teenage stalker. 'I like the sound of her...'

'It's a deal then?' Hope glanced at me before glancing at Dee and Jazzy.

I sighed. 'Ladies, you don't have to do all this. But I do need a better option for getting to work.'

Shaking her head, Dee draped her arm across my shoulders. 'It's not just about the commute, Lia.'

Jazzy nodded. 'We need to find the old Lia Edwards and extract her from her shell.'

Hope pointed to my "Joe wall". 'It's time to let the past go, Lia.'

I gazed up at Joe. I didn't want to let him go.

Chapter 11

Mateo

It was Friday. I'd endured a week of Stella's car share. In that time, I'd come to appreciate the fact I didn't have a teenage daughter like Lauren, I wasn't addicted to reading romance novels involving caddish dukes, I didn't experience hair dye disasters where my hair turned bright orange because I'd relied on someone called Useful Kim, and I didn't snore like Ed. The only saving grace had been the fifteen minutes of decent music each day.

After work, Stella was waiting for me at our usual pick-up point. She gestured to the back of the car. 'He beat you to it.' I saw Ed sprawled on the back seat. He was always fast asleep. The sight of him made me recall what he'd said the other day. 'You know on Tuesday when you were busy yelling at your daughter to go to school in the shopping centre car park – did you hear what Ed said when he woke?'

She shook her head.

'He woke up and asked whether *Roman* was awake?'

'I wonder who Roman is?' She shrugged as her phone bleeped. 'Excuse me a minute, Mateo, there's a call from home. It could be an emergency. I must pull over.'

'Mam,' Lauren's voice filled the car once Stella had parked on a street off the main road. 'Nicole is in Connor's bedroom.'

I turned to face the window. As I'd not experienced Stella's two teenage boys I'd assumed they were not a handful like Lauren was.

'Lauren,' shouted Stella, making me jolt. 'I'm still angry with you for coming home at three in the morning after that party, but I will deal with Connor first. Put him on the phone, please.'

Without putting her hand over the receiver Lauren yelled, 'CONNOR – MAM WANTS TO TALK TO YOU ABOUT YOU AND NICOLE SNOGGING IN YOUR ROOM.'

Rubbing my ears, I wondered whether my hearing would ever be the same again after that outburst. There was the sound of a door being flung open, someone heavy-footed thundering down the stairs, and Lauren screeching in pain. 'Ouch, Connor, don't hit me.'

'Mam,' a young man's voice boomed into the car, 'Nicole and I are watching the football on my bed.'

Stella took a deep breath, and through gritted teeth she growled, 'You and Nicole are both fifteen. Watch the football downstairs because if I get home and find you in that bedroom with her, I will throw a bucket of cold water over you both and ground you until you are thirty.'

He huffed down the phone. 'We're not doing anything. This is not fair. Nicole's mam lets us watch TV in Nicole's bedroom.'

Stella shouted, 'I'm *not* Nicole's mother. I want you both downstairs, now. Where is Nana Ruby?'

'Nana is in the pub, with the old bloke from over the road. The one she fancies. Lauren says Nana's pissed.'

Stella yelped with frustration. 'My mother is supposed to be looking after you lot. Not drinking herself silly in the pub with that bloke across the road.'

I placed my face in my hands. *Blimey, Stella's entire family was a nightmare. Even her mother.*

The phone went dead. Connor had hung up. I tried to not look at Stella, but I could hear her heavy sigh. I turned and she cast me a fake smile. 'If I get to be reincarnated, I am coming back as someone who has goldfish. No kids. Just goldfish.'

Stella's car share was like a form of travelling chaos. *If only the app had signed me up with someone quiet and shy who lived alone, hated talking on the way to work, and did not have any unruly teenage children.*

We set off and Stella decided to put her favourite Queen album on. Slyly, I slipped out my phone as an idea unfolded. *I didn't have to suffer this car share if I didn't want to; there were other car sharers out there.*

Once off the motorway she pulled into a residential area and parked. I watched as she put the handbrake on, turned the engine off and grinned at me. 'Will be two secs. I need to pick up an emergency goody bag.'

She got out of the car before I had time to question her. I watched her go and stand at the bus stop across the road. 'What the hell is she doing?' I muttered. A single decker bus came past, and Stella boarded once it had stopped. 'Where is she going? Why did I join this car share?' I moaned, as Ed stirred in the back. To my relief she got off the bus carrying a supermarket carrier bag. With a wave to the bus driver she hurried back to the car.

Stella placed the bag full of clinking glass bottles on the seat next to a sleeping Ed, and beamed. 'That bus driver Kenny is my friend Josie's boyfriend. He's my emergency delivery service.' She smiled. 'If any of us needs anything quickly and we're too busy to go to the supermarket, we send Josie a text, she sends it on to Kenny and he nips into the supermarket to pick it up on his bus route. His passengers don't seem to mind. I tell you, Mateo, Kenny guarantees same day delivery if he's working, and he uses some of his loyalty points to get money off, so it's a cost saving as well.'

I glanced over at the bag and noticed three screw top bottle tops sticking out. I wondered whether Nana Ruby had put in a wine order for looking after her wayward teenage grandchildren.

Stella started the car. 'It's for my friend, Bev.'

Flicking onto the *Happy Car Sharers* app I requested it find me a new match. I'd had enough of Stella's crazy car share, her family – and now Kenny, the mobile off licence/bus driver. Once the app informed me that it was dealing with my request, I rested my head against the window, allowing the music to flush out my grumpy thoughts and replace them with happy ones. One of my favourite tracks from Queen came on, reminding me of my time as a pianist in a luxury hotel bar. Years ago, I had managed to secure myself a job as a hotel pianist in London. Queen hits were always my go-to songs towards the end of the night. My stint in the hotel was before Natalie came along and turned my life upside down.

As I played, guests would be milling around the bar, clutching drinks, engaging in ambient cocktail chatter, and swaying to the music I played. The joy of being wrapped up in my music beneath a beautiful chandelier, against a vast window with the backdrop of the city at night, was unforgettable. Closing my eyes, I imagined myself back there, trailing my fingers over the black and white piano keys.

'What are you doing tonight, Mateo?' Stella asked. 'Anything nice?'

I tried to say, 'I wish I was playing the piano at the hotel,' but the words, 'I wish I was' must have come out as a tired inaudible mumble. All Stella heard was, 'playing the piano at the hotel.'

'Well, that sounds nice,' Stella exclaimed. Her pencilled brown eyebrows had shot up her forehead.

Sitting up in my seat I cast her a shocked look. What had I just said?

'I've never met someone who plays the piano in a hotel on an evening. Which hotel do you play at?'

My phone vibrated in my pocket. As Stella drove down a side road, I stole a sneaky glance and saw the app had found me another car sharer. Stella's car share was minutes away from ending. It was then that an idea sprang to mind. Tonight, I was going to see Dad and do another piano performance for him before the nursing home served tea. The thought of telling Stella about Dad gave me an uneasy feeling. She'd want me to talk about his Alzheimer's and how much I miss him every day. That would ultimately lead to me getting emotional, and I was not going to do that in Stella's car. *I could just continue with the hotel lie until we got to the high street. I was leaving and there was no need to tell her the truth.*

Stella glanced at me. 'The name of the hotel?'

I desperately tried to think of a hotel name. The street I walked up to get to the high street was called *Travellers Way,* which gave me an idea. 'It's called the Traveller's Rest.'

'Oh, well I haven't heard of that hotel,' she said, running her long pink nails through her hair. 'Playing the piano in a hotel bar sounds impressive though.'

I needed to change the subject, and fast. 'Do you have any plans?'

She nodded. 'I have a hot date later.'

'Huh?' My entire body tensed. I did not want to get into an awkward dating conversation. I kept my eyes firmly on the road ahead and tried to think of a question to divert her away from the subject of her love life. I imagined romance for Stella was probably as chaotic as her car share and family. 'Are you going on holiday this year, Stella?'

To my horror she didn't hear me. 'It's a real challenge to find a decent man these days, Mateo. I am praying that I have hit the dating jackpot with my new bloke.'

I let out an inner groan. What had I done?

'The dating site that I'm on enables you to date someone who looks like your teenage pop star crush. My date tonight is from the Jon Bon Jovi lookalike profiles. By day Wayne is a used car salesman flogging family hatchbacks, and by night he's a guitarist in a rock band.'

'Interesting,' I said, taking out my phone and praying the app had found me someone who didn't use bus drivers to peddle booze for her mates, whose teenage children didn't cause utter chaos, and preferably someone who didn't talk at all.

'Just going to drop this at Bev's house,' Stella informed me as she pulled up alongside a row of terraced houses. 'I will be two secs.' I watched as she grabbed the bag of clinking wine bottles.

Sitting in Stella's car, with Ed snoring his head off in the back, whilst she ran a Dial a Bottle of Wine service to her friends, intensified my agitation.

Stella reappeared from the house. She ran to the car, and five minutes later we finally pulled up on the high street.

The speed at which I grabbed my bag made her gasp. To my dismay, the leather strap was hooked on something under the seat. I tugged and tugged, but it wouldn't free itself. I just wanted to run home as fast as I could, despite my painful ankle. I'd had enough of car sharing.

'What the hell are you doing, Mateo?' Stella cried.

I glared at her. 'My bag is stuck.' I gave my strap an angry last yank and it freed itself.

'By the way,' Stella said, 'Alice has taken my advice. She's decided to go travelling.'

'Really?'

Stella nodded. 'As she's a temp she doesn't have to give much notice that she won't be coming back. I have already found a new person. They start Monday.'

I reached for the car door handle.

'Thanks for letting me drop that delivery off, Mateo. This afternoon I found out that the lady who car shared with me last year, Bev, is in remission. Her breast cancer has finally gone, and I wanted to give her some nice treats. Kenny helped me out as I knew I wouldn't get time to go to the shops. Bev doesn't drink so I got her a few bottles of her favourite Elderflower soft drink, you know the fancy stuff in the glass bottles, chocolates and I also bought her little boy a new toy. I've been worried about her after what she's been through, and she deserved one of my emergency deliveries.'

A wave of guilt crashed over me. Stella was not starting a Dial a Bottle of booze service or taking wine home for Nana Ruby. She had done something nice for someone who she used to car share with. It was time for me to leave.

As I limped home in the rain, I checked out my new car share match. He was called Leonard and described himself as a careful driver who liked silence on the way to work. Leonard ticked all my boxes for a new car sharer, however his driver photo did remind me of Sir Anthony Hopkins playing Hannibal in Silence of the Lambs. I decided to ignore his serial killer vibe, and the absence of any car sharer reviews, and read his profile more carefully later. Smiling to myself, I hobbled home.

After visiting Dad, Harry came to pick me up and took me back to his for a few beers. As he drove, I told him about Leonard and when he'd pulled up at the traffic lights, I showed him Leonard's profile. 'Mateo, stay where you are,' exclaimed Harry. 'I think Leonard's car share will either be boring or terrifying.'

'I like the idea of total silence,' I muttered, feeling my heart sink.

Harry laughed. 'You won't be saying that when Leonard has you tied up in his boot. Have you told Stella you're leaving?'

I shook my head. 'I've not worked up the courage to text her. She's got a new person joining on Monday. Are you going to give me a lift home later?'

Harry shook his head. 'You are staying on the sofa again. See what the new person is like before you go with Leonard. I'll drop you back early tomorrow.'

We were on our third round of beers when my phone buzzed. It was a message from Natalie. My heart began to pound in my chest. My mind whisked me back to the church where I had stood expecting my bride. She was later than planned, and I was starting to perspire. An uneasy feeling crept over me as people started to whisper and the vicar began to pace up and down. When Natalie's mother took out her mobile from her handbag and dashed outside, I knew something was very wrong.

'Mateo, what's up?' Harry asked.

'It's a message from you know who. She wants to "talk and clear the air between us" after what happened last year.' Harry let out a yelp of frustration. 'Why is she doing this now? For goodness' sake, it's been a year. Are you okay?'

'I'm fine. 'Natalie and I ended last year.' My mind reminded me of the day after our disastrous wedding. I had attempted to come to terms with Natalie's six-month affair by drinking so much booze I ended up in Accident & Emergency getting my stomach pumped. Harry found me and took me to the hospital. When I was discharged, he stayed with me for three days, cooking me meals, forcing me to watch football matches on the telly and telling me that I was loved by him and Claire. *Natalie had almost destroyed me.* 'What are you going to do?' Harry asked. I pressed delete. 'It's gone. I deleted it.'

Ghost snuggled by my side when I went to sleep later. She purred in my ear and the way she put her silvery paw over my arm made me feel like she was protecting me. 'Don't worry,' I whispered. 'I will not be loving anyone again.'

In the morning I asked Claire if I could adopt Ghost.

Chapter 12

Lia

Daisy grabbed the hand of her favourite nursery nurse, Keisha. It was hard to not love Keisha with her booming laugh, her pearly white smile, and her zest for nursery life. Keisha pointed to Daisy's new black patent buckle shoes. 'I love your new shoes, Daisy.' A huge smile spread across Daisy's little face, and she squealed, which sent her golden curls into a bouncing frenzy. Bending down, Keisha admired Daisy's new footwear that I had bought for her over the weekend. 'Can I borrow your shoes?'

Daisy burst into a fit of giggles. 'Silly.'

Keisha chuckled. 'Shall we say goodbye to Mummy and go sing some songs?'

Daisy came close to me, and I kneeled so she could plant one of her sloppy kisses on my cheek. Her lips were still coated in toast crumbs from breakfast. I watched Daisy leap for joy then lead Keisha off in the direction of the nursery playroom.

My phone bleeped, reminding me it was time for my first car share with Stella. *Why had I allowed Dee, Jazzy, and Hope to talk me into this?* My nerves were going crazy. The thought of getting into a car with complete strangers and travelling to and from work made me feel jittery.

Then again, the bus wasn't exactly ideal. And the car share was a flexible thing. I could back out at any time. If it didn't work out, I would have to force myself to return to my teenage admirer and the uncomfortable journeys.

Swinging my laptop bag over my shoulder I made my way to the high street where Stella said she would pick me up. The app had informed me that Stella drove a black Ford Fiesta. On Stella's welcome message she said she'd pull in outside the express mini supermarket.

As I got closer, I noticed a male waiting near the express supermarket. From a distance, it looked like the pianist at Dad's nursing home. My heart began to thump. I told myself it couldn't be him as he was probably composing a piano master-piece or teaching music to a load of eager students.

The man looked up as I got closer. *It was him.* His intense dark eyes narrowed as I approached. He took a step back and ran a hand through his curly dark hair. A fluttering sensation took hold of my chest as I took in his strong jawline, his black linen suit jacket, a white T-shirt that set off his caramel-coloured skin, black cargo trousers and retro trainers.

Neither of us spoke. Someone beeped a horn behind us. I turned, expecting to see a black Ford Fiesta, but instead I saw a bright pink Mini with a white roof and silver headlamps. It was being driven by a woman with red hair and massive purple glasses. The word 'Mini' pinged around my head. In a flash my grief for Maria returned. Tears rushed to my eyes, and a lump rose at the back of my throat.

'Lia?' It was the driver of the Mini.

I stared at her. *Was this Stella – my new car sharer? Where was her black car?*

To my horror, the pianist stepped in front of me, opened the passenger car door and got in beside her. She nudged him and I heard her say, 'Mateo, that's Lia. The new addition.' She leaned forward so she could see me. 'Lia, I'm Stella. None of us are morning people I'm afraid.'

'That's okay,' I muttered, 'nor am I.'

Stella nudged Mateo. 'You will need to get in the back so Lia can sit in the passenger seat with me.'

He got out of the car, and I took a generous step back. I could feel his eyes on me as he opened the back door and climbed inside.

'Lia, come sit next to me,' gushed Stella. 'Welcome to my car share family.'

I hesitated and gulped back a wave of emotion. *I was getting inside another Mini after everything I had been through.* Gritting my teeth, I got in and forced a smile at Stella. Her hair was even brighter than in her photo. It was a hot lava red and had so much volume it was brushing against the car roof. She was wearing a pink silk vest and black jeans. Her arms were a golden tan colour, and her nails were long and silver. 'I love your dress by the way, Lia.'

'Thanks.' Stella's car was clean and immaculate. Sweet smelling air fresheners were dotted all over, and my eyes were immediately drawn to the two fluffy pink dice hanging from the driver's mirror. They reminded me of Maria's blue dice, the ones Joe had bought me. I wanted to run away from the car. but somehow, I resisted. Stella followed my gaze and pointed to the dice. 'My kids bought me them. They make me feel young and like a girl racer.' She laughed, distracting me from my grief.

With a trembling hand I reached back for the seatbelt. *I still couldn't believe the pianist was sitting behind me.* Knowing he was there gave me that strange, excited sensation. It was a similar feeling to the one I used to get when I was zigzagging my way past defenders and a whizzy feeling would be surging through my veins. I could smell his aftershave, which was as intoxicating as his piano playing, a mixture of sweet oriental spices against a faint aroma of oranges. Out of the corner of my eye I could see him staring at me. *Why did I feel like this when I was in his presence?*

Stella pointed at her CD player. 'You have read my rules?'

I nodded.

'As you and Mateo live closest to the motorway, the fifteen minutes of listening to music and no talking will start once I've picked you both up.' I nodded, and soon the sound of my favourite U2 album filled the car. It was nice to sink into the car seat, gaze out of the window at the weary commuters queuing for the bus, and let my mind wander. On the way we passed the road that led to Daisy's nursery. I wondered what she was doing.

Stella turned down the music after fifteen minutes. She glanced at Mateo, and then at me. 'Do you know Mateo in the back?'

'Sort of... I've seen Mateo at–'

'The hotel,' interjected Mateo, making me spin around in my seat and stare at him. *What did he just say?* 'We've met before at a... hotel.'

Stella grinned at me. 'Ah, you've seen Mateo play at this mystery hotel of his.'

'Umm... what?' I was confused. *Mystery hotel? What the hell?*

Mateo tapped the back of my seat. 'Yes, Lia is a regular at The Traveller's Rest hotel bar – aren't you?'

My eyebrows shot up my forehead in shock. Me – a regular at The Traveller's Rest hotel bar? I've not been in a bar for nearly two years, and I have never heard of this Traveller's Rest hotel. Also, the name sounded like it was one of those budget hotels, with hard beds and no free biscuits on the kettle tray.

Stella shot me a confused look. 'You frequent The Traveller's Rest hotel bar a lot, Lia?'

'Most evenings,' interjected Mateo.

I turned my head to him and scowled. He smiled and I found myself distracted by his eyes. It was at that point I noticed a man unconscious next to Mateo. His eyes were closed, and he was slumped against the window. 'Is he okay?'

'That's Ed, or the Sleeping Man, as I call him,' explained Stella. 'He's a party animal, and he doesn't get much sleep.' With a nudge she winked at me. 'Tell me – are there any decent single men for me in this hotel bar? She put her hand to the corner of her mouth. 'Side note. I do have a boyfriend, Wayne, but I like to have a plan B up my sleeve when it comes to dating. My mother, on the other hand, who is living her best single life right now, likes to have a plan C, D, and E when it comes to dating.'

'Umm...' I glanced at Mateo as I was sure I'd just heard him groan.

She tapped me on the arm and gestured towards Mateo. 'Is he any good, Lia?'

I cast Stella a bewildered look. 'Pardon?'

Stella smiled. 'Mateo's piano playing, Lia.'

I could hear him groan behind me. *Mateo was amazing at playing the piano, but I didn't want to gush and sound like a fangirl.* 'I like listening to him play.'

'Lia, what brings you to car sharing?'

For a few seconds I hesitated. In my mind all I could see was Maria and Joe waving to me. I wondered whether I should mention Joe. If I did, that would lead to probing questions, which would ultimately lead to me dissolving into tears. I decided to not talk about him. 'Well, I didn't really get on with the buses, so my friends suggested this.'

Stella glanced at me. 'Tell us about yourself, Lia.'

'I have a gorgeous little girl called Daisy.'

She smiled. 'How old is Daisy?'

'Eighteen months.'

'I adored that age,' explained Stella. 'Actually, I adored every age with my three... up until they became teenagers.'

'Are the teenage years bad?' I asked, trying to imagine Daisy as a teenager.

Stella blew the air out of her cheeks. 'I have a daughter and twin boys. They're all teenagers. All were angels until they reached puberty. Don't worry, Lia, you've still got time with Daisy. Does Daisy's father live with you?'

I gulped and gripped the sides of the seat. My face grew hot, and the windscreen blurred. Stella sensed my mood, and to my relief, she didn't chase me for an answer. 'I know what we all need,' she gushed. 'Some of DJ Rick Carter's Breaking Commuter News.' I watched her turn on the radio to a station I'd never heard of – Memory Lane.

'You've just been listening to the Flying Pickets. Here's today's Breaking Commuter News. It's chaos out there everyone. Steve has texted the show to say his wife has driven off on a three-day work conference to Cumbria with his work laptop bag in the boot. A great start to the week for Steve. Andrea's sneezing fit on the bus resulted in the driver telling her he was allergic to early mornings too. Love that, Andrea. Kirsty was supposed to drop her wee sample at the doctors before work, but she's got off the bus to find her wee sample is missing, it's not in her handbag. She thinks it might have fallen out of her bag on the no.72 bus... to be precise, the window seat, fourth row back from the front. It has her name and date of birth pencilled on. Good luck, Kirsty, and can I remind everyone this is not a "track your lost wee sample" radio slot. Kate has texted the show to say the guy she fancies on her morning bus has a girlfriend. Tough times, Kate. Finally, Ryan ran for the bus this morning and heard a ripping sound.

He's sat at his desk at work praying no one asks him to stand up for his team's morning briefing, as he has a large hole in his trousers, and the safety pin he found in his bag is struggling to contain everything. Keep smiling everyone.'

I smiled at Stella who started giggling at Ryan's radio shout-out.

'Sometimes in life when things are not working out all we must do is keep smiling,' she said. 'Even when our journeys seem almost impossible.'

I rested my head back and relaxed. Sitting in this warm car made me feel appreciative. I could have been like those poor souls on DJ Rick Carter's show or even worse, squashed between the bus window and the hooded teenager with his wandering hands.

Mateo, sat directly behind me, shifted his legs, and they brushed against the seat. My heart began to gallop, then my brain reminded me he had insisted on dragging me into his fictitious hotel story.

Chapter 13

Mateo

The person I had been staring at across a crowded back room in Dad's new nursing home was now sitting in the car seat in front of me. As I stepped out of the driver's passenger seat I stole another glance. A breeze had lifted the ends of her long, fly-away red hair from her shoulders. She'd reached up to try and secure the left side behind her ear and I noticed she possessed high cheek-bones, a pink bow mouth, and a few freckles. She was wearing a blue denim jacket over a green polka-dot dress and white trainers.

That stupid lie I told Stella came back to haunt me in the car. I don't know why I didn't explain that I played the piano for the residents of a nursing home. Once again, the thought of talking to Stella about Dad was too much oversharing for my liking. I didn't want to end up getting emotional in Stella's car, so I dragged Lia into my lie.

We were stuck in an endless line of traffic on the outskirts of the city centre. Stella smiled at me via the rear-view mirror. 'Mateo, why don't you tell Lia about yourself?'

'Umm, hi, Lia,' I mumbled. 'I work in finance, and as you know, I play the piano.'

Lia didn't turn around and she remained silent. I sensed she was angry about the hotel lie.

Getting into a conversation with Stella last week about Dad would have meant I would have had to talk without crying, about him being in a nursing home, his illness and my father no longer recognising who I am. The lie enabled me to get out of a long-winded conversation. *I just don't know why I kept it going just now.*

The traffic started moving again. We pulled up at a second set of traffic lights and Stella stared across at the opposite driver. 'It's my nail lady.' In a second, she was winding down her window, and the woman opposite did the same. 'Hi, Katie, fancy seeing you here,' Stella screeched.

'Hey, Stella,' shouted the young woman. 'How are the new nails? Do you like the length?' The lights were going to change at any second, so Stella needed to end the conversation fast. 'I think I might go a little longer next time,' shouted Stella. 'How's your mum now after her operation?'

'Aww, Stella, thanks for asking. Mum's doing great,' said the woman. 'A bit sore as you'd expect. I just hope this operation sorts her bowel out.'

Lia was busy looking at her phone, and Ed was asleep. Neither noticed the lights were now on green, and Stella was too busy finding out how the mother of her nail lady was coping after an operation. *For goodness' sake, couldn't Stella simply drive us to work?*

Eventually, a driver behind hooted us, and Stella giggled. 'See you next week, Katie. Give my love to your mum.'

We were nearly at work when Stella's phone bleeped. 'Excuse me, car sharers, one of my children is on the phone. It could be an emergency. I'm going to pull over. I'll only be a minute.' This was Lia's first car share, but I knew full well

Stella's children were not going to be in the middle of what I would call an *emergency*.

Stella pulled over into a side street and brought the car to a stop. I prayed this wouldn't be awkward for Lia's sake. 'Mam,' boomed a young male voice filling the car. 'I don't have any clean underwear.'

'For goodness' sake, Luke,' exclaimed Stella. 'You know I have a new person in my car. Why do you have to ring me now with THAT sort of thing?'

I could see Lia had turned her head to stare out of the passenger window.

'Mam, you're supposed to make sure I have clean boxers. It's like a basic requirement for a mother.'

There was an uncomfortable silence as Stella glared at her phone which was, hooked to the radio. 'Luke – I work five days a week. At FIFTEEN years of age, you are more than capable of using a washing machine.'

Luke huffed. 'I'm ringing Childline. They'll help me'.

'Good luck with Childline. There are clean boxer shorts in your drawer. I put them in there last night. You were too busy shouting out of your window at that girl you fancy.'

There was the sound of someone giggling in the background. Luke yelped so loudly it made us all jump. 'MAM – Connor has hidden my underwear. He's at the top of the stairs with them. Give me them back, Connor.'

'Luke, put Connor on please.'.

The phone went dead. Luke had followed his siblings, and hung up on his mother.

Stella forced out a smile at Lia. 'I'm sorry, Lia, that you had to listen to that. Luke will be grounded when I get home.'

She started the engine and let out a little sigh. I was tempted to ask Stella whether her standard punishment of grounding her kids was working, as for the past week they'd all been grounded, and none of them had changed their behaviour.

Ed stirred and to my horror, he sat bolt upright, his eyes wide open, which made me yelp in fright. He looked like something out of a horror movie.

Lia glanced at Ed and let out a frightened yelp too.

'Ed – you all right?' Stella glanced in her driver's mirror.

He rubbed his face and turned to me. 'Has Roman woken up? Was that the hospital?'

Oh God, the Sleeping Man must still be drunk. Perhaps one of his party-mad friends was taken to hospital. Could Lia's first car share get any worse?

'I'm sorry,' I mumbled. 'I don't know who Roman is.'

I spent the rest of the journey deliberating in my head whether Lia would stay in Stella's car share after I'd forced her to lie about my fictitious hotel, Stella had struck up a conversation with her nail lady at a set of traffic lights, Stella's fifteen-year-old son had phoned up about his underwear, and the Sleeping Man had woken up like something out of a horror show and frightened everyone.

Chapter 14

Lia

'How did your first car share go yesterday?' Beth, the marketing assistant, asked as I hung up my coat. It was my second day of car sharing. Mateo-related agitation bubbled away inside of me. Beth had been at a conference yesterday, so I didn't get to talk to her. Mateo had still not apologised, or explained why he dragged me into his lie about his hotel story yesterday. To make matters worse, telling Stella I was feeling tired this morning after I had got into the car, prompted her to peer over her giant purple glasses at me with one of those suspicious looks. The kind Dad used to give me when, as a teenager, I would come in from a night out reeking of booze and swear I hadn't been drinking. She glanced at Mateo and turned back to me before asking whether I'd been hanging out in the hotel bar till late with Mateo. Shaking my head, I told her the truth. Daisy had refused to go to bed last night, and I ended up bringing her in with me, which meant I'd had to endure seven hours of sleeping hanging off the edge of the bed whilst little Daisy slept star-shaped.

My fifteen minutes of listening to music were spent worrying Mateo's lie was starting to make Stella wonder whether there was anything going on between the two of us. This car share was something I desperately needed as returning to the hooded teenager and the unreliable buses would be a nightmare. I respected Stella and her rule – the one about no romance between car sharers. It made perfect sense. I vowed to tell Stella the truth the next time Mateo brought up The Traveller's Rest story.

'What's the woman who runs it like?' Beth asked.

My ears were still ringing from Stella's daughter Lauren shouting down the phone about how her brother Connor had stolen her brand new make-up palette and given it to his girlfriend as a romantic gift. 'She's lovely but her car share is an experience.'

Beth had her phone in one hand and with the other, she was twirling one of her brown curls around her finger. She was wearing the black and white polka dot dress she'd bought online last week while we were in a presentation given by senior management. I'd been trying to listen to what the guy was saying about fashion trends for the retired man, but Beth kept flashing different work dress choices at me on her phone, wanting me to give her a thumbs up or down.

'Give me a sec. Just selling some of Jez's clothes online,' explained Beth. 'The ones he left at mine when we broke up, that he can't be bothered to collect. Making money out of an ex-boyfriend's expensive clothes is bringing me so much joy today. It's like he's repaying me for all the crap he put me through. We were together for eight years, so I have a long way to go. I like to think he's sat at work right now wishing he had his suede jacket, the one he bought in a cool shop in London. Little does he know it has just sold for an eye-watering amount.' She giggled and put down her phone. 'Right, I'm all ears.'

'Stella's teenage children are a bit of a handful.'

Beth cast me a look of horror and reached for her vanilla latte. 'Were they in the car as well?'

I shook my head. 'No, but yesterday one of them called her, and she had him on hands-free. He told her he couldn't find his underwear. That was awkward.'

'What the hell?' screeched Beth, shaking her head and causing her curls to bounce with excitement. 'Jez's mother used to lay out his underwear for him and he's like... twenty-seven.' Jez was Beth's ex-boyfriend. She claimed she was well and truly over him, but he came up in most conversations.

Flopping down into my office chair I spun around to face Beth. 'It turned out his brother had nicked his underwear from his drawer. Anyway, he was rude to his mum, claimed he was going to phone Childline, and then hung up on her.'

Beth's perfectly sculptured eyebrows rocketed up her forehead. She grabbed a list from the pinboard behind her head. 'Let me just add this to my *two hundred and twenty-seven reasons why not to have kids* list.' I watched as she scribbled her two hundred and twenty-eighth reason – "*rude teenage sons who are incapable of picking out their underwear. Like JEZ!*" She highlighted Jez's name and underlined it.

'Her daughter this morning screamed down the phone about her brother nicking her make-up and SHE also hung up on her mother.'

I watched Beth raise a hand. 'Let me stop you there.' She turned around to her list. "*Reason two hundred and twenty-nine*"' she wrote, "*teenage daughters who scream at you.*"

Whirling back to me on her chair Beth cast me a look of concern. 'I'm worried about you Lia, and this car share. How is Stella dealing with her wayward teenagers?'

'She threatens to ground them.'

Beth shook her head with disapproval.

'Stella is lovely. She's a mum like me,' I explained. 'She loves eighties and nineties music, which is great.'

'Who are the other car sharers?' Beth folded her arms across her black and white polka dot dress.

I smoothed out my own dress. 'Well, there's a young guy called Ed who sleeps the entire time.'

'Sleeps in the back?' Beth asked, casting me a look of disapproval. 'I would not be happy with that. He sounds a lot like Jez. We'd get to his mother's house on a Sunday afternoon, and he'd fall asleep next to me whilst I had to suffer his mother's lengthy account about her marriage problems with Jez's useless father. Is there anyone else in this happy car share?'

I took a deep breath. 'So, you know I told you about the bloke who plays the piano at Dad's nursing home?'

A mischievous grin swept across Beth's face. 'Don't tell me he's in the car share too?'

I nodded. 'Yes, but he's annoyed me.' I told her about Mateo and his hotel fabrication.

'Does he secretly fancy Stella?' she asked, leaning back in her chair, and chewing on the end of a pencil. 'Maybe he was trying to impress her with his hotel story.' She gasped and sat up straight in her chair. 'Mateo holds a secret candle for Stella and has made up some lie about being a fancy pianist.'

My jaw almost hit the desk. 'That's it, Beth. He's trying to impress her.'

She cast me a puzzled expression. 'If you were going to lie about playing a piano in a fancy hotel to impress someone, you would go for a more majestic name. I mean if these travellers want a rest, the last thing they are going to want to listen to is him on the grand piano.'

'I think he does secretly fancy Stella,' I mumbled.

Beth chewed some more on her pencil. 'Is he good looking?'

Mateo appeared in my mind. 'Very,' I murmured, and then coughed to hide my embarrassment.

Beth studied me. 'A simple yes would have sufficed, Lia. Didn't you tell me that Stella woman has a rule about there being no romance between car sharers?'

Exhaling loudly, I raised my eyebrows. 'That rule will never be broken by me, Beth. One of the guys in Stella's car is unconscious, and the other likes making lies up about how I spend my evenings. I hate him already.'

She laughed. 'You know what they say about love and hate?'

Playfully swiping her I turned back to my desk and hid my hot cheeks with my hair. Joe's face appeared in my mind and within a few seconds I was so overcome with guilt I went to the toilet and cried.

After lunch, we had a campaign to work on for a new range of men's elasticated waist trousers, but Beth insisted on making me practise confronting Mateo about the hotel lie and getting him to apologise profusely to me. We did several role-play scenarios across the desks where she was me and I was Mateo. At times I did sense she was mixing Mateo up with her ex-boyfriend Jez, as she launched into a full-scale tirade about how lies involving fictitious hotels were one step away from lying about what happened on his best mate's stag do.

The stag party where a girl Jez had met messaged him on Instagram. Beth had found the message, which had read: *"I don't mind having some fun again with you and you can still keep your dull girlfriend."* Even though Jez claimed he hadn't done anything Beth had finished their eight-year relationship.

Once the working day came to an end, I walked to the bus stop where Stella said she'd pick us up. Mateo had got there before me. His hands were stuffed deep into his trouser pockets, his eyes fixated on the café across the road. A group of tired office workers were at the tables and chairs outside the café enjoying a coffee before their trek home.

All my role-playing ideas vanished as I began studying his side profile. He had a Roman nose like mine, which I liked. It was large and distinctive. His hair was mahogany brown, short at the sides and back, but curly on top.

'Will you be at the nursing home tonight?' Mateo asked, making me jolt with surprise. I noticed how he was focused on the people at the café opposite. My heart began to pound like a drum.

'Yes.'

There was a lengthy pause between us.

'Thank you for keeping my secret.' He didn't look at me.

'Why is it a secret that you play piano at a nursing home? Oh, and by the way, that is a poor choice for a hotel name.'

He slowly turned his face towards mine and frowned. 'You don't like The Traveller's Rest?'

I shook my head. 'If you're trying to impress someone by making out you play the piano in a swish hotel you should have come up with something a little fancier.'

'I'll remember the next time... I'm trying to impress someone.' He cast his eyes back across the road.

'You haven't answered my question,' I said. 'Why are you making up a lie? Why aren't you telling Stella you play the piano in a nursing home?'

Stella beeped her horn and pulled up alongside us. He opened the back passenger door, climbing in without giving me an answer.

I climbed into the front seat with mild agitation and decided that I would not be listening to him play the piano when I visited Dad next.

Chapter 15

Mateo

The queue for takeaway coffee snaked out of the café. Checking my phone, I saw that there were ten minutes before Stella would arrive. *Why the hell was there such a queue?*

The guy in front of me turned around. 'Some idiot at the till has dropped their bag, and there's stuff all over the floor. The barista is helping them, which is annoying. I guess we all stand here like lemons and wait for our coffee.'

Stuffing my hands in my pockets, I shook my head. 'I hate waiting for coffee.'

'Me too. This is going to take ages.'

We both stood there for what felt like an eternity. 'I'm going to get some coffee at work. Good luck, mate.' The guy left his space in the queue and ran across the road to catch an oncoming bus. I checked my phone again. Six minutes until Stella would pull up. I wondered whether the guy had the right idea. There was always the coffee shop next to my office. In a few seconds, I made my decision and walked up to where Stella met me and Lia. When I got there Lia wasn't to be seen. Stella pulled up a few minutes early with a sleeping Ed in the back. 'Lia not here?' she asked.

'You're a bit early.' I opened the back door and climbed in beside Ed, who didn't even wake up to acknowledge my presence.

Stella was about to leave when she saw Lia in her wing mirror. 'Ah, here she is.'

Lia got into the front seat. 'Morning,' she said, smiling at Stella. 'Sorry I was late; the café was very busy.' I could see she was holding a paper cup with a plastic lid.

'You had more patience than me, Lia,' I piped up from the back. 'I waited for ages. Some idiot dropped their bag and the barista decided to help them pick up their stuff rather than carry on making coffee.'

Lia turned around and scowled. 'That was me, Mateo. I was the *idiot* you are referring to.'

I wanted the ground to open and swallow me whole. Stella cast me a look of concern in the driver's mirror. 'Let's all calm down by listening to the wonderful INXS.'

After we'd all listened to INXS in silence, and I'd cursed myself a hundred times for the coffee story, Stella turned on the radio.

'*You've just been listening to Sister Sledge. Here's the Breaking Commuter News. Helen is on the train to work and has just emptied a salt sachet into her coffee instead of sugar. Emma has parked in her work car park and realised she has forgotten to drop one of her children off at school. He's still in his car seat. Loving your work, Emma. Pixie has seen her boss kissing his new girlfriend on the train platform and has a nine o'clock meeting with him. She wishes she could unsee his kiss, which reminded her of a washing machine's slow spin. Let's all think of Pixie and her nine o'clock meeting.*'

I found myself smiling for the first time at DJ Rick Carter's morning news.

'*Finally. Sharon wants to wish Stella a happy birthday. Stella will be in her car listening as Sharon says she's our biggest fan. Happy Birthday from me too, Stella.'*

Stella let out a jubilant shout. 'It's my birthday today and Sharon got me a shout-out from the one and only – DJ Rick Carter'.

Lia and I both said, 'Happy Birthday,' in unison.

'Did you get anything nice?' Lia asked, as Stella turned down the radio.

Stella ran her hand through her hair. 'Connor and Luke forgot despite me telling them six hundred times, Lauren got me some red hair dye, my mother got me a bottle of vodka and Sharon my best mate got me something unexpected.'

Knowing Stella, this unexpected gift could be anything.

Stella was busy describing Sharon to Lia. 'She has had more jobs than I've had hot dinners, she's a magnet for gossip, a whirlwind on the dance floor and a storm-drain when it comes to drinking.'

I found myself praying Sharon never joined Stella's car share.

Stella continued. 'Sharon has this laugh, which is so loud it can be heard a few streets away, and no matter what life throws at her she still hauls herself to her feet with an ear-to-ear smile.'

'She sounds fab,' gushed Lia. 'How did you come to know Sharon?'

'We've known each other since a legendary day back in comprehensive school when Sean Routledge announced to the entire school during assembly that he was two-timing the both of us.' Lia gasped and I tried to block out the phrase 'two timing' as it was making Natalie's face flash into my mind.

'As we were both in different social crowds at school, Sharon and I hardly knew each other. Whilst Sharon and I stared in horror at each other, everyone crowded around us and chanted, "Fight, fight, fight!"'

'Oh no,' Lia gasped. 'What did you do?'

Stella turned to her and grinned. 'Before we knew it our fight was arranged at the back of the tennis courts. Some of the sixth-form lads had started taking cigarette bets on who would win. Sean got so excited at the prospect of two fifth-year girls fighting over him he bet all his cigarettes on me beating Sharon. A few hours later, Sharon and I faced each other on the tennis courts surrounded by a giant swarm of schoolchildren. For a few seconds we both stared at Sean, who couldn't believe his luck, and then back at each other. We realised we were too good for Sean, so we burst into fits of laughter and hugged each other. Sean lost all his ciggies, and I got a wonderful best mate.'

'Love it,' affirmed Lia.

Stella chuckled. 'Earlier, Sharon presented me with my birthday gift. I always look forward to her present offering, which has not changed for years: a bottle of Prosecco, a little box of chocolates, a delicious-smelling candle, a selection of celeb magazines and some fizzy bath bombs. This birthday, Sharon replaced all that with... an A5 hard-backed diary.'

'A diary?' Lia asked.

Stella nodded. 'Do you have a close friend who never gives up on something about you and won't let you *ever* forget about it? Sharon has been going on about something she reckons I am talented at for years and I should be pursuing it as a life goal.'

Lia sighed. 'I have several friends like that. My best mate Dee is a Sagittarius and–'

I heard Stella gasp. 'Your best mate is a Sagittarius?'

'She is, and I know Dee will *never* give up on something she thinks I should be doing.'

Stella cast me a look of sympathy. 'Good luck with Dee.'

I was curious as to what it was Lia's best mate wouldn't let go of.

'Sagittarian women are not to be messed with. I can't keep

up with all that energy and life force they put out into the world. My mother is a Sagittarius, and the amount of energy she's putting into her new relationship with the bloke who lives opposite me is staggering.' She fiddled with her large gold hoop earring. 'Saying that, she did go all in with that chap from the DIY shop not so long ago. She even bought herself a drill from him the next day.'

In the back of the car, I prayed Nana Ruby never joined the car share.

Stella continued. 'Sharon came over this morning, on her way to work, to give me the present. She claims out of the two of us I have always been the *wordy* one.'

Lia looked at her. 'Are you good with words?'

Stella nodded. 'When I was a teenager, I wrote for the school magazine. Sharon still goes on about how funny my agony aunt column was to read, and she thinks I should be a famous author. She reckons I could be the forty-something version of Bridget Jones.'

'Why don't you?'

'I haven't got the time, and the thought of writing in a diary makes me feel uncomfortable after what happened to Florence at work. Diaries can be dangerous things.'

'Really?'

'Daily journaling resulted in Florence self-publishing her first spicy romance about a handsome *naked* gardener (her neighbour, who she could see from her upstairs window). She blamed her diary for everything that followed. Her father discovered she'd written a book, and he proudly read out the first chapter at a family gathering.'

Lia broke into a giggle. 'Did her father know about her preferred literary genre?'

Stella shook her head. 'He read four pages, by which point the gardener was mowing the lawn in the buff and kept asking the woman he was working for to join him in her shed for some... *special seed sewing.* Her father stopped reading as the woman sprinted to her shed. Thank goodness he stopped before the shed antics began. Florence was so embarrassed she pretended to faint, and spent the rest of the gathering locked in the bathroom with a bottle of Prosecco.'

'Will you write your diary, and will it one day turn into a novel?' Lia asked, making me let out a silent groan. Did Lia have to encourage Stella?

With a shrug, Stella pulled into the street where the car share ended. 'I am undecided. I'll let you know. If I ever do write a book about my life, it will cover the wild times, the good and bad decisions I have made, my romantic highs, a few ugly truths, and of course, my big comeback.' She grinned. 'Just think, in years to come when I get my diary published you two might catch sight of my book on Amazon or in bookshops. You can say to whoever you are with – "I used to car share with that famous author." You might even make a purchase to relive your car sharing memories.'

As I left the car, I decided that I couldn't think of anything worse. Stella's novel would remind me of Stella's unruly teenagers, her chaotic driving, her constant oversharing and the stupid mistakes I made with Lia.

My phone bleeped with a voice message as I walked towards my office. It was the mechanic who had come out to see how much it would cost to fix Dad's car, a gleaming white 1976 Triumph Spitfire that lived in my garage. There was something wrong with the engine. It kept making an odd sound.

Dad loved his car. She was his pride and joy. Before he became unwell, he would spend hours driving her up and down the country lanes. Whenever I popped over to see him, he would be in the garage peering under her bonnet. He also spoke to her a lot. It made me smile as sometimes he would sing a love song to her as he polished her body work. I knew he wasn't well when he started forgetting where he'd parked her. He'd return home on the bus and call me in a panic about his car having been stolen.

The price the mechanic was quoting made me pull my phone away from my ear. I walked into work muttering about mechanics being daylight robbers.

Chapter 16

Lia

'How's the car sharing?' Beth asked, placing a takeaway vanilla latte on my desk. 'I haven't had an update for a few days.'

'Stella started today's journey by talking about her pet hates, namely: people tapping her on the shoulder, her mother –otherwise known as Nana Ruby – being in the pub when she's supposed to be looking after her grandchildren, and the man in her office who always eats a fish curry at lunchtime, which stinks out the entire room.'

Beth nodded. 'Stella's teenagers sound like a nightmare so I can see why Nana Ruby is hitting the pub.'

I recalled Stella talking about her mother's latest romance. 'Nana Ruby is a bit of a live wire. She's dating the chap who lives across the road from Stella. Apparently, Nana Ruby has a new boyfriend every month.'

Beth's eyes widened with surprise. 'Stella deserves some sort of medal for dealing with her kids and her mother.'

I continued. 'Stella asked us about our top three pet hates this morning.'

Beth took a sip of her cappuccino. 'Ooooh, I love things like this. I would have said... Jez, his mother, and all his ex-girl-friends.'

'You should have heard what Mateo came out with.'

Beth inspected her nails, which were sky blue and had tiny white daisies on them. 'Tell me.'

'Football, weddings, and mechanics.'

Beth grinned. 'I can see he's pressing all of your buttons.'

'Well, I'm glad I now know he hates football because that makes me feel better for not liking him. He's not someone I would ever be friends with.'

I watched Beth's perfectly sculpted eyebrows come together in a V shape. 'Hang on... you don't like football anymore, so why would that bother you?'

'I don't think I could be friends with someone who actually hated the game.'

Beth nodded. 'What about his piano playing, though?'

'I think the piano playing is the only good thing about him.'

'And his good looks?' Beth smirked at me.

'All right, he has two good things about him.' My face felt warm.

Beth took another sip of her coffee. 'I wonder why he doesn't like weddings or mechanics.'

I shrugged. 'I love mechanics so that's made me hate him more.'

'What were your pet hates?' Beth asked, hugging her coffee.

I held up my hand. 'I'm going to caveat what I said with... I shared my pet hates *after* he'd shared his, so you know the context.'

Beth's eyes widened. 'Tell me. I love passive-aggressive car-share drama. What did you say?'

I took a deep breath. 'Liars, curly-haired men, and people who hate football.'

A snort of laughter burst out of Beth. 'Brutal. What was his reaction?'

I thought back to Mateo's face after I'd informed him and Stella of my pet hates. I'd expected a look of defiance, but his eyes were wide, and his mouth was agape. 'He was definitely shocked by what I'd said.'

'Ignore him. Jez always gave me a shocked face. It's a ploy to make us feel sorry for them.'

I recalled Mateo talking about his cat Ghost, after my pet hate outburst, which had rendered both him and Stella silent for a good five minutes. He'd recently adopted Ghost from his best friends, apparently. 'He has a cat,' I added, 'so that's another good thing about him.'

'Careful,' warned Beth, 'you might end up liking him.'

Rolling my eyes, I switched on my laptop. 'Chances of that happening are zero, Beth.'

In the background, I could hear Beth pick up the phone. 'Hello, Beth, speaking... I'm sorry, I'm on my way to an urgent meeting. I'll get back to you tomorrow.' She swivelled around on her chair. 'I'm just going to make a TikTok with the handsome new guy who has started in the post room. I'm going to upload it and tag Jez.'

I turned my attention to Mateo. His dislike of weddings made me curious. *Was it a fear of commitment fuelling that pet hate, or did he just not want to get married?*

After getting some fresh air at lunch I came back to find Beth scrutinising her phone. 'What's up?'

'Jez's mum has posted on Facebook. I am trying to figure what's going on.' She sat back in her chair and stared into space.

'Are you still friends with his mum on Facebook after everything you've been through?'

Beth stared at me as though I'd said something daft. 'Lia, of course I am still Facebook friends with his mother. Without her Facebook feed I wouldn't know what Jez was up to.'

'What does it say?'

Beth frowned at her phone screen. 'She's proud of her son's inner strength. I can't think what he'd need to be strong about.' She let out a heavy sigh. 'He's now blocked me on all his social media. I couldn't tag him in the TikTok I made earlier, and I am clueless as to what's going on with him. How can I help her with him when he blocks me?'

My afternoon at work went at a glacial pace. I must have checked the time on my laptop a hundred times and wondered why the day was going so slowly.

Stella was waiting for us both. I'd come out of my office later than Mateo as Beth had accidentally spilled cold coffee all over her desk, and I helped her to clean it up. I was a little way behind him. As we made our way towards Stella's pink Mini, I tried to focus on Mateo's pet hates, and not get distracted by his broad shoulders and tanned neck. I noticed his limp had improved.

The sleeping man called Ed was awake in the back, which was a shock. He grinned at Mateo and me as we climbed into Stella's car. 'Hey, guys. I'm Ed.'

We all stared at him for a few seconds. We'd only ever seen him asleep.

With a flick of his floppy brown fringe, he continued. 'I know it must be weird seeing me awake, but I have had some very good news.'

I studied his face. His bloodshot eyes were set against two purple rings. He was clutching his phone, and his hand was trembling. 'Thanks Stella, for letting me sleep in the back of your car to and from work, and for not asking too many questions. I really appreciate it.'

She smiled at him. 'I don't blame you Ed for partying all

night long and burning the candle at both ends. You youngsters go out until dawn and then you have a full day of work to do. My daughter Lauren will be doing exactly what you're doing, mark my words.' She let out a nervous laugh. 'Lauren's currently trying to party all hours and pass her A levels. If that daughter of mine spent more time in her bedroom studying than out for all hours at parties, then she might have a hope in hell's chance of passing.'

His bushy brows knitted together, and he sat bolt upright in his car seat. With a frown he stared at Stella. 'Do you think I've been asleep because I have been out on the town every night?'

'I'm sorry, Ed. I just assumed...' She fiddled with her purple glasses.

His face softened. 'It's all right, Stella. I can see why you'd think that.' He turned his phone over repeatedly in his hands. 'My boyfriend Roman lives in California. Two months ago, we were in a car accident.' Ed took a deep breath. 'He's been in a coma, ever since.'

My jaw nearly hit the car floor in shock. Stella looked like she had been frozen in time, and Mateo's eyes widened dramatically. Ed placed his phone in his lap and began tapping his fingers lightly on the top of his knees. 'I was in the car with him when the accident happened, but I was unhurt, which has made me feel terrible. His family has been at his hospital bedside every day since it happened. I couldn't afford to stay out there so I had to come home.'

'Oh, Ed,' gasped Stella, 'I'm so sorry. That must be so hard.'

Ed nodded. 'His parents don't know he's gay. They think I'm just a friend. They tried to restrict the amount of time I was spending at his bedside.' He stopped to gaze out of the window. 'His sister goes to see him on an evening. She's always believed that hearing my voice would wake him. So, she started taking her laptop along. I get up at 2am every day to talk to Roman via

Amber's laptop. That's why I'm so tired. I can never go back to sleep once I have been talking to him.'

'You sit and talk to him through a laptop?' Stella asked, with a look of shock.

Ed nodded. 'It was a bit odd at first... me talking to my unconscious boyfriend. They'd done tests to show there was still brain activity, so I had a small glimmer of hope.'

In a flash, I was back at Joe's bedside in the hospice. He was on end-of-life care, and he spent much of his time asleep. I used to sit by his side, holding his hand, and talking about how I hoped he could make it until Daisy was born. Ed's face went blurry, and I could feel myself starting to tremble.

'Are you okay, Lia?' Mateo asked.

Nodding, I turned away to rummage in my handbag for a packet of tissues. They were not in my bag, and fat tears began to plop onto my bag. My sleeve stemmed a few, but soon it sounded like heavy rainfall. I felt a tap on my shoulder. Mateo's hand travelled between the seat and the door. Inside it was a small unopened packet of tissues.

'Lia – is everything all right?' Stella asked, as I tried to pull myself together. I sniffed and hid my face with my hair.

Ed continued. 'Anyway, I got a call an hour ago from Amber. Roman is showing signs he's waking from his coma.' He sniffed. 'Earlier he opened his eyes, and he seemed agitated, which is a sign. He's done the same again since, and he's moving his hand.'

'Oh, Ed,' gushed Stella, turning back to him, 'that's wonderful news.' She ran a hand through her red hair. 'That must have been so hard.'

Ed shrugged. 'I love that guy, and I'd do anything for him. It's going to be tough getting him back to full recovery. We still don't know whether there has been any brain damage.'

Stella nodded. 'I am going to keep everything crossed, Ed.'

'I'm going to fly back out to California soon Stella, so I won't be needing my spot in your car much longer.'

She nodded. 'I understand, Ed. You need to be with Roman. Just let me know when you're planning to leave. It's been a pleasure to have you in my car, even though we did refer to you as the *Sleeping Man.*' Starting the car she put the radio on. 'Right, let's get you all home. As we are in a celebratory mood I'm going to put on DJ Trish.'

'DJ Trish?' Ed asked.

Stella smiled and turned on the radio. 'Memory Lane is my favourite radio station. In the morning I listen to DJ Rick Carter.'

Ed shook his head. 'I've never heard of him.'

Stella sighed. 'DJ Rick Carter appeals to the mature listener, Ed. In the afternoon it's DJ Trish.'

'It's that drive home, and I am here with all your favourite eighties and nineties hits. Let's find out who has been messaging the show. A big shout-out to Joe, who has just asked his fiancée to marry him. She said yes so huge congrats, Joe.'

Sadness engulfed me. Reminders of Joe were everywhere. I pressed my face against the car window, cried quietly into Mateo's tissues, and tried to suppress the memories of Joe in his last few days.

After Stella had dropped us off on the high street, Mateo turned to me with a kind smile. 'You can keep the tissues.'

He held my gaze, and I found my dislike of him wavering slightly. Then I reminded myself of how he had made out to Stella that I spent my evenings at that fictitious hotel of his and still had not apologised, plus he hated football and mechanics.

'Goodbye, Mateo,' I said, with a cool tone, and walked away.

Chapter 17

Mateo

'I'm waiting for my wife and son Mateo to visit,' Dad announced to me. He was sitting in his chair, wearing his blue jumper and beige corduroy trousers. His grey hair was as chaotic as mine. A TV game show was on in the background, and several residents were staring blankly at the screen. An elderly woman was talking loudly to her friend in the corner of the day room about a cake her daughter-in-law had baked and brought in for her. I hid my smile when I heard her describing how eating it was "like chewing on a brick". She also added she'd never liked her daughter-in-law.

As always, Dad reached out his hand to me. 'Can you tell me when the bus is due?' Bending down, I stared into his blue-grey eyes, and he focused them on my face. I saw a flicker for a second. I liked to believe it was a millisecond of recognition. Under the heavy blanket of confusion was the person who I still loved dearly. I lived for that flicker.

Mum died when I was three years old, so it had just been me and Dad for over thirty years. I think that's why after four years I was still struggling without him.

My neck and shoulders ached as I sat beside Dad.

Polishing his car was my way of getting through a particularly stressful time. Each day, I dumped my bag in the hallway after work, and headed for the garage. There was something meditative about polishing. It calmed me down. Earlier, I had polished and thought about Lia. She must have been through something similar to Ed. Seeing her so upset had made me feel for her.

'Once my wife and Mateo arrive, we're going to the concert in the park,' Dad gushed, bringing me out of my head. 'There's a wonderful pianist we listen to.'

'That sounds nice,' I said, stroking his hand. 'I'm sure the bus will be here soon.' When he first started getting confused about things like dates, names of people and places I'd correct him, and when he started speaking from the past, I'd try to bring him back into the present. It was frustrating and upsetting for me, but I soon realised it was even more distressing for him. Now, I went along with whoever he thought he was.

Under my arm, I had the photo album I'd made for him when he started to become unwell. On my visits, I often brought it with me. Dad loved going through it, even though he couldn't recognise any of the faces. I took out the album and watched as he broke into a huge smile. 'What do you have there?'

I watched him stare at the front cover, which had a photo of his Spitfire Triumph. 'Wow – that's a beauty,' he exclaimed, giving me a burst of happiness. This was one of what I called, *Dad's special moments*. He didn't know it was his car, but he still marvelled at it, and that for me was everything. We worked our way through the rest of the photos, and he said the woman on the fourth page with her long black hair was pretty. It was Mum.

'Are you playing tonight, Mateo?' Sharon asked, coming to stand next to me once Dad had closed the album. She gestured to the crowd of excited faces behind her.

I got to my feet and nodded. 'Let's get this show on the road.'

Dad smiled and began tapping his hands on the arms of his wheelchair. He gazed up at Sharon. 'Can I go to the concert now? My wife and son Mateo will meet me there.'

I pushed Dad down the long corridor to the back room and parked him by the piano. Sharon was pushing Lia's father's wheelchair. I watched her park him next to Dad. He removed his headphones and nodded at me. 'Listening to you is the highlight of my day.'

'Thank you.' I smiled at him and noticed how alike he and Lia were facially. He had the same large brown eyes. As I arranged my sheet music, and Sharon helped more residents into the room, I thought about Lia. I sensed I wasn't her favourite person. I found myself hoping she would appear at the back room later.

I was about to start my final song on the piano, and there was no sign of her. *She'd probably changed her mind, after everything that had gone on between us.* I had steamrolled Lia into pretending she knew me from the hotel, and I did feel guilty. The coffee incident hadn't helped, and my pet hates only seemed to make her glare at me. *She could be texting Stella, to say she would look for another car share, and I would not get the chance to apologise and explain.*

'Ready when you are,' called out a tiny grey-haired lady at the front who always knitted throughout my songs. She threaded her lemon-yellow coloured wool across her knitting needle and nodded for me to start.

I closed my eyes for a second and gathered my thoughts. Taking a deep breath, I began to play and let the music soothe my anxious state. As I played, I thought about Ed talking to an unconscious Roman thousands of miles away, and how awful that must have been for him. I asked myself whether Natalie would have done the same for me. The answer filled me with instant sadness. *She would probably have been too busy with her gym classes and Zane.* I broke off from my train of thought, looked across at the doorway and there Lia was, holding an excitable Daisy. My heart leaped for joy at the sight of her. For a few precious seconds, I held her gaze. I was rewarded with a smile, and I forgot about Natalie. I promised myself I would make more of an effort with Lia.

Chapter 18

Lia

By the time I'd dropped Daisy off at nursery and walked up to the high street I found myself gasping for a vanilla latte. The barista recognised me. I was the customer who had knocked her handbag off the ledge, spewing its contents everywhere. He asked me whether a tiny blue car keyring was mine as he'd found it after clearing up. It was the keyring Joe had bought me when he'd bought Maria. I thanked the barista and held it tightly in my hand whilst he made my coffee. I slipped the keyring into my bag, picked up my latte, and tried to keep control of my emotions.

'Hello, Lia,' Mateo said, as I approached Stella's pick-up point.

I looked up with surprise.

'How was your dad last night?' he asked.

'He's a changed man since you started playing the piano.'

'Really? In what way – good or bad?'

'Good. Before you started playing, he used to sit in the corner and stick his headphones on,' I explained. 'Trying to get him to talk to me was a struggle. The stroke he had a few years

118

ago robbed him of so much. He's now bright eyed, talkative, and complimenting your piano playing.'

'That's nice.' I noticed how Mateo's face had lit up.

'Listen, Lia, about *The Traveller's Rest* thing...'

I took a sip and raised an eyebrow at him.

He stuffed his hands in his pockets and shifted his weight from foot to foot. 'Dad and his Alzheimer's is a sore point for me. Talking about it in front of strangers is hard. I feel like I am breaking myself into tiny pieces each time.'

His voice cracked, and I could sense his vulnerability.

He carried on. 'I lied initially to Stella, because I didn't want to answer awkward questions about Dad. Before his memory started to disappear, he was an amazing man. He drove a classic sports car and he was the life and soul of any party. It's so hard to talk about him now.'

I gave him a knowing nod. 'I can relate. Up until my dad had his stroke, he was an avid hiker at weekends, a lover of open-water swimming, and always had a holiday planned. Mum died when I was young so there's only ever been Dad. He never married again but had a string of female friends. The stroke replaced my energetic and life-loving father with a sad old man, who spends most of his time sitting in a chair by the window in the day room, listening to the radio on his headphones. It used to break my heart. It still does.'

'I'm sorry I made you lie for me,' Mateo said, gently. 'It was wrong of me, and I can't imagine what you must have thought. I wasn't trying to impress anyone with my rubbish hotel name.

There was a time I did play piano in a hotel, but that was years ago.'

'How's Ghost?' I asked, trying to distract myself from his eyes.

'Her resting bitch face scares me,' he said, making me laugh.

'Ghost is now in control. One day she will tie me up in my sleep and never let me escape. Do you have any pets?'

'A cat called Burrito. Daisy and I both report to him.' We smiled at each other as Stella drove up beside us.

'Thanks, Mateo,' I said, as he reached out to open the car door for me. His arm brushed against mine.

'Ed's not here,' announced Stella, 'he claims he's WFH, but I think he's sorting out his plane tickets for California. Roman has made a lot of progress, and earlier was whispering what Amber thought sounded like "Ed". I had a tiny cry over his text and had to reapply my mascara. That's why I am a few minutes late. Morning, both.'

Mateo opened the back door and climbed in. I was about to climb in the front when I noticed a book lying on the seat. It was titled *A Rogue's Rules for Seduction* by Eva Leigh. The book was full of Post-it notes, which made me giggle.

'Shove my latest read in the glove compartment,' said Stella. 'I could see myself in that book. I thought the heroine did a good job at taming that handsome rogue, but I would have done it in less time.' Stella sighed, which made me laugh again. Her clothes and hair were a bold burst of colour. She was wearing a vibrant red double-breasted blazer with gold buttons, a white top, and cream skinny jeans. In each ear were two giant gold hoop earrings, and around her wrist was a collection of gold bangles. We all listened to fifteen minutes of Oasis.

'How was Daisy this morning?' Stella asked, after the fifteen minutes of music had ended.

'Full of life, and she kept making silly faces at me.'

Stella grinned before switching on the radio for our daily dose of DJ Rick Carter and his breaking commuter news.

'Here's the latest Breaking Commuter News. Brace your-selves, listeners. Karen has emailed in to say a work colleague sat next to her on the train earlier and showed her a photo of her new

man. *Karen feels bad as the first words that came out of her mouth were not, "Oh, he's nice," – instead they were, "Oh, God, that's my ex-husband!" Our thoughts are with you, Karen. Mick fell off his bike, this morning. A handsome motorist got out to ask if he was okay, and according to Mick it was love at first sight. They've swapped numbers, listeners. Let's all think of Mick and his possible new love interest. Here's a great song from Ocean Colour Scene.'*

'Poor Karen,' murmured Stella, tapping away to the music. My phone bleeped to signify a message. Before I looked at it, I knew who it was from. It was a text from Angel.

> I'm not feeling very well. I'll give my next visit a miss. I don't want to spread any germs.

There wasn't time to give Angel much thought. A flashing warning light on her dashboard made Stella yelp. The car began to lurch towards the passenger side. 'Oh, God, I think have a flat tyre. I am so sorry, guys,' Stella said with a groan. She pulled onto the side of a residential street, behind a van, and shot out of her car to study her wheel. Mateo and I got out too.

'The breakdown van will take forever,' Stella groaned again. 'I don't need a flat tyre this morning. Mateo – do you know how to change a tyre?'

'Huh – ummm... I could try, but I can't remember the last time I changed one,' he said, shooting her a look of fear.

Joe's face appeared in my mind as Stella leaned against her pink Mini looking troubled.

'Have you got a spare wheel?' I asked, as she put her head in her hands.

Stella lifted her face and nodded. 'Yes, I have. I bought this car a few months ago. The guy I bought it from told me it had a spare, but I have no idea where it is or how to change it.'

I took out my phone and Googled her pink Mini. 'This is a 2006 Mini Cooper – right?'

Stella nodded.

'It should be underneath the car.'

Out of the corner of my eye I could see Mateo was staring at the church opposite. His face was white. It was like he'd seen a ghost.

Stella came to stand by me. 'You sound knowledgeable about cars, Lia.'

A memory of Joe waving at me to come and pay attention to his car tutorial on how to care for Maria came rushing back. 'My boyfriend Joe was a mechanic. He taught me all the basics with cars.' Before the emotion could take over, I knelt to inspect the flat tyre. Feeling underneath the wheel arch, I could feel a sharp nail protruding from it. 'Is the boot open?'

Stella nodded. Rising to my feet I went around the car, lifted the boot, and took out the black floor trim panel inside. Underneath, there was a handle and a tool to unlock the wheel carrier. Joe had told me that often with Mini Coopers, the spare tyre had to be lowered until the tyre tray could be pulled out from underneath. Carefully, I unlocked the handle and began lowering the tray with the black handle. Once the tyre was within reach, I brought it out. 'We will need to check the tyre pressure of this once I have fitted it.'

To change the tyre, I would need a car jack and a wrench. *This was the point where my great idea could fall apart.* Thinking on my feet, I stepped out into the road and saw a van driver parked in front of us. He was busy eating a sandwich. After knocking on his van window, he wound it down. 'Yes, luv?'

'This is a long shot, but do you have a car jack and a wrench? We have a flat tyre, which I can change, but...'

He began to cough and splutter on a bit of his fried sandwich. 'Sorry, what did you say?'

'A jack and a wrench?'

He cast me an odd look. '*You* need a car jack and a wrench?'

'I need to change a tyre.'

His shocked expression sent irritation coursing through my veins.

'Can *you* really change a tyre?'

My sarcasm decided to join the discussion. 'No, I just felt like wasting my time by asking you.'

After a few seconds, he tumbled out of his van. 'You are in luck as this is my mate's van, and he's a mechanic.'

Instinctively I glanced up at the sky. *Perhaps Joe was helping me in some way.* Excitement raced through my veins. 'Is your mate around?'

The man shook his head. 'He's broken his leg and is stuck at home. I'm borrowing his van.' After a lot of banging around in the back of the van he emerged with a wrench and a jack. 'Do you want some help?'

I smiled. 'Can I see how I get on? If I need a hand I will shout.'

Stella and Mateo watched me return to her car with shocked looks on their faces.

After taking a deep breath, I recalled Joe's tyre changing lessons, which he often did in our driveway or when he had work to do at the garage on a Sunday. I would get a coffee from the café across the road and would watch Joe work on cars. He'd always talk me through what he was doing, as he reckoned I would make a great mechanic.

Once I'd got Stella to apply the handbrake and turn on her hazards, I tasked Mateo with finding me a large stone or brick from the undergrowth. He came back with a heavy stone, which I used as a wedge behind the right rear wheel. I recalled Joe telling me to secure the opposite wheel to the one with the puncture as I needed to ensure the car didn't roll whilst jacked up. It was tempting to start levering the car up, but Joe always said it was safer to loosen the wheel nuts whilst the car was still on the ground. Using the wrench, I began loosening each nut by turning it anti-clockwise. Once I was happy, I positioned the jack in the right place. I could hear Stella whispering to Mateo, 'She looks like a pro,' as I jacked the car up. Unscrewing all the wheel nuts and gently pulling the wheel towards me, I glanced at the van driver, who was watching open mouthed.

Once the flat tyre had been removed, I rolled the spare tyre along, and lifted it against the hub. Everyone stood behind me in silence and watched as I made sure the wheel nuts were snug and tight on the new wheel. Once happy, I lowered the car to the ground using the jack. After a final check of the nuts, I turned to them with a grin.

'She's done it,' gushed Stella, who began jumping up and down on the spot. Brushing dirt off my black jeans I silently thanked Joe for his valuable wheel changing lessons.

The van driver looked like he was in a trance as I handed him back the jack and the wrench.

Mateo came alongside me as I admired my tyre change. 'Nice work, Lia.'

'Thank you, Mateo.'

He checked the time on his phone. 'I was hoping you'd be a bit longer with the tyre change. At this rate I will make the work meeting I didn't want to go to.' His cheeky grin made me smile.

As we drove away, Stella tapped me on the shoulder. 'Lia – you are a superstar.'

'Joe was the superstar,' I mumbled, and cast my attention out of the car window.

Stella placed her hand on my arm and whispered, 'It gets easier.'

'Does it?' I croaked.

She cast me a kind smile. 'It does.'

'How do you know?' I whispered back with watery eyes.

'I'm sensing I have been where you are. I see myself in you, Lia. Believe me it gets easier.' She smiled. 'Right, we need to get the tyre pressure checked, let's do that now.'

Chapter 19

Mateo

'Are you still planning to leave Stella's car share?' Claire asked, as I placed a pint of beer in front of her. It was Friday night. We were sitting in our favourite pub.

Harry and Claire had persuaded Claire's mother and father to babysit their seven kids.

I sat down and took a sip of my pint. 'No, I have changed my mind about Stella's car share. It still feels like chaos on wheels, but it's growing on me.'

'Would this decision have anything to do with the woman from your father's nursing home joining?'

'Lia is her name, and no, she wasn't the reason I changed my mind.'

Harry laughed. 'You're still a crap liar, Mateo.'

My face became hot. 'We're just friends.'

Claire playfully swiped Harry. 'Stop teasing your best friend.' She smiled at me. 'It's great to hear you're making new friends, Mateo. I thought you didn't like Stella, the lady who runs the car share?'

Stella's face appeared in my mind, her mass of crazy red hair and those ridiculously sized glasses. 'You must look past the chaos with Stella. When I first met her, I got so caught up in her whacky approach to life and parenting that I didn't see the kind and thoughtful person behind all that.' I recalled the caring look Stella had given Lia once we'd all climbed back in the car. Lia had been upset about something, and Stella had comforted her. She'd then put on some great music, and encouraged us to sing our hearts out for the rest of the journey. Later, during the return trip home, we were all still jubilant and singing away to The Beautiful South. Lia had glanced at me a few times, and I'd noticed her happy smile. The sight of it had sent a warm glow up my spine. *Stella had been right about good music being a form of therapy.*

'What about Lia?' Harry asked, with a mischievous smile.

'She's a nice person. Her little daughter is called Daisy. Her father is in the same nursing home as Dad's. She has a cat called Burrito, she likes The Beautiful South, and she can change a flat tyre.'

Claire grinned and held up her pint. 'Please can we toast Stella and Lia.'

Harry nudged Claire and laughed. 'You should ask Lia for lessons on car mechanics.'

I took a deep breath. 'Stella's car broke down opposite the church where I was supposed to get married last year.'

Harry reached out and tapped my arm. 'How did it make you feel?'

The memory of seeing the little white church again, and the urge to be violently sick, came rushing back to me.

'If it hadn't been for Lia changing the wheel, I don't know what would have happened.'

Claire changed the subject. 'Is there anyone romantically on the scene with Lia?'

I shrugged. 'I don't know. She's been through something painful recently; I'm thinking a possible breakup. I also know she doesn't live with Daisy's father.' Leaning back in my seat, I ignored Harry, who was grinning at me. 'For now, it's good being Lia's friend, and anyway, I'm not looking for anyone romantically.'

My best friend coughed into his hand, muttering 'rubbish' as he cleared his throat.

'How's the ankle?' Claire asked.

I stared down at my ankle. 'It must be better as I have stopped noticing it.'

'Have you heard anything more from Natalie?'.

I shook my head. 'Not since I deleted her text. There's this guy in Stella's car share who is called Ed, and he sleeps for the whole car ride.'

'You told us about him,' Harry nodded. 'As I said, Ed is a wise man.'

'Well, this week he woke up and revealed why he sleeps so much. His boyfriend has been in a coma in California, and Ed spends the entire night talking to him through his boyfriend's sister's laptop. He's been doing that for two months in a bid to wake him. This week Roman, his boyfriend, began coming out of his coma.'

Claire gasped. 'Oh God, I bet he wondered whether Roman would ever wake up.'

'As he told us about his love for Roman, I found myself thinking about Natalie. If she had been in a coma thousands of miles away, I would have done what Ed did for Roman. Would she have done the same for me?'

I felt Claire's hand on mine as I continued. 'For a few years, I was under her spell, and I would have walked through fire for her. I even put aside my dreams of being a songwriter and got myself a steady job in finance.'

Harry rubbed my shoulder. 'Come on, you can't dwell on ifs and buts. Natalie was a lesson.'

'What do you mean?'

'My advice is to stay in control of your own life. Even when you're in love.'

Claire stared at her husband. 'Plumber turned agony aunt now, are you?'

Harry shrugged and sipped his pint. 'It's true. My mother wanted me to go into the Army because Dad had been in the forces. She also wanted me to marry her best mate's daughter and not the rebellious, sexy, dirty minded Claire Golding from number forty-two.'

Claire rested her head on Harry's shoulder.

Harry continued. 'I've always wanted my own business, a large family, and I always wanted to marry Claire Golding. What I am saying, Mateo, is you have one life. Decide what you want to do and go for it.'

I recalled Stella saying something similar when she was talking to Alice.

'How's Ghost?' Claire asked. 'I know I ask you every half hour, but I am fond of her.'

I smiled. 'She's like my cat wife. At night we sleep side by side, and she has one paw over me the whole time. When I get home from work it takes her a good hour to forgive me for leaving her all day.'

Claire grinned. 'I love Ghost, bless her. She used to be cat mates with Dave, you know that giant ginger cat I fostered a few years ago.' The memory of Dave thumping me around the head with his huge tail would never leave me. 'How can I forget Dave?'

'Ghost and Dave always slept on the same shelf, and they followed each other around the living room. She wasn't the same after we found Dave a home.' Claire fiddled with the corner of a beer mat. 'I used to say to Harry that Ghost and Dave were in cat love.'

Harry returned with a round of drinks and rolled his eyes at me. We both grinned at Claire as she took her pint from Harry's tray.

Chapter 20

Lia

Daisy giggled as I carried her home from nursery. Ed had brought us doughnuts for the journey home from work as it was his last week in Stella's car share. It must have been the sugar rushing to our heads as we all sang our hearts out to Deacon Blue. I had saved some of my doughnut to share with Daisy as we trekked back to the house. I encouraged her to lick her sugar-coated fingers, which she did, and that produced endless giggles.

In my hallway, I removed her yellow jacket and smiled as she raced into the living room. After her tea I bathed and dressed her in clean sky-blue PJs with sunflowers on them. She looked so cute and smelt of blueberries due to the new bubble bath I'd bought her. I promised her a bedtime story. We made our way into her bedroom and sat on her pile of cushions. She snuggled into the crook of my head, and I pressed my lips against her silky blonde curls. 'I love you, Daisy, so much.'

Later, when Daisy was asleep, Dee called on FaceTime. Curled up on the sofa, with my legs tucked under me, I grinned at her as she appeared on my screen. Her black hair was piled on top of her head, and she was wearing an oat-coloured face mask.

In the background, I could see her partner Shona sitting in their kitchen, working on her laptop. Prior to Shona, Dee was seeing a guy who worked near her office. It wasn't really a relationship. She described it as a weekly hook-up. One night she went to visit him at his flat. On the way up to his floor she got stuck in a broken-down lift with Shona. They were stuck in the lift for six hours. When the engineers finally got the lift doors open, Dee and Shona were sitting in the corner of the lift kissing. Up until this point Dee had never been interested in women. That was seven years ago.

I like Shona because she stands up to Dee. My best mate likes to get her way a lot. Shona also brings out the best in her. She's a huge supporter of Dee's football, and she encouraged her to study for a degree via the Open University.

'Well?' Dee said, as I giggled at her face mask. 'How is the car share?'

'Good, and guess what? I changed a tyre last week.'

Dee grinned. 'No way?'

'Stella's car had a flat tyre, so I changed it. I was so proud of myself.'

'Lia, you are such a car queen. Do you remember that amazing football tour, the one where you and Hope scored a ridiculous number of goals...'

Dee never failed to amaze me with her skill at squeezing football into every conversation. I remembered Stella talking about how powerful Sagittarian women can be, which made me smile. '...The one where we had to stop on the motorway and have an emergency wee stop in the bushes, and we came out from the undergrowth to find some fella had pulled in beside our minibus with his flat tyre?'

I remembered back to my tyre change on the side of the

motorway. 'That was funny. Mitzi and Jazzy were hoping they could chat him up while I changed his tyre.'

Dee stared wistfully out of her window. 'We all had such fun on our football tours.'

'DEE,' I said, in an assertive voice. 'This convo is supposed to be about car sharing.'

She grinned. 'Okay, tell me about the other people in the car – do you get on with them?'

'Stella's great, and...'

Dee studied my face. 'I'm sensing the other person is... male?'

I laughed. 'If I said no, would you believe me?'

Dee shook her head with such vigour it made her hair escape from her clip and her face mask begin to crack. 'You have a look about you. There's a twinkle in your eyes.'

Joe's face from my "Joe Wall" caught my attention. The sight of him grinning into the camera tugged at my heart. 'I'm not planning to meet anyone else.'

'Whoa! Where did that version of Lia who was laughing a few seconds ago go?'

'What do you mean?'

Dee took a deep breath. 'I saw a glimpse of a new Lia when you were laughing. Her eyes were bright. The second you glanced at your "Joe wall", your face changed dramatically.'

I stared at Dee. 'It didn't.'

Dee grabbed her iPad with both hands. 'Joe didn't want you to stay single for him.'

'I want to as he was the best thing ever to happen to me.'

Dee pressed her face up against the screen. 'True, but he told you to move on – didn't he? I was there – remember?'

My mind whisked me back to the week before Joe passed away. I'd been practically living at the hospice as I didn't want to miss a single second with him. Dee and Shona had come to visit. Dee went to sit in the armchair next to his bed, and Shona gave me a huge hug. I remember Joe reached out and took Dee's hand. 'Dee, Lia must not put her life on hold for me. I want you to make sure of it. I don't want her to stay single for me.'

I'd leaned over and tapped him on the arm. 'Joe, don't talk like that.'

He'd turned to me with a serious expression on his face. 'I mean it, Lia. You and my unborn daughter deserve a life and happiness.'

Dee had nodded and gently squeezed his hand. 'I've got this. Don't worry.'

He looked directly at her. 'Take her out, Dee, and introduce Lia to new people.'

Back then, the thought of him not being around was too much for me, and tears began to bubble away. I felt his hand on my arm. 'I'm not going anywhere just yet so don't worry.'

'You've got to get Lia through labour, Joe,' laughed Shona, 'so don't think you're going anywhere soon.'

We'd all laughed, and Joe had managed a sleepy smile.

Dee took a slurp from an iced coffee beside her, which brought me back to the present. 'How's your dad?'

I smiled. 'He's good.'

Dee nodded. 'That's fab, Lia.' She took another slurp of her iced coffee. 'Mitzi texted me to say Alex has put up a post on the Gram to say that he's rethinking his plans to stay in New Zealand. She thinks he might be coming back to the UK.'

'Really?' *My heart ached. How I wished Joe was here to hear this. He would have loved to have had his best mate back in the UK.* I remember the day Alex broke the news he was leaving with Georgina. Joe had been quiet and sad for weeks afterwards. No matter how many times I took him out for a few beers, cooked him his favourite meal, bought him new running gear and organised for all his mates at the garage to take him away on a boy's weekend, he couldn't seem to muster a smile.

'She's hoping he comes back and coaches the Tigresses again. If he does you should come back to training.'

I groaned. 'Dee, I've told you, I'm not coming back to football. Anyway, Petra is the coach.'

Dee rolled her eyes. 'She's got no time for the second team. She pays more attention to training the first team. None of us can remember winning a game under her. I am serious, Lia, we've forgotten how to win a match.'

I shook my head. 'I'm sure you lot have won matches recently.'

'Lia, you have avoided every conversation about football since Daisy was born. I haven't brought up our dreadful performance. We've not won a game for ages. It's also not a laugh anymore like it used to be with Alex. He was so funny, and he was the one who made you team captain. Best decision ever. Alex believed in you, Lia. You had a great connection.'

'Alex and I were good friends because of Joe. That's why we got along so well.'

Dee swept back her black hair, which was in danger of sticking to her face mask. 'I remember at Joe's funeral, when he pushed your dad's wheelchair, and walked alongside you in the church. Alex is a good guy.'

A lump grew at the back of my throat, and I could feel my eyes becoming watery as I remembered that dark day.

'He went over to visit you when he came home to see Georgina's parents last Christmas.'

'Yes, he did pop in for a cup of tea with Georgina. I wasn't great back then. I just sat in a trance. They didn't stay long.'

Dee nodded. 'Mm hmm... If Alex does return, I think he will be good for you.'

'Why are you looking at me like that?' I saw something flicker across her eyes.

'Lia, I think you and Alex have always had a strong connection'.

'Yes, we did, because of Joe.'

Dee widened her eyes at me. She leaned closer to her screen and whispered, 'Don't tell Mitzi, but I always thought Alex had a thing for you.'

I gasped. 'No, he didn't, Dee. Alex and I were just good friends. Anyway, my friendship with Mitzi is important to me, and I'm not looking for anyone romantically.'

Dee's eyes twinkled with mischief. 'Aren't you, Lia? I saw your face light up like a lantern when I asked you about the other person in your car share.'

'He's called Mateo and last week I didn't like him. This week he's started to grow on me.'

'Oh, really?' Dee said, with a smirk.

I rolled my eyes. 'He doesn't like football.'

Dee asked Shona to put a slice of toast on for her before turning back to the camera. 'Well, they say opposites attract. Anyway, you won't have that issue with Alex.' She erupted into a fit of giggles.

'Dee, nothing will happen with me and Alex. Anyway, I'm not going back to football.'

Chapter 21

Mateo

It was Ed's penultimate day in Stella's car share. He'd decided not to go to sleep. After the fifteen minutes of music, Stella asked for an update on Roman. 'How's he doing?'

Ed smiled. 'He's making good progress. I'm so proud of him. He can respond to small commands like lifting his hand or wiggling a foot, and he can mumble names, but he has a long way to go. Roman will have to learn to walk again, and he might need some help with his speech.'

'How did you and Roman meet?' Lia asked, turning around to smile at Ed.

Ed ran his hand through his hair. 'We met on a beach just off the Pacific Coast Highway. Near Santa Monica. I was travelling and trying to get over my ex-boyfriend at the same time.'

'Wow – that sounds like a beautiful place to meet,' Stella gushed.

He nodded. 'The beach was spectacular. We first met in the sea though.'

'OMG a swim meet-cute,' gasped Stella.

'A what?' I asked.

Stella rolled her eyes in the mirror. 'Mateo – a meet cute is in all the romance films where the couple first meets.' She fiddled with her earring. 'That swim meet-cute would never happen to me. In my head, I am a graceful dolphin, but when I took the kids to Benidorm Lauren said I thrashed about like an angry sea lion. The trouble is, when you're in the sea and you look back at the shore to see your sixteen-year-old daughter cavorting with several Spanish boys, one of your fourteen-year-old boys nicking someone's inflatable beach ring, and the other fighting with the son from the German family who had their sun beds next to yours, you find yourself getting frustrated with the water and wishing you'd stayed on dry land to control your kids.'

I silently questioned Stella's use of the word, "control". From what I'd witnessed in this car share, she had none.

Ed laughed. 'Well, Roman saved me from drowning, and dragged me back to shore. Stella, I too was not blessed with aquatic abilities. I'm a dreadful swimmer and I should not have even thought about going for a swim.' He chuckled. 'I got caught in this riptide, which took me away from the beach. It was scary. Anyway, Roman appeared and he got me back to shore. The rest is history.' He sat up in his seat. 'Roman saved my life back then in so many ways. Look, I know this is a bit deep for ten past eight on a morning, but...'

For once in this car share, I was happy with going deeper. Ed had a good story to tell.

'Ed – as car share organiser,' said Stella, 'I think on a Tuesday we need to go deep in terms of a conversation because the weekend seems so far away. We need conversations like this to take our mind off it being only Tuesday.'

'Roman not only rescued me in the sea, but he also taught me to love someone again.'

'That's so sweet,' said Lia.

I noticed how different Ed looked; energised and full of excitement beside me. 'I do believe in destiny, guys. Roman and

I were exactly what the other needed. It was like we were destined to be placed in each other's paths. I was destined to scare myself to death by swimming in the sea, coughing up a lung, sinking like a stone, watching my short life flash before my eyes, and being saved by a handsome guy called Roman on that day.'

Stella pulled up at the traffic lights. 'I'm afraid my ex-partner was not what I needed all those years ago when I accidentally knocked his pint over him in the pub.'

'It doesn't always work,' explained Ed. 'Thanks to Roman I'm a changed person from the guy he met on a beach. You know, my father loves to make model boats out of tiny pieces of wood. When I was a kid, I would watch him meticulously glue each one and finally he would have his model. That's what Roman did to me. He picked up all the pieces of me and glued them back together, one by one.'

His words pinged around my mind until a memory from years ago unearthed itself. I was in a pub, frantically writing song lyrics onto the back of a beer mat, whilst Harry was laughing at me. Hot on the heels of that memory was the chorus to my old song, 'The Pieces of Us'.

Ed gazed out of the window. 'Roman knew I needed rebuilding before any romance happened between us. I respected him for that.'

Stella made an 'Awww!' sound. 'Tell us how Roman did that, Ed?'

'Well, he encouraged me to stop drinking, and to have some therapy about my ex-boyfriend. He cooked me good meals, listened a lot, took me to see some bands, and showed me what good fun surfing can be. The romance came afterwards. Once I felt all my emotional wounds were starting to heal.'

Memories of what happened after the wedding chaos came rushing back. Harry and Claire rebuilt me by dragging me over to theirs for good food, arranging Xbox competitions against Harry and Raff, taking me on long walks in the park with the kids, and no matter what state I was in they always took me to the pub every Sunday evening.

'I love that,' exclaimed Stella. 'Where do I find a Prince Charming who is good at model building?'

'What about Wayne?' I asked, recalling Stella telling me about her Jon Bon Jovi lookalike boyfriend.

Stella chuckled to herself. 'Wayne is good for posing on stage at the social club his rock band plays at on Friday nights, letting me run my hand through his long curly hair, and taking me on hot dates. That's it.'

Her phone started bleeping. 'Excuse me, everyone, I have an emergency call from my children, so I need to pull over and take it.'

Ed nudged me and whispered, 'I hope everything is okay.'

'What with?' I whispered.

'Her children. Their emergency call to Stella.'

Poor Ed, I thought, *he's going to wish he'd stayed asleep.*

'Mam,' a teenage male's voice boomed into the car.

'Luke, no bad language as I have people in the car. What's the emergency?'

'My TikTok has gone viral,' he shouted. 'Nana Ruby said to call you to ask whether I still need to go to my GCSE exams?'

Stella let out a yelp of frustration. 'Wait till I speak to Nana Ruby!'

'Mam, it's gone viral,' he shouted, making us all place our hands over our ears. 'Do you know what viral means?'

'Luke,' hissed Stella, 'go to your GCSE exams. NOW.'

'Nana Ruby said that if I am famous, I don't need qualifications.'

'Do not listen to Nana...' The phone went dead, and we all found interesting things to study inside the car.

Ed nudged me and mouthed, 'What the hell was that?'

Stella checked her hair in the mirror, rearranged her glasses, and started the car . 'Lia, put the radio on. I need a distraction from my family.'

'In Breaking Commuter News, Lizzie has texted the show to say she's forgotten to give her husband a lift to work. He has a broken ankle, so can't drive. She got distracted in the kitchen and left without him. Jack has emailed the show to say he accidentally cut his director up on the motorway earlier and is now in the office car park wondering whether his director recognised him. He is being interviewed by that director at 9am for a new job. Jack has phoned his Nan, to ask her opinion. Jack's Nan thinks it will be fine and the director was probably mouthing, "Be careful, Jack!" and nothing rude. Jack – good luck with the interview, and tell your Nan she's a superstar. Alice has texted in to say she's leaving on a jet plane for Australia, and she wants to send a big thank you to Stella and her car share. Blimey, Stella is becoming popular on my show.'

We all let out a cheer, and Stella beamed with pride.

Ed groaned. 'Does this mean I have to get DJ Rick Carter to shout-out Stella?'

We all laughed and chorused, 'Yes, Ed.'

'Are you doing anything nice tonight, Stella?' Lia asked.

Stella turned to Lia and grinned. 'Wayne is taking me out on his motorbike.'

'You've been on a motorbike before, Stella?' Ed asked.

'Yes, but never on the back of my boyfriend's bike. I've even got myself a new outfit for the date.'

'What sort of vibe are you going for?' Lia asked.

'Head to toe leather biker chick,' giggled Stella. 'Useful Kim is coming over later with my outfit.'

'Useful who?' Lia asked.

'Useful Kim. That's what everyone calls my friend,' explained Stella.

I let out what I'd thought was a quiet groan, and Ed glanced at me. In my mind I recalled Useful Kim: her blue hair, her jeep packed full of dodgy goods, and that day during my first week of car sharing when Stella's hair had looked like a giant tangerine. She'd used Useful Kim's hair dye, and something had gone wrong. Stella was tearful for the entire journey, and insisted I kept assuring her it wasn't that bad, I had a hunch the motorbike gear would cause issues.

'She's one of those people who can get you whatever you need.' Stella pulled into her normal drop-off point.

'Does Useful Kim do travel rucksacks?' Ed asked. 'I need one before my flight at the weekend.'

I tried to get Ed's attention by shaking my head, but it was too late. He was a nice guy, and even though I was only going on a hunch, I didn't think he should resort to buying Useful Kim's goods. Stella was already speed-dialling Useful Kim.

As Lia and I got out of the car I tried to get Ed's attention.

'What are you up to, Mateo?' Lia asked, casting me a puzzled look.

'Oh... nothing. I have seen some rucksacks on offer in town, so he doesn't have to bother with Useful Kim.'

Lia grinned at me. 'You're up to something. I know it.'

As we walked, she kept laughing at me. It was so nice to see her happy against the backdrop of an azure sky and golden sunlight. The image stayed with me all day.

Chapter 22

Lia

Struggling to get Burrito through the door of the vets and into the waiting room, along with a grizzling Daisy and her buggy, was a tougher challenge than I'd anticipated. Burrito was a heavy chap, and he didn't take kindly to being hauled to the vets in a giant cat basket.

Before, I would stick Burrito in Maria and nip up to the vets whilst Dee looked after Daisy. It was so much easier carrying him inside as he liked being held. Due to his size, other cats and dogs didn't worry him in the waiting room. He would sit on my lap and give other animals death stares. Most of the time dogs didn't know what to make of Burrito, and kept away from him. All this was much easier than lugging him up the road in the drizzling rain with a screaming Daisy in her buggy. Burrito also hated being caged, so our journey was punctuated with hisses and growls. All of which made Daisy cry.

Bursting into the vet's reception room with Daisy, Burrito's cage swinging precariously by my side, I had to take a few seconds to compose myself. Burrito let out a ferocious growl, and the receptionist cast me a concerned glance. I cursed myself for not booking his vaccination on a weekend when I could have persuaded Dee to run us up in her car.

Glancing around the vet reception I saw that it was empty except for a man on his hands and knees on the floor, trying to encourage a grey cat to come out from underneath the row of plastic seats. His curly dark hair looked familiar. 'Mateo?'

Bumping his head on a seat he turned around. It was Mateo, and I noticed a relieved look flash across his face. He got to his feet. Daisy stopped grizzling, and pointed at the grey cat. 'CAT!'

Burrito was now going crazy, and headbutting the door of his cage. A piercing growl mixed in with a 'Miaow!' made Mateo and I jolt. He stared at my cage. 'What on earth have you got in there?'

'Burrito – the cat who thinks he's a dog. What's happened?' I asked, placing Burrito's cage away from the other cat, who was roaming behind the chairs. Bending down, I peered at Mateo's cat. She was so pretty with blue-grey fur, giant paws, and a beautiful face. 'You must be Ghost.'

He nodded. 'My best mate told me not to open the cage in the reception room.'

I smirked at him. 'You listen to your best friend then?'

Mateo shook his head. 'Ghost was giving me these loving eyes. She made me feel sorry for her so I thought she could sit on my lap and look pretty.'

With a laugh, I knelt and held out my hand towards Ghost. Her purr sounded like a small engine. She rubbed her furry head against my hand.

'She refuses to come out from behind the chair,' Mateo explained, as Daisy started to screech. She was clearly desperate to join in the fun instead of being strapped into a buggy.

'Have you tried moving the chair, lifting her up, and sticking her back in her basket?' I asked, glancing back at Mateo. He nodded, and made a facial expression like he was in pain. 'She doesn't want me to do that...'

With a laugh I returned to giving Ghost some love. 'Mateo, you can't give her a choice. She must go back in her basket.'

'She glares at me.'

I tried to stifle a laugh, but it escaped. 'Who is the boss in your relationship?'

Without hesitation he said, 'Ghost.'

Burrito let out a low grumble, and Mateo went to check him out. 'Blimey, he's massive, Lia.'

'He's a big boy,' I exclaimed. 'The vet reckons he's the biggest cat he's ever seen.'

Mateo crouched down and stared at Burrito. 'He looks very familiar.'

'Really?'

Mateo nodded. 'My best mates Harry and Claire used to foster unwanted cats. Claire gave up on fostering, as it all got too much, so she ended up adopting about six cats. Harry and Claire live on the other side of the city. Ghost was one of their cats. They once had a cat just like Burrito.'

'Unlikely to be the same cat if they live on the other side of the city. Right, where's Ghost's basket?'

Mateo dragged it to the side of me. In a few seconds I had grabbed Ghost, and plopped her gently into the basket. There was a hiss or two, but I took no notice.

As I got to my feet, I found myself brushing against Mateo. We were standing closer than intended. Daisy distracted us by babbling, and the moment was gone.

The vet came out of her examination room to call in Ghost.

'Good luck,' I said, as Mateo carried in Ghost's basket.

The receptionist smiled at me. 'Thank goodness you got that situation under control. I was struggling not to march over and put that cat in its basket myself. I've never seen such a performance.'

'He's a new pet owner,' I said, soothing Daisy by pushing her buggy back and forth.

By the time Mateo and Ghost came out Daisy was out of her buggy, sitting on Burrito's cat basket, babbling away to herself.

'Do you want me to watch your buggy?' Mateo asked.

'Would you?' I said, hoisting Daisy onto one hip and grabbing Burrito's cage. 'That would be great. How was Ghost?'

'She hates me,' mumbled Mateo, staring down at an angry face peering out of her basket.

'Oh well, it's been nice knowing you,' I said with a giggle, and staggered in to see the vet.

When I came out Mateo and Ghost's baskets were on chairs, and he had Daisy's buggy by the side of him. 'How was Burrito?'

'Well, he's going to be really annoyed with me when he gets home; the vet wants him to lose a few pounds. He scares me when I'm late putting his food down so I think he might pin me down until I give in to feed him.'

'Nice knowing you too, Lia.'

Once outside the vets I was filled with relief as it had stopped raining. Mateo and I said goodbye and walked away in our separate directions, clutching our cat baskets, and in my case also pushing Daisy in her buggy.

'Do you want a hand?' Mateo called out, rushing back towards us.

My old independent streak made me shake my head. 'There must be an easier way. All I need is a cunning plan.'

He watched me as I took Daisy out and attached some reins to her, which she loved. I then placed Burrito's basket in the buggy and did what I could to strap him in. He wasn't best pleased, and hissed at me, but it was a good plan.

Mateo grinned. 'I like your plan. Well, have a safe trip home.'

I walked off with Daisy toddling beside me whilst I pushed an angry cat. At the corner of the street, I turned back, and Mateo had stopped to look at me. We both gave the other an awkward wave, and hurried away.

Chapter 23

Mateo

'Mateo, you do realise I am on the school run right now, which involves seven children, seven lunch boxes, four PE kits, a lot of chaos and a mental breakdown?' Claire shouted down the phone at me. I was in the café, waiting for my coffee before I went to meet Lia and Stella.

Lia's cat Burrito had been on my mind all night. He looked exactly like the cat Harry and Claire had fostered called Dave. I remembered staring into those huge eyes years ago and hearing Harry joke that his cat would guard the house against burglars. The urge to call Claire and check was strong. It never crossed my mind that she was on the school run. In the background I could hear a noisy school playground, a father yelling at his son to stop hitting his school friends, and a child crying about their lost PE kit.

'I know, sorry,' I said, tapping my card and paying for my coffee. 'This is important.'

Claire groaned. 'Reggie, please put your coat on, and don't drag it across the floor. Mateo, how important is this query – on a scale of one to ten?'

'Nine point five.'

'Go on then. What is it?'

'Dave the cat. Do you remember which home he went to?'

'Mateo, do I sound like someone who can remember, during the bloody school run, who a cat was adopted by three, maybe four years ago? I couldn't even remember that my fourth son was on a school trip today and needed a signed permission slip.'

She chuckled down the phone. 'Mateo, I will text you later, goodbye.'

'Morning,' Lia called out as I approached Stella's meeting point. 'Did you and Ghost make it home safe?'

'We sure did. Ghost is still not talking to me,' I chuckled. 'She glared at me out of the window as I left this morning. What about the big guy?'

Lia giggled. 'He spent the night sulking under a bush, and refused to come inside. This morning he must have forgiven me as he came in for his breakfast, but when he saw his new diet portion, he was not happy at all.'

'Poor Burrito.' I took a sip of my coffee and we grinned at each other.

'It was a nice surprise seeing you in the vets last night,' she said, twirling a strand of coppery red hair around her finger. I spotted Stella's pink car coming up the high street and my heart sank. *I wanted more time alone with Lia.*

'Wonder how Stella's date went last night,' Lia muttered as we watched a thunderous looking Stella pull up alongside us.

'Morning, both,' Stella grumbled as we climbed in.

After the fifteen minutes of music, Stella turned down her Oasis album. 'Ed, how's Roman?'

Ed nodded. 'Still the same, but all good. I can't believe this is my last car share.'

'We're going to miss you, Ed,' said Stella.

I leaned across and shook Ed's hand. 'Glad we got a chance to get to know you, mate.'

Ed grinned. 'The feeling's mutual.'

'I'll miss you, Ed,' said Lia, 'it won't be the same looking in the back and not seeing you asleep.' Ed laughed.

'How was your date?' Lia asked Stella.

I noticed Stella glancing at Ed in the mirror before answering. 'Great,' she said.

'Did your friend get you the outfit you wanted?'

Stella squirmed in her driver's seat. 'Sort of.' My suspicion was that Useful Kim had either not delivered Stella's date outfit, or it had not been what Stella wanted.

Ed piped up from the back. 'I can't believe your friend Kim has managed to get hold of that rucksack I wanted.' He smoothed his unruly brown hair. 'She's quicker than Amazon.'

Stella nodded and I noticed she was gripping the steering wheel a little tighter.

I needed to change the conversation. 'So, Ed, when do you fly?'

'Sunday. I'm looking forward to it, although Amber has told me not to get my hopes up; Roman is still very ill and he has such a long way to go.'

'How long will you stay over there?'

'My father is American, and I was born over there, so I have dual nationality,' he explained. 'My mum is over here in the UK. I can stay longer over there in the States, and I have handed in my notice over here, so I've not got any UK commitments. My priority will be Roman.'

Lia turned around. 'Does his family know you are going over?'

Ed nodded. 'Yes, they still think I am a friend though. I'm cool with that. Amber is letting me crash at her place, so everything is going to work out. All I need now is my new rucksack, and I can start packing.'

I could hear Stella muttering something under her breath.

'Did you say something Stella?' I asked. She glanced over her shoulder at me and gave me what can only be described as a death stare.

My phone bleeped. It was a text from Claire.

Dave was adopted by someone called Joe Carter, four years ago.

There was a second bleep, and a photo of Dave appeared on my phone. There was no mistake – it was Burrito. *Who was Joe, and was he still in Lia's life?*

We all got out on the high street to say goodbye to Ed. Stella hugged the life out of him, which at first made me roll my eyes. I muttered away to myself about how Stella should rename herself Oprah. It was then that I noticed Lia staring at Stella and Ed. I followed her gaze and saw that Ed was wiping his eyes, and Stella was holding out tissues to him. 'Roman needs you to be strong. It's going to be hard, seeing him emerging from his coma, but he needs you so much.' She took out her phone. 'You have me on WhatsApp, so message me if things get tough. Ed, you're not on your own.' He pulled her into another hug. 'Stella, your support and friendship means so much to me.'

She placed her hands on his shoulders. 'Ed, in life it doesn't matter where you're going, it's who you have beside you.'

The way Stella spoke to an emotional Ed reinforced my growing belief that Stella was more than a crazy car share lady with ridiculously sized glasses, and chaotic children. She was becoming a good friend to us all.

Chapter 24

Lia

I t was coming up to my one-month anniversary of joining
Stella's car share family. In that time, I'd got used to sitting
inside a Mini again, and I was no longer haunted by the loss of
Maria. Without Ed the car share journeys became a daily
mixture of chaotic calls from Stella's children, singing at the top
of our voices to great music, hearing tales from Stella's love life,
and trying to get shout-outs from DJ Rick Carter on the radio.
Stella didn't advertise for someone to replace Ed, so it was just
us for a few weeks. I still hadn't spoken about Joe. Neither Stella
nor Mateo had probed, and I liked them so much more for that.

Meeting up with Mateo on the high street, sharing funny
stories about our respective cats before Stella arrived, and travelling to work whilst singing along to the sounds of the eighties
and nineties had become something I looked forward to. We did
the same on the way home. In the evenings when I went to visit
Dad I would stand and listen to Mateo play his piano while
Daisy danced.

Dee came over most weekends, and she began to share tales
from football training. I resisted at first, but over time I found
myself grinning at her joking about Mitzi complaining non-stop

about Petra, Flo's dreamy state about her new love interest, Hope getting faster despite slacking at training, and Gee getting angrier in her goal net. Talk of Alex had subsided, as there had been no posts on his Instagram, and Mitzi had met someone new on Tinder. Although Dee reckoned this Tinder guy was a distraction while she was busy manifesting Alex's return.

Everything changed with an announcement on DJ Rick Carter's radio show. It was a damp and grey Monday morning, and we were all a little irritable. Stella had waited up half the night for her daughter to come home from a party, Mateo had been up late playing his piano, and Daisy had cried a few times in the night, too. After fifteen minutes of music, Stella had switched on the radio.

'*Listeners, this is a change to our usual slot as I need your help. Bert, eighty-three, has messaged my show in the last few minutes to say he's due to marry his childhood sweetheart Violet, eighty-three, in the city centre at the registry office at 9am. The issue he has is that his taxi has broken down, and he's stranded on the side of the road. Violet had a lift with her daughter and is already in town. Is there anyone out there who can help Bert?*'

Stella and I looked at each other. We both knew we had to help. Within a few seconds I had tapped out a text to the radio station and pressed 'send'.

Five minutes later, Mateo tapped me on the shoulder from the back. 'I've been thinking. Do you think we should help Bert?'

Stella laughed. 'You need to be faster than that, Mateo. Lia's already texted the show.

I turned around to grin at him. 'We're going to save Bert's wedding.' The look on Mateo's face made my smile fade. In those few seconds before my phone started vibrating, I stared into his eyes, and I saw a look of vulnerability and pain. There was no time to think about what I'd seen. The researcher from the radio show was calling me. DJ Rick Carter had picked us to help Bert. 'Stella,' I said, putting the researcher on speakerphone. 'We've been picked to rescue Bert, and save his wedding.'

We approached the broken-down taxi. The driver was having a cigarette whilst leaning against a lamppost. A little old man beside the driver was waving at us. I got out as soon as Stella pulled in so that he could sit in the front. 'Ah,' he gushed, 'my pink chariot awaits.'

'Bert, get in and buckle up,' shouted Stella. 'We've got a wedding to get to.'

Bert had fluffy cloud-like white hair, twinkly blue eyes, and a warm smile. He was wearing a smart, dark pinstriped suit with a gold tie. As Stella sped off, he turned to Mateo and me in the back. 'It's lovely to meet you all. Thank you for rescuing me.'

'No problem, Bert,' I said. 'Glad we could help. Are you a fan of DJ Rick Carter's show?'

Bert shook his head. 'It was Violet's daughter who is a big fan. She's always trying to get her name read out on the way to the school she teaches at. I think she has a soft spot for the DJ.'

Stella tapped Bert on the shoulder. 'Tell Violet's daughter to join the queue for DJ Rick Carter. I'm at the front. He's what I call a hot silver fox.'

Bert looked at her and ran a hand through his hair. 'Like me then?'

We all laughed. Sitting close to Mateo in the back of the car was electrifying. His citrus aftershave made my nostrils go wild, and he was wearing a crisp white shirt, which made him look even more tanned. I could see his defined arm muscles straining against the shirt, and I couldn't help but notice his beautiful hands. His fingers were long and slender, and his nails were well trimmed. Mateo smiled and I felt something stir inside me. It was like he had awoken something in me that had gone into forced hibernation. My Joe related guilt tried to counteract the warmth spreading over my body by wrapping itself around me and squeezing the air out of me... but what struck me was that the guilt didn't feel as powerful as it had done when I had first met Mateo.

On the way to the city centre, Bert relaxed in the front of the car. Stella asked him about Violet. 'She is still, in my eyes, the pretty girl from years ago, who served me in her father's sweet shop with her silky black hair tied up with a red ribbon, and her smile that was full of mischief and excitement,' he explained. 'I have been in love with Violet since I was a boy. The first mistake I made was listening to my mother about how a wild girl like Violet, wouldn't make a good wife. The second mistake I made was allowing my mother's friend to set me up with her daughter Esther. Don't get me wrong, I was a good husband, and we have three lovely children and six grandchildren. Sadly, Esther died ten years ago. Violet left town to go work in a posh hotel in London after I'd started courting Esther, and we never saw each other again until last year.' He took out his handkerchief to mop his brow. 'I have a wonderful granddaughter, who took me to London to see the sights, and as we were admiring Buckingham Palace, someone tapped me on the shoulder and said, "Hello, Bert." It was Violet, who was sightseeing with *her* daughter. We swapped addresses and phone numbers. We spoke on the phone every day. At Christmas, I asked her to marry me.' He smiled. 'I realised I didn't want to spend any more time away from her.'

We were all silent. He shook his head. 'If I have any advice for young folk like you three–'

Stella interrupted him. 'Bert, I'm so glad you've included me in the "young folk" category.'

He grinned at her. 'You're not a day over twenty-five – are you?'

'Bert, you are always welcome in my car share,' sighed Stella.

We all giggled and Bert continued. 'God rest Esther's soul; she was a wonderful wife and mother. I did love her dearly, but I never forgot the love I had for Violet.'

The rush hour traffic was heavy. I could see Bert checking his watch. *We were in danger of missing his wedding.* Mateo piped up beside me. 'Stella, I know a secret route into the city centre. You turn off at the lights and keep going.'

Stella nodded. 'Mateo, please be navigator.'

He smiled. 'I can't believe I am saying this, but you might want to get into racing car driver mode.'

With Mateo's help Stella managed to get Bert into the part of the city nearest the registry office with six minutes to go.

Bert beamed at all of us. 'I can't thank you all enough.'

'It was a pleasure, Bert,' gushed Stella. 'Have a wonderful day with Violet.'

'Oh, I will,' he beamed.

We watched him walk in the direction of the registry office. As Stella was turning the car around, I spotted a schoolgirl dressed in a maroon football shirt, gleaming white shorts, maroon footie socks pulled up to her knees, and trainers. Under her arm was a football, and over her shoulder was her bag. The city stadium was nearby, and I wondered whether she was going to a youth football event. She caught my attention. It was like seeing a younger version of me. I was whisked back to the non-uniform days at school when me, Hope, Dee, Mitzi, and Gee would wear football kits to school. The boys would laugh at us, but we didn't care. We'd ask them for a game, and as they all fancied Hope, we'd end up scoring a lot of goals.

The girl looked amazing. In a few seconds my love and passion for the game came back to me. I wanted to get out of the car and join whichever football event she was taking part in. Tears rushed to my eyes at the sight of the girl. Mateo was staring at me. I could feel his eyes on the back of my head. Stella drove off in the opposite direction, and I watched the girl get smaller and smaller. As I turned back to Mateo he stared at my face. 'Are you all right?' he asked, softly.

Joe's face appeared in my mind. Running with a football would remind me of him, kicking a football would make me think Joe was in the crowd watching me, and scoring a goal would be so painful as I would want to go hug him. The flood-gates opened. Stella spotted me in her driver's mirror. 'Lia – you, okay?'

I wiped my eyes. 'I'm fine. It's probably all the emotion with helping Bert.'

Mateo placed his hand on my arm. 'You don't look fine.'

Stella pulled into a side street, and turned around in her seat to face me. 'Talk to us.'

'I've played football all my life... I gave it up for good when Joe... when my fiancé died,' I sobbed.

'I'm so sorry,' Mateo whispered.

'Lia, I'm sorry too.' Stella cast me a friendly smile.

A hot tear trickled down my cheek. 'Football reminds me of Joe.'

Stella reached over and rubbed my arm. 'Hey – it's okay, Lia. I understand.' She grabbed a packet of tissues from her door and handed them to me.

'I saw a girl in her footie gear when we dropped Bert off.' Tears streamed down my cheeks. 'Football was a huge part of my life,' I sobbed.

'Who did you play for?' Mateo asked.

'The Tigresses. They're a local women's team. We were not

professional. Just a group of women who enjoyed playing football.'

He nodded. 'I have heard them being mentioned on the radio.'

Stella reached for my hand, and covered it with hers. 'I'm sensing you've just realised you still love football?'

It was like her words had cracked me open like biting into a strawberry cream in a chocolate box. In a few seconds, I became a gooey and tearful mess. Mateo reached out and placed his warm arm around my shoulders. Without hesitation, I leant against his broad chest. He smelled so good, and I could hear the rhythmic beat of his heart.

'Lia – would Joe have wanted you to stop playing?' Stella asked, rearranging her glasses.

I shook my head, and sat up quickly at the sight of Mateo's damp shirt where my wet cheek had been. 'No, he wanted me to keep playing, but once he'd gone it was so hard.'

'How long ago did Joe die?' Stella asked.

'I was a few weeks away from giving birth to Daisy when he passed away.'

Stella cupped my hand with hers. 'Lia, I'm so sorry. You've been through hell. I've been where you are right now. I lost my first love Tom, so I know how it feels.'

I stared at her. 'Really?'

She nodded. 'He died suddenly when Lauren was three months old. He was her dad. It was an undiagnosed heart problem. He collapsed whilst playing rugby. Tom and I were both twenty-five.'

'I'm so sorry,' I said, placing my hand over Stella's. Her eyes had become pink and watery.

'Lia, I want you to know it did get easier. What worked for me was talking about it, and getting all the dark thoughts, painful memories and anger out into the open. Don't do what I did and allow grief to take you hostage.'

I gulped and fiddled with the ends of my hair. 'What do you mean?'

'I locked myself away in my tiny council flat with baby Lauren. Every day, I closed all the curtains, and sat in darkness. It was all I wanted to do in my new world without Tom. I stopped seeing my family and my friends. A neighbour did my food shopping, and I became a hermit.' She smiled. 'Lauren has always loved night-time. As a child, she would never sleep at night. I think she got used to a darkened world.'

Staring down at my hands, I reflected on what she'd said. *Why did her words about grief taking her hostage resonate with me? Had I been doing the same?*

Stella sat back in the driver's seat. 'Grief can make you so sad you end up building a little world for yourself in all that pain when you should be letting it go.'

She reached over to me. 'Find your version of Roman, who will help to rebuild you.

Right now, you are a million pieces of tiny wood. You are one of the boats Ed's father is about to make. Find someone who will pick up all your scattered pieces and glue you back together.'

'I don't need anyone to rebuild me,' I muttered.

Stella turned to face the windscreen, and put her seatbelt on. She looked at me through the rear-view mirror. 'You have been waiting for your old self to return for too long. You must return to football, Lia.'

The thought of returning to football stayed in my head. It was still there after I'd finished work and travelled home with Stella and Mateo. After I'd put Daisy to bed I sat on the sofa, and allowed myself to think about football – properly – for the first time in a very long while.

Chapter 25

Mateo

Lia took up permanent residence in my mind. When she leaned in to me in the back of Stella's car, I noticed her hair smelt of berries, and it brought back happy memories of Dad taking me blackberry picking when I was a kid. He'd say things like, 'Be careful, Mateo, don't squash them,' and, 'At this rate we'll be having berry fruit juice,' as I clutched my plastic box and grabbed at the juicy fruit.

She had rested her head against my chest and had allowed me to encircle her with my arms. I couldn't remember ever having such a tender moment with Natalie. I had met my ex-fiancée in a bar. She'd stood out with her blonde hair, legs which seemed endless, and piercing icy blues. That was the night I'd been drowning my sorrows over Dad's Alzheimer's diagnosis. All I wanted to do was block his rapidly declining health out of my head, and find something or someone to focus on. Natalie quickly became a distraction for me as Dad's memory was slowly eaten away. Natalie was good at helping me numb my pain. She loved to party, eat out at fancy restaurants, and go on expensive holidays. However, she rarely helped me with Dad or came to visit him in his home. She was keen to fit our lives into managed compartments. Her compartments were exercise, her wardrobe, and her social life. Mine were bringing in the money so we could live in a ridiculously expensive house, playing my piano when she was out as she hated it, and Dad. We never wandered into the other's compartments. The only deep conversations we had were when she had an idea about our next long-haul holiday destination, or how much money I could be earning if I went for a promotion.

Looking down at Lia's trembling shoulders, and feeling her damp cheeks on my arms had made me pull her closer to me and try to take away her pain. This was new to me. Something I'd never gone through with Natalie. I couldn't recall a time when Natalie was upset and needed consoling.

Later that day, I'd gone home in a Lia fuelled daze, and started to compose my first piece of music in three years. For the first hour, I'd alternated between crying and playing. It was surprisingly cathartic; later, I slept like a log for ten hours.

Lia didn't mention football for another few days. Stella and I left her to stew in her thoughts whilst we discussed our favourite biscuits to have with a cup of tea, our favourite UK seaside destinations, and our favourite Wham! and George Michael hits.

Stella was growing on me. She was still chaotic, and at times unable to control her teenage children or her mother, but I was starting to see how much she cared for others. I also felt guilty for judging her so much in the early days.

Lia was at the bus stop before me, sipping on her coffee as I crossed the road to meet her. 'Hello, Mateo,' she beamed, which made my heart break into an early morning gallop. 'How was your weekend?'

'It was all right. I have been composing a new song.' I'd

spent several hours writing some new lyrics and playing around with a melody.

Her eyes twinkled. 'Will I get to hear it at Cherry View nursing home?'

'You might do... if you're lucky.'

'Do you write a lot of your own stuff?'

'I stopped writing music for three years so this song I've written is my first for a long time.'

She looked genuinely interested in what I had to say, which made my heartbeat go even faster. 'Oh, why?'

'Well...' I paused. Did Lia really want to hear why I had stopped playing the piano and writing music? Up until now I'd avoided any discussions about my past life, the wedding or Natalie. My mind brought back a series of memories from writing and creating my new song. I'd played with such intensity, and the process of creating a beautiful song had filled me with warmth and happiness all weekend. The world had become a lot brighter.

Lia's expectant look brought me back to reality, and it was then a thought occurred to me. *Lia and I were similar, in that we'd both given up something we loved during a dark time in our lives. We'd both shut out our passion, and punished ourselves even further.* I held her gaze and promised myself to get her back to the sport she loved. 'I gave up the piano when someone who I thought loved me, broke my heart. I told myself I could never go back to playing it.'

Lia's doe eyes widened.

'I returned to playing the piano a few weeks ago and it's been the best thing I have ever done.'

'I haven't been back to football since Joe got diagnosed.' She nudged a loose stone with the toe of her white trainer. 'I thought I could forget football, but it's...'

'Part of you,' I whispered.

She nodded. 'Yes, it is part of me, and it's still got a hold over me.'

'Music is a part of *me*,' I explained, rolling up the jacket of my linen suit. 'If you looked at my blood you would see musical notes running through it.' A faint smile from her spurred me on. 'Looking back now I should have carried on playing the piano through the shit times instead of letting it gather dust.'

'Would it have helped?' she asked.

I nodded. 'Without a doubt – yes. Lia, I think football will help you.'

We stared at each other for what felt like an eternity, and to my surprise she stepped closer to me. Stella's horn made us both jump. As we turned to face the road, Lia's fingers touched my hand for a few beautiful seconds.

Stella had a teenage girl sitting alongside her who resembled the girl from the shopping centre car park. This must be the infamous Lauren. When Stella pulled up it was clear she and Lauren were arguing in the car. Lauren had poker-straight black hair, the longest eyelashes I had ever seen, and big dark eyes. As Lia and I climbed into the back we noticed Stella's hair gelled back, and it made her look fierce. She grimaced at Lia and me. 'I've entered my eighties hair era.' Before we could reply she glared at her daughter. 'Lauren, why are you wearing a belt instead of a skirt for school?'

With a flick of her black hair, Lauren glared at Stella. 'It's a skirt. Not a belt.'

Stella fiddled with her glasses and peered at her daughter's skirt. 'Where is this skirt? I can't see it.'

'I'm seventeen, Mam. I can wear what I want. Stop being narky! It's not my fault about what happened at the weekend.'

As Stella pulled away from the kerb I reached out and placed my hand next to Lia's on the back seat.

Stella was ranting at the wheel. 'I told Useful Kim I wanted a club DJ for the twins' sixteenth.'

'Mam, you were never going to get a club DJ for thirty quid.'

Stella let out a heavy sigh. 'It was so embarrassing for the boys when that DJ said he was taking us all back to 1965.' She ran a hand through her hair. 'At least Mum enjoyed herself.'

Lauren let out a frustrated yelp. 'Ugh, why did Nana Ruby have to slow dance with that old bloke from across the road? So embarrassing. Why can't she be like other people's nanas? Lexi at school says her Nana is as good as gold, she plays bingo, has a flutter on the horses, wears ankle grazing dresses and likes a bottle of cider or two at Christmas. My nana turns up to her grandson's party looking like a seventy-year-old Spice Girl, knocks back the martinis, and dances with him across the road.'

Stella nodded. 'Nana Ruby is a handful, and she does make me tear my hair out, but she's happy, and isn't that the important thing? Would you want Nana Ruby to be sad?'

Lauren shrugged. 'No, but Nana Ruby could think of others when she's out partying.'

As her daughter gazed out of the window I heard Stella mumble under her breath, 'I could say the same about someone else.'

Lauren turned back to her mother. 'That DJ was terrible. When will you learn Useful Kim is not *useful?*'

Lia smiled and placed her warm hand beside mine.

Stella turned on the radio. *'This is DJ Rick Carter, and you were just listening to Duran Duran. Here's this morning's Breaking Commuter News.'*

Lauren scowled at her mum. 'What the hell is this?'

'It's my favourite DJ, Rick Carter and the local radio station, Memory Lane.'

'Violet has contacted the show to say a huge thank you to Stella and her car share gang for helping Bert her new husband

get to the registry office on time last week. They had a wonderful wedding day, and are finally together.'

Stella, Lia, and I all cheered and clapped. Lauren grunted, and tapped at something on her phone. 'Mam, I'm looking at his Instagram.'

'Whose Instagram?' Stella asked.

'DJ Rick Carter's. He looks like someone you'd date.'

Stella sighed. 'Thank you, Lauren.'

'Why are all his photos of him in ripped vests and tiny shorts?' Lauren exclaimed.

We watched Stella tap her daughter on the shoulder. 'Let's leave DJ Rick Carter's Instagram pics for me to look at in private when I am not with all my car sharers.'

Once Lauren had been deposited at school, Lia offered to sit in the front with Stella. 'Are we doing our fifteen minutes of no talking, Stella?'

Stella beamed at the wheel. 'Hearing Violet's shout-out was great. I'm so glad Bert got there on time. As I am now in a celebratory mood, and no longer annoyed about the birthday party, shall we just chat?'

'I'm thinking of going back to football training,' Lia announced, making me sit up in the back of the car.

Stella glanced at her. 'Really?'

Lia nodded. 'Football is a part of me.'

Stella punched the air. 'This is progress. Go for it, girl!'

Lia turned around in her seat. 'Both you and Mateo have helped.'

'Good work, Mateo,' gushed Stella, 'now we have to get Lia to physically attend a football training session.'

I heard Lia let out a heavy sigh. 'It's not going to happen overnight, Stella. I need time to think about going, and someone will have to look after Daisy.'

'While you are at training, you mean?' Stella asked.

Lia nodded. 'She'll be in her buggy, so it will just involve standing by her buggy and getting her to wave at me.'

Stella grinned. 'Mateo and I will look after Daisy.' She winked at me in the rear-view mirror. 'We can also come and give you some support. Set a training date, and we'll go from there. Baby steps.'

Chapter 26

Lia

Dee shrieked when I rang from work to tell her I was going to return to football training. She screamed down the phone, and then shouted to Shona who was in the kitchen. I could hear both cheering. It reminded me of the times I used to watch football at their place and Liverpool, which was Dee and Shona's favourite team, would score. I had to pull my mobile away and wait till they had both calmed down.

'Who has performed a miracle, and persuaded you to come back to training?' A breathless Dee croaked down the phone.

'Mateo and Stella from the car share...'

'WHOA,' cried Dee. 'Who the hell is... MATEO?'

Heat blossomed over my face as I heard Dee say his name. In the background, I could hear Shona saying, 'Dee, that's a Spanish guy's name.'

'He's the guy in the car share. I told you there was someone else apart from Stella.'

Dee cackled down the phone. 'I love the sound of this car share. When are you coming to training? Thursday?'

I took a deep breath. 'I am going to try, Dee. You know how hard it has been for me to even think about football.'

'We know, Lia.'

'I have also done zero exercise for a long time.'

Dee laughed. 'Hope does nothing in training, and she's getting faster. No one knows her secret. You'll be fine.'

Shona grabbed the phone from Dee. 'Lia, it will be like getting back on a bike. Your ball skills will not have deserted you.'

Dee took the phone back. 'This is good news as Petra wants us to start playing more matches.'

The thought of playing in a match was a step too far; it made me freeze. Joe appeared in my mind. He was cheering me on from the stand. My heart ached.

'Just training for now, eh, Dee?'

Once I'd said goodbye to Dee, I spun around in my office chair to face Beth. 'What the hell have I done?'

Beth was staring at me with a gaping mouth. 'You're going back to football?'

I nodded and let out a heavy sigh. 'Crazy, or what?'

She rubbed her forehead as if the conversation she'd heard had been a dream. 'Lia, that's wonderful news. I take it Mateo has made an impression on you?'

'Sort of,' I mumbled, thinking back to our conversation early that morning. 'He made me realise that football will always be part of me. If you opened one of my veins, you'd probably see tiny footballs floating through there.'

Beth nodded. 'If you opened my veins, you'd see tiny daggers with Jez's name imprinted on them.'

To my dismay time went quickly. Before I knew it Thursday evening had arrived. Taking out my old leggings, sports T-shirt, and football boots from the back of the wardrobe was harder than I thought it would be. With a trembling hand I stared at them for ages wondering whether I had the strength to go through with it. I made the decision not to look at myself in the mirror as the sight would probably unleash a thousand tears. Joe would not be there in the background admiring my bum in my leggings, and making cheeky comments about how tight my T-shirt was.

As I put Daisy into her buggy I looked up at my "Joe wall". My old friend, guilt, came rushing back. The memory of my hand placed next to Mateo's on the back seat materialised. Our hands had touched, and I had felt a powerful sense of calm.

What was I doing? The trouble with Mateo was that he was like a huge magnet drawing me to him. The more I got to know him the stronger his magnetism got.

A rap at my front door made me jump, and Daisy squeaked. It was an overexcited Dee. She burst into my house, and began smothering Daisy with kisses. Daisy squealed with laughter, and kicked her tiny legs.

'Come on,' said Dee, bounding around my living room like an energetic child. 'I'm so excited about this. I might cry when I see you in training, sweating away with the rest of us.'

'Please don't cry, Dee,' I said, with a grimace. 'This is not going to be easy. To make matters worse, Stella and Mateo are coming to watch Daisy for me.'

Dee stared at me. 'It's becoming more likely that at some point tonight, I will pee myself with joy.'

Giving her a playful swipe, I bundled her out of the door, and passed her Daisy's buggy. While I locked up, I could hear Dee racing down the street with Daisy.

Mateo and Stella were standing by her car in the football ground car park. Stella waved frantically as we approached. The sight of Mateo in a vintage tanleather jacket, faded blue jeans and retro trainers made my heart go berserk. His hair was even curlier tonight, and he was giving me a breathtaking smile.

I introduced them all and handed over Daisy in her buggy. Stella smiled and grabbed the buggy handles. We watched her peer at Daisy with her huge purple glasses on and her tongue out.

Dee practically frog-marched me onto the pitch where a huge cheer erupted. Within seconds, I was mobbed by a crowd of familiar Tigresses faces. 'LIA!' they all screamed, cheered, and screeched. Petra began blowing her whistle to get everyone's attention, but I was being hugged by Hope, kissed on the cheek by Mitzi, lifted off my feet by Gee, praised by Jazzy and filmed by Flo on her phone.

Training started with the usual laps of the pitch. Somehow, I made it around the first lap, but on the second lap I saw Petra unleashing a load of footballs. In a few seconds my eyes were scanning the side of the pitch for Joe. It hit me like a punch to the guts. *Joe would never be there again, waving, and cracking jokes with Dee as we passed. It was too much.* I wanted to run away from the pitch. Dee shouted to me as I broke free from the pack, and ran off towards the back of the old shed where Petra stored all our kit.

Tears streamed down my face as I leant against the far side of the shed, out of sight, and placed my hands on my knees. *It had been a mistake coming back. I shouldn't have let Mateo and Stella talk me into it.* I cried and cried until a pair of warm hands were lifting me up, turning my body around, and strong arms were wrapping themselves around me.

Through blurry eyes I looked up and saw Mateo's handsome face staring back at me. He gently pressed the back of my head into the crook of his shoulder and held me close until my tears dried up. 'It's too hard, Mateo,' I sobbed. 'Joe's gone forever.'

'Remember what we spoke about earlier on in the week, Lia?'

I nodded.

'Football was your passion, and it still is. Joe would not want you to give it up and deprive yourself of the love you have for it. Would he?'

'No,' I said, softly.

'Strange as it sounds, getting back to football will help you move on.'

Lifting my head from his shoulder I tried to fight a huge urge. His lips looked almost perfect. My head was a swirling cloud of Joe grief and new electric pulses. What I needed was something physical to take away the pain of Joe. I wanted to feel Mateo's lips on mine.

Closing my eyes, I leaned in to kiss him.

Chapter 27

Mateo

Lia will never know the amount of self-restraint it took for me not to kiss her. Ten seconds after I'd pulled away and said to her, 'Lia, you need to go play football,' I felt like an absolute fool. She stepped back, her dark eyes flashing with anger. I watched in horror as she scowled and strode off in the direction of the training pitch. Ed's voice echoed in my mind. *Lia needed rebuilding before any romance could happen between us.* A kiss from me was not what she needed. I could tell she was still in agony over losing Joe, and I also knew getting her back to football was far more important. Football was the glue that would help piece her back together.

At first, I thought she was going back to training, but I watched her say something to the coach and shout at Dee, 'Sorry, I shouldn't have come tonight, it was too much.' She ran off the pitch, grabbed Daisy's buggy from Stella, and hurried away.

'What the hell did you say to her?' An angry Dee came marching over to meet me as I made my way back towards a shocked Stella. 'You assured me you would get her back on the pitch. If I knew this would happen, I would have talked to her myself.'

Stella came between us, raising her hands. 'Can everyone calm down? This was always going to be a highly pressurised event for Lia. Maybe we should all be thankful she turned up tonight. I think it's going to take tiny steps.'

The next day, Lia didn't show up for Stella's car share. To make matters worse there was no sign of her at the nursing home.

On Monday, I sat in the front by Stella, feeling like an idiot. 'Lia's still not feeling very well, she'll be back tomorrow,' Stella explained before pulling out onto the road.

Why the hell hadn't I succumbed to the urge and kissed her? I had ruined everything now. Stella and I listened to her eighties soft rock playlist. I zoned out and wondered what Lia was doing, and whether she'd talk to me ever again. Sinking into the car seat I stared out of the window. Once the fifteen minutes of no talking had ended Stella began chatting to me about her recent diary session where she'd used up ten pages of her new diary just thinking about her ex-partner Rob, the father of her boys. 'Rob has always worked in a tropical fish shop, and he struggled to remain faithful to me for years,' she explained.

I wondered what had drawn Stella to Rob the philandering tropical fish expert. 'Were you into tropical fish at the time you met him?'

Stella cast me a puzzled stare. 'Mateo, I met Rob a few months after Tom had died. I was lonely and in pieces due to grief, plus I had a tiny baby to look after. Looking after colourful fish was not at the top of my priority list back then. Don't get me wrong, I am sure there are lots of tropical fish fans out there, but the fish world does nothing for me.' She flicked her red hair to one side. 'Sharon got me a babysitter one night and dragged me out of my darkened flat to the pub where I met Rob. He was a laugh, a charmer, and back then he was attractive.'

After accelerating into the fast lane, she continued. 'The conversation we had with Ed about his dad's model boat analogy really resonated with me. Rob's idea of rebuilding me after Tom's death was to get me pregnant with twins three months into the relationship.' She pressed her strappy gold sandal to the floor and the car lurched forward. 'I love my boys, you know that, Mateo,' she explained. 'I wouldn't change them for the world, but I could have thought of better ways to glue me back together after losing Tom.'

I sensed she was trying to convey a message to me. 'Rob told me he reckoned I needed something else to cuddle as well as baby Lauren. I just hope Lia meets someone who takes the role of rebuilding her seriously, and does not think a quick shag will fix her world.'

Frustration and anger bubbled up inside me. *I wasn't like Rob, and my actions from last Thursday night proved that. I could have kissed Lia, but I respected her too much. She needed football, not romance.*

The next morning, I stood by myself outside the express supermarket for ages thinking Lia was going to miss car sharing again. Out of nowhere she came rushing over to Stella's car the second it pulled up. Lauren was in the front seat, so Lia and I were forced to sit together in the back. Lia kept her face almost pressed against her window as Stella started the trip to Lauren's school before going on to work.

'Mam, Connor has dumped Nicole,' gushed Lauren, tapping on her phone. 'I never liked Nicole.'

Stella gasped. 'What? Really?'

Lauren nodded. 'He said she was getting too serious for him. She wanted him to tell her his favourite baby names.

I heard Stella let out a loud sigh of relief. 'That's good news, Lauren. I was worried they were spending too much time together. She wasn't good for him, and I lost count of the number of times I caught her in his bedroom'.

'She spent all that money on him for his sixteenth birthday.'

Stella came to a stop at a set of traffic lights. She turned her head to the car opposite, at the lights, and gasped. 'Lauren – Connor! Who the hell is that young woman driving him in that car?' Stella began to frantically wind down her window. 'CONNOR,' she shouted. Lauren let out a shriek of laughter as she watched her brother stare in horror at them both.

I groaned. This was all we needed – more teenage chaos from Stella's children. Sneaking a look at Lia, I was surprised to see her staring back at me. Her eyelids looked puffy, and her eyes were red rimmed.

'What are you doing, Connor?' Stella yelled, as I slid my hand over the seat towards Lia's.

Connor waited for his electric window to go down. 'Oh... Hi, Mam. Fancy seeing you here.'

'WHAT ARE YOU DOING IN THAT CAR?'

'Connor, you loser!' shouted Lauren.

'MAM...' he shouted, but was interrupted as his female driver roared away from us as the lights flicked to green.

Lauren flashed her phone up. 'That's his new girlfriend Eva. She's in the sixth form and has just passed her test. He's got pics of her on his Instagram page.'

Stella glared at Lauren. 'He's dating an older girl now?'

Lauren nodded. 'He's a player, Mam.'

'You wait till I get hold of him,' growled Stella. 'He's got GCSE exams coming up. These girls need to stop luring him away from his studies.'

'Mam, you can't get hold of him when he's six foot three..'

It was then that Stella took an unexpected detour to her

children's school. The second the handbrake was on in the carpark and the ignition was turned off, Stella was out of the car. Lauren leapt out of the car screaming, 'Mam, don't embarrass him.'

Lia turned to me when Stella and Lauren's shouts had drifted off into the distance. 'Sorry for taking things too far last week. I misread everything. I feel such a fool...'

Sweat began to gather on my forehead. Blood thundered in my ears. *Had I given her the wrong signals by hugging her? If I was honest, it hadn't just been a friendly hug, it was full of warmth and... oh God... it had felt like something else. I wanted to be sick.*

'Lia, listen to me...'

She continued. 'Letting Joe go has been harder than I thought. It's going to take some more time. I'm going to look for another car share.' I watched her turn back to the window.

'No... please, Lia, I didn't want this.'

'It's for the best Mateo.'

Stella yanked open the car door. 'Lia, fancy sitting up front with me? All three of my children have annoyed me in the space of ten minutes.'

Lia scrambled to get out of the car. *She wanted to get away from me.*

Stella let out a heavy sigh once back in the driver's seat. 'Connor is now dating a sixth former who will lead him astray, I have no doubt about that. Lauren can't keep her mouth shut, and Luke...' She sucked in a huge lungful of air. 'Luke's obsession with becoming a TikTok influencer is causing him to miss revision sessions. His teacher cornered me as I was shouting at Connor, to say if Luke spent less time on TikTok talking to his massive following, and more time on schoolwork, he might just scrape a pass in his GCSEs.' She took out her phone. 'On top of all that, Wayne has just dumped me by text. He's met an attractive fifty-year-old female lead of a rock band, and can't stop thinking about her. People always go on about men running off with beautiful women in their twenties and thirties, but the real danger right now is from hot fifty-year-old chicks who know what they want and have amazing bodies.' She looked at Lia. 'Can you get my Boyzone CD out? I need to hear their beautiful and calming voices.'

Placing my head in my hands I let out a silent groan, and wished the ground would open up and swallow me whole. I wanted the best for Lia. That's all I wanted. *If only she knew how strongly I felt about her*. She was vulnerable. Behind the football shed she had looked broken. All I wanted to do was put her back together, like Roman had done with Ed.

Lia remained unusually silent, gazing out of her window. I was feeling like an evil git. At one point I caught Stella glancing from Lia to me via the rear-view mirror with a puzzled look on her face. We pulled up to a set of traffic lights by the shopping centre and Stella frowned at me in the mirror, and then to Lia. 'Is there something going on between you two that I need to know about?'

Both of us murmured, 'No,' in unison.

Stella ran her hand through her hair. 'Do I need to remind you of my car rules?'

'Absolutely not,' snapped Lia.

I shifted uneasily in the back of the car. Being stuck in a car with someone who thought I was a heartbreaking shitbag was torturous. There was nowhere for me to go, and I couldn't say anything either.

Lia was on her phone, and through the headrest I could see she was on the *Happy Car Sharer* app. My heart sank. She was going through with her decision to change car sharers. *I couldn't let this happen*. Beads of sweat gathered on my forehead. We joined a long queue of stationary traffic leading into the city centre. *What the hell was I going to do?*

It was then an idea occurred to me. I took out my phone. I would need some help from Claire. She would be in the middle of the school run, dropping off her seven children, and would shout at me again... but seeing Lia happy would be totally worth it.

Chapter 28

Lia

I hurried away from Mateo as soon as we got out of Stella's car. The embarrassment of having tried to kiss him made me walk faster.

'LIA,' he shouted, 'Wait... please... I need to talk to you.'

Last Thursday evening at football training had been an absolute disaster. *How awkward it must have been for him to have seen my pouting lips travelling towards his.* Shame mixed with embarrassment crept over my exhausted body. I'd spent the weekend replaying the incident in my head. I made sure I went to see Dad earlier in the afternoon on Sunday, so I didn't have to face Mateo.

All the girls from the Tigresses had messaged me to say they understood how hard it had been for me to even turn up at the training pitch. They all hoped I'd be back soon. The thought of returning there made me feel sick.

To my dismay, he caught me up. 'Lia, please give me two minutes to explain.'

I hid my face with my hair as he gently reached out for my hand. 'Please, Lia.'

His hand was warm and inviting, which didn't help. Neither did the shot of electrical-like charges it sent up my arm.

He stood in front of me, his chest heaving. 'Lia, look at me.'

His dark eyes located mine. There was no escape.

'Can you get someone to look after Daisy for an hour after nursery tonight?'

'Mateo, you embarrassed me at football...'

He wasn't listening. 'Is there a friend who would pick up Daisy and have her for an hour or so?'

I cast him a puzzled look. Hope sprang to mind, or Dee. 'I could text someone – why?'

'I want to show you something,' he explained. 'Don't decide on whether to leave Stella's car share until after tonight. Promise?'

He looked so handsome. His dark hair was unruly and curly. He was wearing a blue fitted shirt, which emphasised his broad chest, and beige jeans. I wanted to be angry with him, but I was also curious about what he wanted to show me.

'Will you come with me straight after Stella has dropped us off?'

'Ummm,' I mumbled, flicking my eyes to the floor, and staring at my white trainers. *Did I really want to spend time with a man who I'd embarrassed myself with?*

'Lia, I cannot stress enough how much I need you to say yes.' There was a pleading tone to his voice.

I took a deep breath. 'All right.'

He'd raced away by the time I lifted my face.

Beth was painting her nails bright pink when I walked into the office. She looked up with a smile of relief. 'Thank goodness you're back. It's been hell here. Are you feeling better?'

'Yes, why has it been hell?'

Beth grimaced. 'I had a one-night stand with one of the lads from the post room.'

I gasped. 'The one you made a TikTok with?'

She nodded. 'He was in a club at the weekend and kept complimenting me on my dance moves. Jez never said anything about my dancing.'

'Oh... I see.'

Crossing her legs, she let out a sigh. 'I'm not going to lie; it was a turn on.'

I hurried to my desk, and tried to look busy so Beth wouldn't go into details. She groaned whilst painting her last fingernail. 'We went back to my flat and in the middle of our passion I screamed his name... well I thought it was his name... but apparently, I shouted... "Go faster, Jez."'

I snatched the office phone and pressed it to my ear. 'Beth, I've got to make a call.'

She carried on. 'He got over that and we ended up having some more fun. I got his name right, but then I got carried away with a black marker pen.'

'What?' I stared at her in horror.

She looked like she was going to be sick. 'We were pissed, and I got carried away. While he was sleeping, I wrote, *"I LOVE Beth Roy"* on his forehead.'

I gulped.

'It was permanent marker, Lia.'

I didn't know what to say. My eyes widened in horror.

'He had a strop and left my flat. So, I came into work on Monday and read a company news article about how the CEO, Margo's son, has started working with the company, and wants to work his way up.'

I stared in horror at Beth. 'Oh, God?'

Beth nodded. 'That's right, he has started in the post room. He's the one who now has my name on his forehead.'

She gestured, and grimaced at her laptop screen. 'Margo has cancelled my coffee 'career' chat with her.'

Thankfully, Beth's work issue with the lad from the post room distracted me all day. It was mostly spent googling ways he could get the marker removed. I had little time to think about what Mateo was planning.

'Right, I'll see you both tomorrow,' Stella said, pulling the car to a stop. 'Have a good evening.' She watched us both cross the road. I wondered whether she'd picked up on the awkwardness between me and Mateo. Neither of us had talked much on the way home.

Dee and Shona were going to pick Daisy up for me. I hadn't told them where I was going as that would have created questions I couldn't answer. So, I said I had to stay late at work.

'Where are we going?' I asked. Mateo was striding ahead. He was carrying a large plastic bag, along with his work satchel.

'You'll see.'

We turned into the road which led to the training ground, and I stopped. Every muscle and limb in my body froze. 'Are we going where I am thinking we're going? Because if so, I'm off home.'

'Trust me, Lia.'

He stopped and turned to me. 'Just give me five minutes of your time. After five minutes you can leave.'

The second I stepped onto the training ground my heart began to pound against my chest. At one end of the grassy pitch was a group of youngsters doing ball control skills with a coach. There were a few parents dotted about watching their children. Scanning the perimeter, I searched for Joe. My breathing quickened.

'Lia, look at this.' Mateo's voice distracted me. He guided me towards the opposite end. He put down his plastic bag on the grass and opened it. I watched as he removed a pair of old football boots and a brand new ball. 'I've taken a guess on your shoe size. Your feet look the same as my friend Claire's. Size 5. These are her old boots, as she used to play when she was a girl. I didn't know that until earlier today.'

My mouth hung open as he handed the boots to me. 'Put them on please. Luckily, you're in wide trousers today so you should be okay. Oh, and here's a pair of new sports socks.'

'What are you doing?' I murmured.

He rose to standing, and placed his hands on his hips. 'You didn't embarrass yourself last Thursday, and you didn't misread my signals.'

'What?' I stared at him. His dark eyes were intense, and glued to mine.

'Lia, right now you need rebuilding, and that's what I'm going to help you do. Now, get the boots on, and show me what you can do with this new ball.'

I did what he asked. Leaning against the goalpost I put on the football boots. They were old, but they were clean and the right size. Once laced up, I noticed he'd cleared away our stuff, which had been blocking the goal net. He'd also unboxed the yellow ball. Without hesitation he rolled the ball to me. Instinctively, my feet become bouncy just like they used to be all those years ago, as I received the ball with my right foot. 'Oh God, I can still receive a ball.'

'Can I let you know now that I have never liked football?' admitted Mateo.

I grinned as I kept the ball in front of me and broke into a slow run with it at my feet. Repeatedly, I kept pushing the ball four to five yards in front of me. In my head I could hear Alex shouting from the sidelines in training when we used to practice running with the ball. I passed it back to Mateo who made a mess of receiving it. He laughed and rolled it back to me.

Excitement and adrenalin surged through my veins as I received the ball, changed direction, and ran towards the net. My heart leapt for joy as I hammered the ball into the corner of the net. Closing my eyes for a few seconds I savoured the rush of warmth and passion that was travelling around my body. *That kick awoke something inside of me.* I raced into the net, collected the ball, and did the same thing until my legs got tired.

By the time I'd finished, Mateo was sitting on the grass opposite, grinning at me. 'Wow – that's some smile you've got on your face, Lia.'

My whole body was tingling. I felt alive. My exhaustion had disappeared, and if it wasn't for my lack of fitness I would have happily carried on. 'I love football. Always have done.'

'Do you think you could return to training?'

I nodded and he began to clap. We stared at each other, and it was a struggle not to hug him. After I'd changed back into my trainers, he walked me home. 'Still want to leave Stella's car share?'

'Still thinking about it,' I said, with a mischievous smirk.

I got to my old blue gate, and we came to a stop. 'Thanks for tonight, Mateo.'

He ran his hand along the top of the gate. 'Rebuilding you, Lia, is my aim right now. That's what you need. Please don't think I don't care about you, because I do.'

As he walked away my chest felt like there were a thousand football fans all cheering and clapping inside it.

Chapter 29

Mateo

L ia was already at our meeting point as I approached. She turned and gave me the biggest smile I'd ever seen. It was one of those ear-to-ear smiles, which light up an entire face. 'I still can't believe you got me kicking a ball last night,' she gushed. 'Last night I dreamed about footballs and goal nets.'

'Well, that's good to know,' I said, feeling proud of myself for taking steps to free Lia from the past. 'When I returned to the piano all my dreams had a soundtrack to them.'

She smiled, and waved at Stella, who was pulling up along-side us. In the front of the car was a teenage boy who glared at us from the front passenger window. He had a mop of black hair, and a grumpy expression on his face.

Lia and I climbed into the back.

'This is Luke,' explained Stella. 'He has a dental appoint-ment about his braces.'

'Mam, please don't say anything,' he snapped. 'It's bad enough being in this car let alone listening to you broadcast to the world that I have to wear braces.'

Stella sighed. 'Lia and Mateo, as you can see Luke is not a morning person.'

He glared at his mother. 'Mam, I'm not any kind of a person.'

Stella turned to her son. 'Are you this miserable on TikTok, Luke? Because if you are I question why you have got such a large following?'

He shrugged. 'You don't understand.'

'No filming in the car, either. Do you hear me?'

Luke looked out of the window, and I could hear him muttering something under his breath.

As we set off, I noticed Stella kept glancing at me and Lia in the back.

She put on The Beautiful South for the fifteen minutes of no talking. It dawned on me halfway into the journey that Lia and I were different to the two car sharers who had been in Stella's car yesterday morning. There was no frosty atmosphere between us. We were now sitting in the back, relatively close together, and we couldn't take our eyes off each other. Last night, watching Lia kick a ball around and shoot at a goal had changed something inside of me – and her. Her happy glow this morning was so sexy, it was a struggle not to ask her out on a date. I had to keep reminding myself that this was only the start of her journey. At the edge of my mind a worry sent up a flare. I remembered Stella reminding us about her car rule about how romance between car sharers was not allowed. Lia and I were not engaged in a romantic way yet, but the way things were heading...

Would she really ask one of us to leave if she had her suspicions? I dismissed the thought, and returned to catch Lia casting me a sneaky glance.

Stella switched on the radio.

'You've just listened to Whitney Houston. Here's the Breaking Commuter News for today. Someone called Sparkle has texted to say that yes, she will go out on a date with the handsome

dude (*her words, not mine*) *who sat next to her on the train to work this morning and when she wasn't looking, stuck a Post-it note on her coffee cup to ask her out. Sparkle, I can't guarantee this handsome dude is listening, but if he is – result. Rich has messaged us to say he ate his breakfast bap on the train too fast and ended up coughing. The woman he's been getting friendly with slapped him on the back in case he was choking, and now he's in love. For goodness' sake, listeners, this radio slot is becoming like a dating announcement service. Good luck to both Rich and Sparkle.*'

I walked Lia to her office after Stella had dropped us off. 'I'm going out at lunch to buy some new gear for football,' she revealed.

'Good for you.' I grinned as a young lad, racing to get to Lia's office, bumped into me. 'Sorry, mate,' he said, holding up his hand. My eyes were drawn to his forehead, and the black words plastered across it. Before I could read what was written on it, he rushed away.

I turned to Lia. 'Did that guy have something written on his forehead?'

She leant in to whisper, 'I'll explain in the car later.'

She took out her phone. 'I have just got a text from Petra the coach. She's over the moon I have decided to give it another go after last week.'

'This is the start of your new life, Lia.'

She nodded. 'Who was the friend who lent you the football boots?'

The memory of Claire hurtling into the city yesterday to drop off her old football boots made me smile. 'My best friend Claire, who is married to my other best mate, Harry. They have seven kids.'

'Seven?' Lia raised her eyebrows.

'Yup, seven, so she's always busy... and I'm always calling or texting her with requests that initially make her scream and shout at me, but when she calms down, she always helps me out. She's the one who used to foster unwanted cats. Anyway, after yelling at me down the phone, reminding me that it was her only day off and telling me she was not going to spend it digging out boots from her wardrobe, she found her old boots and brought them to me at lunch.'

'That's some friend,' chuckled Lia. 'Listen, you know yesterday when Stella made that comment about us reminding ourselves about her car share rules? Are we in trouble, do you think?' She twirled a strand of her long hair around her finger, and gazed up at me with her bright brown eyes. 'I mean, there's no romance going on between us – is there?'

'For now I'm focusing on getting you back to football,' I murmured, finding it excruciatingly difficult to not go against everything I'd said last night. The urge to cup her face with my hands and kiss her was strong.

She murmured back whilst staring at me, 'That's exactly what I thought. It's good that we're clear on that.'

My day at work was good as Linda, who sat opposite me, had lost her voice. She could only croak and whisper, which was great for me. I got so much work done.

I met Lia at the doors of her office at the end of the day, and we walked to Stella's car. When we got to the meeting point Stella was waiting for us. Lia sat up front with Stella, and I sat in the back.

'How was your day, Lia?' Stella asked.

She groaned. 'Yesterday I spent a lot of my time trying to sort out a mess my friend at work, Beth, has got herself into. Today, Beth was distraught at her desk and thinks her career is over.'

'This sounds interesting,' said Stella. 'What sort of mess are we talking about?'

'A mess involving a permanent black marker, a guy from the post room, a one-night stand, the company CEO, her son, and Beth's career aspirations.

Stella shook her head with bewilderment. 'My mind is boggling so you better tell us.'

Lia explained about Beth's revelation about the black marker and the poor guy from the post room who had turned out to be the CEO's son. It was he who had bumped into me in the street earlier that morning.

To my surprise Stella rattled off a huge list. 'Baby oil is good, plus sea salt, coconut oil, and make-up remover.'

'You sound knowledgeable, Stella,' I said, from the back.

She nodded. 'I once wrote a terrible word on Rob's forehead the day after I found out he'd slept with one of my so-called friends from Pilates.'

Lia stared at Stella. 'Did it come off?'

'Yes, it did, but it took a lot of scrubbing. We had to get it removed as it was the day before his uncle Jack's funeral, and he could not have stood in the church service with that written on his head.'

'Oh...'

'About two months later we were at his house, and he confessed to sleeping with my ex-hairdresser. I always carry a black marker with me. Let's just say I let him carry on drinking, and watched him fall asleep. By the time I'd finished with the black marker, his face looked like it had been tattooed. I left and we never got back together.'

'Does every woman nowadays carry a permanent black marker?' I asked, with a look of horror on my face.

Stella and Lia both laughed. We were interrupted by Stella's mobile, which began bleeping. 'Excuse me a minute, I need to pull over and take this call. It's Rob my ex, and it could be an emergency. He's meant to be picking up Luke and Connor.'

'Stella,' boomed a man's deep voice. 'I need to talk to you.'

'Rob, is this an emergency because I have people in my car, and you are on hands-free – are the boys with you?'

Rob coughed down the phone. 'They're with your mother in the pub.'

Stella's voice was very close to sounding like a hiss. 'Why have you given them to my mother? She always takes them to the pub. I thought with you they'd have a change of scenery.'

He coughed again. 'Calm down. They're all playing pool. Do you have Useful Kim's number?'

I heard Stella exhale loudly. 'You rang *me* to ask for Useful Kim's number?'

'The mobile I have for her is ringing out and she's not picking up,' he growled. 'I have a problem with those pregnancy tests she got Chantelle. They were faulty.'

Stella gasped. 'You and Chantelle want to have a family? When were you planning to tell me this? To be honest, Rob, you have only been seeing her for a few months, and I think you–'

'CHANTELLE IS PREGNANT,' Rob yelled down the phone, making everyone jolt in their seats. Lia was staring at Stella's car phone, and Stella looked like she was in a trance.

'Your dodgy friend's tests told us she was not pregnant, even when Chantelle was throwing up every morning, and she couldn't stand the smell of my shop. I don't want another child, Stella.'

I heard Stella muttering something under her breath before she said, 'Sorry, Rob, bad line. Will call you later.'

With a sigh she turned on the engine and muttered some words under her breath. In the past I would have kept quiet during one of Stella's chaotic telephone calls, or moaned to myself, but I found myself sitting up and asking, 'Are you okay, Stella?' I felt sorry for her having an ex-partner like Rob.

She looked at me in the mirror and cast me a grateful smile. 'Thanks, Mateo, I'm all right. Nothing shocks me anymore with Rob.'

Chapter 30

Lia

My feelings for Mateo had intensified after he'd encouraged me to return to the sport I loved. Seeing him outside the express supermarket on a Monday morning had become one of my favourite weekly pastimes. I sensed he felt the same as we'd both started getting to Stella's meeting point ten minutes earlier, and we always burst into lively conversation.

It was a grey and overcast Monday. Stella gave Mateo and I one of her disgruntled looks as we climbed into her car. They were normally reserved for the start of the week, other drivers on the roads who annoyed her, and the antics her teenage children got up to over the weekend. I assumed her bad mood was to do with all of that and the fact that her ex Rob was having a baby with his girlfriend.

'Hi, Stella,' I beamed after sliding into the front passenger seat beside her.

She grimaced and glanced at Mateo in the back of the car. 'Do you two have anything to tell me?'

'About what?' Mateo asked.

'Breaking my car share rule, by any chance?' She peered at

us over the top of her glasses. 'I had my suspicions last week. One minute you're avoiding each other, replying to questions with frosty answers, and the next you're staring at each other like a pair of lovesick teens.' She took out her phone. 'As you know, my children disobey everything I say. Well, Luke recorded this, and I'm afraid it's confirmed what I know.'

It was a TikTok of Mateo and I gazing into each other's eyes in the back of the car. The caption read – "She's so PENG 🔥 – why is she with him?"

The video had clocked up 898 views. I stared at the phone screen. 'Peng?'

Stella cast me an uncomfortable look. 'It's a teenager term. I think it means you look... nice. He's a teenage boy, and he takes after his father. What *I'm* talking about is the look you two are giving each other. That there is the look of love.'

'It's not, Stella. Mateo and I are just friends.'

'I like a bit of romance, I do,' explained Stella. 'The trouble is, romance in the car makes an awkward journey for everyone, and I like my car journeys to be... calming.'

Out of the corner of my eye I could see Mateo's eyebrows shoot up his forehead. Her car shares were not what I would describe as a calming experience.

Stella continued. 'And *not* a rollercoaster of emotions.'

'I can assure you, Stella,' explained Mateo, 'Lia and I are just friends.'

She turned to me. 'Lia?'

I nodded. 'Just friends. I promise you, Stella.'

Her face softened. 'I trust you. Sorry, I had to mention it, but I wouldn't like to ask one of you to leave my car share.'

My head became awash with memories of the bus and the hooded teenager. *I wouldn't like to return to those days. But what would happen if Mateo left?* As much as I found myself drawn to him, I didn't feel I was ready to not have him sat beside me in Stella's car.

On the way to work, Stella played her soft rock hits from the eighties playlist. I tried my hardest not to turn around and look at Mateo. My phone bleeped with a message shortly before Stella arrived at our drop off point. It was a text from Angel.

> I might come down in a few weeks. Let me check my diary and I will get back to you.

I stared at her text. Irritation bubbled inside of me. *Why did she even bother to text me when we both knew full well the chances of her having a break from her glamorous lifestyle to come and visit Dad and me were zero?*

'Everything okay, Lia?' Stella asked, waiting for the traffic lights to change.

'Just my sister, Angel, annoying me.'

'Does she live nearby?'

I shook my head. 'Manchester.'

'Do you see her much?'

My finger flicked onto Instagram, and to Angel's profile. 'No, she's got a busy life in Manchester.'

Stella nodded and tapped her nude-coloured nails against the steering wheel. My eyes wandered over Angel's array of Instagram photos: beautiful hotel rooms, sun drenched beaches, her and a man sipping cocktails, and one of Angel sitting between a load of glamorous young women.

'Does she not want to see her little niece?'

I sighed. 'Angel barely knows Daisy. As I said, Angel has a busy life, working in PR for celebrities, staying in luxury hotels, and going on holiday with her rich boyfriend. She also struggles with seeing Dad.'

Stella cast me a puzzled look.

'Dad had a stroke a few years ago. His left side is paralysed, and he can't look after himself. Angel finds it upsetting to see him.'

'He's still her father,' Stella said, with a look of disapproval. 'Is there just you and Angel?'

I nodded. 'Mum died when we were little.'

Stella gripped the steering wheel. 'Have you talked to her about this?'

Shaking my head, I fidgeted in my seat. 'I've been avoiding it.'

'Why?'

'If I'm honest, I've not had the energy to argue with her, because that's what would happen. It's been easier to just ignore her fake promises of coming to visit.'

Stella peered at me over the top of her purple glasses. 'So – what are you going to do?'

I shrugged. 'I don't feel strong enough to argue with her.'

Stella nodded. 'One day you will summon the strength to talk to her. Whether she acts on that will not be your problem. What I have learnt over the years is that you can't control people, especially family.' She fiddled with her earring. 'The trouble with family is that you believe you can change them. You can't. They must be the ones who choose to change. I just hope Angel realises what she's missing out on before it's too late.'

'I'm not sure she will ever realise that. Angel only cares about herself. Always has done.' As children, Angel had always been self-centred. She was the baby of the family, and after mum died, everyone took pity on her. Dad has since admitted that he spoilt Angel as a child, and he should have paid more attention to me. He claimed I always got on with things and was very independent whereas everything was a drama for Angel, and if Angel wasn't happy, he would bend over backwards to change that for her.

'All Angel cares about is her swanky life and her Instagram feed.' I flashed Angel's Instagram grid. 'My sister lives in a beautiful, curated world.'

Stella flicked her eyes back to the road after glancing at Angel's feed. 'Lia, Angel is a different person to you. She's got her own way of handling things. I think you need to lower your expectations, and stop expecting Angel to be like you.'

I thought about what she'd said. *Perhaps I was expecting Angel to be like me. If I was Angel, I would be making regular visits to see Dad and my sister.* I wouldn't be avoiding him.

Stella dropped us off near our offices. Once she was out of sight, we both turned to each other and tried to talk at the same time. 'About what happened in Stella's car,' I said. 'I need–'

He stopped me. 'Now is not the best time for either of us to leave Stella's car share. She's been good to us both, and I think you and I need to get to know each other some more first.'

'Mateo, that's what I was going to say.' I giggled.

He grinned. 'Beat you to it. I did struggle not to laugh when she called her car sharing *calming*.'

'Me too. I know it's far from calming inside that car, but Stella has grown on me, and I think she's like the rest of us, just trying to make her way in life. I also think Stella has been put in our lives for a reason.'

He nodded. 'To make me think twice about buying anything from Useful Kim.'

I laughed as we walked towards our offices.

Chapter 31

Mateo

It was Friday morning, three weeks since I had taken Lia to the training ground. I watched a new Lia come bouncing over the road towards me. She looked like a different person. Her eyes were wide with excitement and her red hair was curled, tumbling down in gentle waves, and framing her face. It had been like watching a butterfly emerge from its cocoon. Her friend, who also had a little girl the same age as Daisy, had volunteered her husband to look after both the little ones while she and Lia went to football practice.

We'd all forgotten about Luke's revealing TikTok video and Stella's interrogation. Our car share trips had returned to being fun and lively. Lia had persuaded me to sing along with Stella or share amusing work stories. I'd come to realise that when Lia was happy, I was happy.

'Hello, Mateo,' she beamed, coming to stand by me.

'How was training last night?'

She grinned. 'I'm not going to lie, Petra nearly broke me physically as I am still so unfit, but me and the girls had such a laugh, and I felt amazing walking home.'

Seeing her radiating with happiness filled me with a warm

sensation. It was a struggle not to open my arms, lift her up and twirl her around in celebration, but I managed to keep hold of my emotions.

'Stella's new person starts today, don't they?'

I nodded. 'Hope they know what they're letting themselves in for!'

Lia laughed. 'It is certainly an experience. I hope the new person is ready for Stella's teenagers.'

'I'm praying for someone like Ed, who sleeps a lot,' I admitted. Lia gave me a playful swipe. 'Stella said they were only a temporary car sharer, so I won't have to do much talking.'

Lia tilted her head to one side. 'I bet when we get in that car you and the new person will hit it off immediately.' She smiled and studied my face. 'You know that great day a few weeks ago when you started...' She paused. 'What was the word you used? It wasn't helping me... it was?'

'Rebuilding you. I think the idea came from Ed though.'

'Yes, that's it, rebuilding me.' Lia nodded. 'Like his dad used to piece together his model boats. Well... I have been wondering whether *you* need rebuilding. I mean I do recall you talking about someone breaking your heart last–'

Instinctively, I held up my hand to stop her. She was the focus now, not me. *I was doing fine,* I told myself, ignoring the fact that I still couldn't walk past the little white church without feeling sick. I also kept reliving the memory of happily playing a song I'd written for the church audience before my bride arrived. It was like a form of slow torture. *Everyone in that church must have talked about my failed wedding for months.* 'Oh look, here's Stella,' I said, as relief at avoiding that conversation flooded me.

Lia grinned and waved at Stella. In the front beside her was someone with short black hair. They were talking to Stella, and had the back of their head pressed against the front passenger seat window.

As they turned around in their seat to glance at me, I froze. The person was an older woman. Her face was fully made up, complete with purple glittery eye shadow, heavy blusher, and bold pink lips. I recognised her instantly. It was Kay, my wedding planner from last year. She was Stella's new car sharer.

Natalie had been insistent on using a wedding planner when she began planning our wedding. It was a few days after I'd proposed. Looking back now I don't think marriage was the answer to our deteriorating relationship. Asking Natalie to marry me was, for me, a last-ditch attempt to stop her spending so much time at the gym, to prove to the world everything was great between us, and to paper over some worrying cracks that were appearing.

One of Natalie's friends highly recommended Kay, who apparently was on hand throughout *her* big day, but didn't require a formal invite or a place at the dinner table. Natalie's friend had said Kay went above and beyond the call of duty to ensure everything ran smoothly.

I gulped and hoped that she'd forgotten who I was. *Surely, she must have had more jilted grooms over the past year. Kay must organise hundreds of weddings. She can't possibly remember every client.*

'Mateo?' Kay said, 'How are you doing?'

My heart sank. Neither Stella nor Lia knew about Natalie and my wreck of a wedding ceremony. It was not something I'd planned on talking about.

Stella glanced in my direction. 'Do you two know each other?'

Kay cast me a sympathetic smile. 'We do know each other, don't we, Mateo? How have you been?'

Stella grinned at me in the mirror. 'Is Kay another one of your fans from The Traveller's Rest hotel bar?'

Lia nudged me with a puzzled look.

There were no words. I was in utter shock at Kay being in the car. My silence made everyone stare at me. The only sound was from outside; two school kids were arguing about a can of Pepsi, and an old woman was shouting at her husband about wanting to go in the betting shop.

Kay took it upon herself to update the car. 'Mateo was a client of mine last year.'

Stella's face snapped around in my direction. 'You're married?'

Lia let out a shocked yelp. 'Mateo, you're married?'

Kay let out a deep sigh and with a bleak facial expression, which she must reserve for jilted people and funerals, sadly shook her head. Anger and frustration at Kay's lack of client confidentiality bubbled away inside of me. *I was now going to have to explain what happened.* 'No, I'm not married. I was going to get married last year, but my fiancée, my now ex-fiancée, I should add...' My neck was itching like mad. I paused to loosen my shirt collar. 'Didn't... turn up...' My voice sounded delicate and brittle. 'to the church.'

Kay gave a knowing nod. I could hear her muttering, 'Terrible... just terrible.'

Stella raised her hand. 'Let's leave that there for now. Right, Kay, that's Lia and as you know, that's Mateo. Have you read my car sharing rules?'

Kay nodded. 'I only need a lift for a week or so. I have a large wedding in a hotel in the city to organise.' She gave me an odd look.

We set off, and Stella put on Breaking Commuter News.

'You have just been listening to Simple Minds. Here's today's Breaking Commuter News. Steve's done the school run and one

of his kids threw up in his new car. Lou's train has been cancelled, and her boyfriend has texted to say he's broken up with her. Let's all think of Steve and Lou today. Keep smiling, everyone.'

I leant back into the seat, and for the first time since I started listening to Breaking Commuter News, I felt comforted that others were having a crap day like me. Lia touched my hand. I gave her a weak smile before directing my attention outside the car window. *It was at times like these I wished Dad was at the other end of a phone, and not in Cherry View nursing home, unaware of my existence.*

My mind replayed the events from last year. When Natalie's mother had rushed out of the church with the mobile pressed to her ear, and the congregation became a sea of murmurings and whispers, it was Dad who I'd wanted to go to. He'd not come to the wedding as he wouldn't have known where he was or who I was. I remember when the news broke that I'd been jilted. It was Dad who I wanted by my side. My lovely father who used to move mountains to get to me when I needed him. Blinking back tears, I remembered when I broke my arm on a school trip in the Lake District and Dad drove for hours to reach me. He appeared and pulled me into one of his huge bear hugs. I wiped my eyes with the back of my jacket cuff and thought, *'Dad, I miss you and I hate feeling so alone.'*

Stella turned down the music to signal the end of no talking. 'So, Kay, do you normally drive to work?'

Kay nodded. 'My car broke down last week and the garage told me it is going to take a while to fix.'

She went on to describe the oil leak, and I zoned out until Lia's fingers wrapped themselves around mine and gently squeezed. Her touch soothed the pain inside my chest.

Chapter 32

Lia

On the return journey from work Mateo was quiet. He didn't smile or say goodbye to me later, after Stella had dropped us off. He walked away down the high street with his head bowed. My mind was awash with questions. *What had happened between him and his fiancée at their wedding?*

With Mateo on my mind, I collected Daisy from nursery, and together we caught the bus to see Dad. I was hoping to see Mateo. On the bus, I decided I would try to catch him after his piano performance. Two stops before Cherry View nursing home I realised how little I knew about Mateo, which had to change. As we made our way down to the back room, I could hear Mateo playing the piano with such intensity. Once inside, I became spellbound by his performance. His eyes were shut, his face damp with sweat, and he was completely absorbed in a dramatic piece of music. I couldn't help but notice how his fingers danced back and forth across the keys. The music came to a dramatic end as he slumped over the piano, breathing heavily. There was a smattering of claps and the little grey-haired lady, whose tiny feet didn't touch the floor, let out a thundering whistle of appreciation.

Daisy was making an old man smile by giggling and spinning round and round. I grabbed her hand before she was sick, and waited for Mateo to notice us. He didn't look up. Instead, he began to play another piece of music with a trance like look on his face.

Four songs later he was still playing, and residents were being wheeled out for their tea. Mateo was overrunning his allotted time. Dad waved at me as he was wheeled past. 'See you in the day room,' he said. Daisy blew him one of her kisses and he cast her his best wonky smile.

I waited until all the residents had gone. It was just, me, Daisy, and Mateo. He seemed oblivious to the fact that his audience had left. From what I could see, Mateo was hurting, and this was his way of dealing with the pain. Daisy let go of my hand and began to wander through the forest of chairs.

Placing a hand on his shoulder I brought him out of his thoughts. I gestured towards the rows of empty plastic chairs, and he stopped playing. His dark eyes were glassy, and his cheeks were damp. After gesturing for him to shift up on his piano stool, I sat next to him. My thigh brushed against his, and he touched my boot with his trainer. Waves of sensations travelled around my body.

'Did you know, Mateo, I'm good at football... well I'm getting better, I'm fab at singing my heart out to songs in Stella's car, and I'm great at listening.'

His face softened. He laid his hands on the piano keys and began to play a beautiful, aching piece of music. 'It's all in the past. I don't know why I'm still so worked up about it.'

'Try me?'

He took a deep breath, and carried on playing. 'She left me standing at the altar last year. On the way to the church...' He paused like it was painful to force out the words. 'She made the driver stop, she got out and... into the car belonging to the guy she'd...' I watched him hang his head. 'Secretly been having an affair with.'

I couldn't believe what I was hearing. 'Mateo, I don't know what to say... I'm so sorry; that must have been traumatic for you.'

He rubbed his forehead. 'I can't stop reliving the part where the church congregation is staring, whispering, and pointing fingers at me. I still feel like such a fool.'

'They probably felt sorry for you.'

Resting his fingers on the keys, he chewed his lip. 'Everyone knew I was making a stupid decision by asking Natalie to marry me, and I ignored them. Like a stupid idiot.'

'You loved her, Mateo. That's what people saw. You wanted to marry her, because you loved her.'

He nodded and laid his hands in his lap. 'I'm lucky. I have two great best friends who have got me through the last twelve months. Even though I wanted to hide from the world, drink myself stupid and deprive myself of the piano. They kept dragging me out on day trips with their kids. They'd cook me good food and talk to me for hours. Some people must go through what I have been through on their own.' He looked at me. 'How did you handle losing Joe? What I've been through feels insignificant compared to you losing the person you loved.'

'When he died, I locked us away. I plastered a wall in my living room with hundreds of photos of him, and I deprived myself of football. I kept replaying everything that happened, in my mind.' I waited for the tears to come. After any sort of Joe conversation, I always struggled to contain my emotions. This time, I felt an ache in my chest, but there were no tears.

'What's up?' Mateo asked. 'You've gone quiet on me.'

I smiled at him. 'That's the first time I've been able to talk about Joe without crying.'

'Lia, that's great. The football practice must be working.'

Shaking my head, I held his gaze. 'It's a mixture of that, Stella's car sharing... and having you in my life, Mateo.'

Gently, he brought down the lid of the piano over the keys. I felt his body turn towards mine. He looked achingly beautiful with his crazy curly hair, his deep brown eyes, and his toned arms. Holding my gaze, he smiled. 'I appreciate you coming to see me,' he whispered, leaning closer and pressing his forehead against mine. 'I want to kiss you so badly right now... but...'

'But what?' I whispered, yearning for his lips to be over mine.

He closed his eyes. 'I don't want to rush you into anything, Lia. You've been through such a lot, and you're only at the start of your journey.' Pressing his forehead against mine, he whispered, 'You are someone who I could easily fall head over heels in love with, and I guess after what happened to me last year... I'm trying to stop myself from rushing in.'

I placed my hand over his on the stool. 'So, we're sticking to noses touching foreheads... until when?'

He smiled. 'I haven't worked that bit out yet.' I followed his lead and pulled away.

'We're both in need of rebuilding – aren't we, Mateo?'

He nodded.

'I also know very little about you,' I said, as Daisy came over and rested her head in my lap. 'We better go see Grandpa before he goes to bed.'

Mateo smiled at Daisy. 'Another time, Lia. See you on Monday for Stella's car share?'

'Definitely.' A huge smile swept across his face, which gave me a fluttering sensation. It was then that an idea occurred to me. 'Why don't you come and watch me play football on Sunday... if you're not doing anything?'

'I'd love to. The training ground?'

I nodded. 'Be nice to see you.'

As Daisy and I walked up the corridor towards the day room, my phone bleeped. It was a text from Dee.

> OMG – Alex is back, and he's coming to football on Sunday!

Chapter 33

Mateo

Natalie's email was waiting for me when I woke up on Harry and Claire's sofa. She'd sent it in the early hours. The sight of her email address made me shiver. She'd titled it, *"Please Read, Mateo."* My thumb hovered over it. *Did I really want to read what she'd written? Did I want anything more to do with her after what she did to me?*

Claire appeared with Reuben, Reg, and Raff. They were all yawning and rubbing their sleepy eyes. The boys went over to their pile of toys, and Claire came to sit at the end of my makeshift sofabed. 'Harry's still in bed, moaning about his head and how you made him drink beer,' she chuckled. 'How are you feeling?'

I sat up, holding my phone. 'I was all right until I saw Natalie had emailed me in the early hours.'

Claire shot me a puzzled look. 'Why? Have you read it?' She ran her hand through her black hair, and outstretched her hand. 'Do you want me to read it?'

'No, I feel strong enough to look at it,' I said, clicking on it. My eyes darted to Natalie's email, and I scanned the content.

'She wants to apologise to me again. She feels bad about what happened. It's time to draw a line in the sand, apparently... She hopes one day we can be friends. Oh... and she wants to tell me she's getting married to Zane at the end of the month. At the same church.'

'What the hell?' Claire said, as I flashed the screen at her. 'Oh God, Natalie has no shame. The apology is a start, but why does she feel the need to tell you about getting married?'

Letting out a sigh I took my phone back and pressed delete. 'I think it's time to block her.'

Claire nodded in agreement. 'It's a guilt thing on her part. She's finally feeling guilty for what she did to you, and to make herself feel better she's acting like you are long-lost friends.' Rising from the sofa Claire stretched. 'Coffee, Mateo?'

My head was stuck back in the past. A memory from the day after the wedding had come to the front of my mind. Natalie and Zane had come to Harry and Claire's house to make sure I was okay. They wanted to inform me they were going to America. I was on the sofa, feeling rough after drinking myself into a right state. Harry had gone to the door with Claire behind him.

'You and Harry met Zane, once – what was he like?'

Claire stuffed her hands into her pyjama pockets. 'You mean Harry pinned Zane against the wall and told him if he ever set foot in our garden again there would be trouble. I don't think it was a friendly meet and greet. Natalie did a lot of shrieking, and I did a lot of shouting.'

'I'm curious – what was he like?'

Claire shrugged. 'He looked like a gym dude. Short hair, tanned, and athletic looking. It was funny as despite all this guy's workouts and chiselled looks, Harry, a man of limited exercise, lifted a squealing Zane off the ground at one point.'

She turned towards the kitchen. 'Mateo, that part of your life is over now. Forget it.'

'Yeah, you're right.'

'What you need is a coffee. Oh, and Harry told me you are going to watch Lia play football today – that right?'

'It's just a practice session, but yes I am.'

While the coffee machine grunted and gurgled, I sat and thought about what it was about Zane that had made Natalie choose him over me. Reuben and Reg began to argue over the cereal box, while Raff watched.

Claire broke up the fight. 'Raff, please pour out cereal for your brothers. Ronnie, stop hitting Reg,' she said, before handing me a coffee. 'Mateo, stop digging up the past in your head.'

'I'm not.' Silently, I admired her ability to multi-task.

She tilted her head to one side. 'Take a seat,' she said gesturing for us to sit at the kitchen table. 'Mateo, I know you. I could see you from the kitchen, deep in thought about Natalie and Mr Plastic.'

'Mr Plastic?'

She laughed. 'Yes, that was the nickname Harry and I gave him.'

'What do you mean?'

'He looked like there was nothing else going on inside his head, but thoughts about his appearance. Once he got back in the car with Natalie, he spent ages checking himself out in the mirror.'

We both chuckled. Raff gave his mum a cuddle. Claire rested her head on his shoulders. 'This son of mine is my angel.' Raff smiled before leaving her to go and rugby tackle Reg, who was busy carrying his bowl of cornflakes over to where the milk carton was stood. Claire rolled her eyes as cornflakes were scattered everywhere and Reg started shouting. She turned to me, seconds before erupting with anger at her boys. 'Natalie has found her ideal man, Mateo. Mr Plastic. She was also a bit plastic, Mateo. All about her looks. Nothing else. You can do a lot better. Don't feel sad; feel relieved. Now, if you mention either of them again, I will set all my naughty children on you.'

I smiled as she shouted at Reuben, Reg and Raff and made them get down on the floor to pick up every single cornflake.

Later, Harry dropped me off near the training ground. 'Do you want me to come with you? I am a smooth talker with the ladies.'

I smirked. 'Harry, I don't need a chaperone.'

He ran a hand through his mass of russet hair. 'Claire's a lucky lady.'

I laughed and leapt out of his van. He hung out of the window as he watched me walk off. 'Go get 'em, tiger.'

I ignored him, stuffed my hands in my jeans pockets, and made my way to see Lia. Above my head was a cloudless blue sky, which made me smile. *Claire was right. I had to stop digging up the past. The future was what I needed to focus on.*

When I got to the training pitch Lia looked over from a crowd of footballers and came rushing over. She looked incredible in silky black shorts, a white T-shirt, and with her hair pulled back into a ponytail. She sat with me on the grassy verge that hemmed the pitch. 'Hello,' she beamed, lighting me up inside.

'Will I see you score any goals?'

She shrugged. 'Bit too early for that. I'm very unfit. Not sure what training we will be doing. It's nice to see you, Mateo.'

'Great to see you too.' We looked at each other until someone blew a whistle.

'Better go,' she giggled, 'see you in a bit.'

Stretching out my legs, I took my shades out of my shirt pocket, put them on, and watched the team mingle around a female coach. Lia kept looking over in my direction. I couldn't take my eyes off her amazing legs as the coach got the team weaving in and out of cones.

A shout made everyone look up. I looked over to see a tall man waving to the team. The whole team let out what only could be described as an excited scream, and within seconds, the bloke was being mobbed by a team of footballers. For a good five minutes, women were shouting with glee, hugging him, and chanting, 'ALEX... ALEX... ALEX.' Then my heart ground to a halt. The man spotted Lia and to my horror, he lifted her into the air and twirled her around. She was laughing and everyone was dancing around them.

The session became increasingly difficult to watch as the tall man seemed only interested in Lia. At the end, she jogged over to see me. 'What did you think of my ball skills?' she asked, gushing with excitement.

'You were amazing,' I said, hiding my discomfort.

She bent over to get her breath. 'Our old coach has returned from New Zealand, and we're going to grab a coffee with him. You're welcome to come along.'

'I'm going to head off,' I said. 'Late night last night so could do with a lie down.'

'Who's your friend, Lia?' a loud voice boomed behind her. I looked up to see the most heroic looking tall man walking towards us. He had a chiselled jaw, shiny hair, and huge biceps. He looked like one of the men from Natalie's gym, who she used to pose with on her Instagram page. Back then I wasn't the jealous type as I had no reason to think she'd ever cheat on me. She'd told me her last relationship had naturally run its course and she and her ex had remained friends.

Once standing next to Lia, he pulled her into his side and grinned. 'I've missed you, Lia Edwards.'

It was the way he looked at her that made me uncomfortable. I sensed they had history together. The look he cast me said it all.

Chapter 34

Lia

Alex was staring at my "Joe wall" when I came in carrying in two mugs of tea.

It was late Sunday afternoon. Earlier, everyone had descended upon the local café not far from the training pitch after practice. As Shona was looking after Daisy for me, and had insisted, I stayed behind and went to the café with everyone. We all listened to Alex's tales of the amazing life he'd left behind in New Zealand. He and Georgina had lived at the top of South Island, within driving distance of Wharariki Beach. From his phone pics, which he passed around, it looked stunning. When Georgina wasn't working, they'd spent a lot of their free time hiking, playing with a mad looking dog they'd adopted, and surfing. It had looked idyllic, and I wondered why he had left all that to come back.

He'd made a beeline to sit next to me in the café, which was nice, but it made me feel anxious.

When Alex had left all those years ago, Joe was still alive, and I was Captain Lia Edwards of the Tigresses. Alex and I would regularly mess about on the pitch like two kids. We'd be joking about the other's football skills, and Joe would be laughing at us on the pitch line. After training in the pub, the three of us would always sit together. We were a unit.

Earlier in the café, Alex had insisted on draping his long arm over my shoulders and leaning in extra close, which made my shoulders and neck tense. I don't know whether he felt I needed his displays of affection, but I found them uncomfortable. Mitzi wasn't happy, and kept sending frosty stares at us both from the end of the table. Anxiety and frustration bubbled away inside of me. I could feel his warm breath on my neck.

Placing the tea down on the coffee table I looked at him smiling at each photo of me and Joe. *Perhaps I had been wrong to feel irritated with him in the café?* Everyone was so excited at seeing Alex our much-loved football coach. He was not only a larger-than-life character, but he was also a six-foot-three, athletic, tanned, and exceptionally handsome man. His dazzling white smile lit up any room, and his booming laugh made everyone giggle like a load of pop crush groupies.

We all had so many memories to recall with him. There had been so many messy football tours, which always involved Alex sneaking off with one of the ladies from the opposition in the bar afterwards, Alex dancing in the centre of a load of pissed footballing ladies, and Alex shaking his hips on the dance floor of a nightclub. He was like our own personal celebrity. In the café, all the team wanted to know everything about him, and there was a lot of jostling for his attention. *I should have known coffee with the Tigresses and Alex was never going to be a calm affair.* However, despite everyone around me making him laugh, flicking their hair, sending him cheeky smiles, all I wanted to do was go home, let Shona go, and be alone with Daisy.

He turned to me now, with pink, watery eyes. 'These photos are great... Joe would have been so proud of you for doing this.'

I watched as he pointed to each one in turn. On some, he joked about Joe's hairstyle, on others, he was able to recall what he was doing at the same time, and on most he just stared at the photo until his cheeks were damp. Emotion rose inside of me, when I heard him whisper, 'I miss you, mate, so much.'

'I miss you too, Joe,' I said, my voice breaking into a series of sobs. I felt Alex's arm snake around my waist, and even though I resisted at first, he pulled me closer to him.

'Joe,' he croaked, focusing on one photo, 'I'm going to look after your girl Lia, and Princess Daisy.' We both turned to glance at her fast asleep on the sofa in a new, bright pink Disney princess dress that Alex had bought her. She'd been so excited we couldn't get the dress on her fast enough. Once she'd run around the living room giggling at Alex and waving the tiny silver crown he'd also bought her, she'd collapsed on the sofa.

He ran a hand through his floppy brown hair. 'Yes, mate, I'm back for good from New Zealand.'

I pulled away from him, to grab a handful of tissues. He gestured for me to return. 'Come back here, Lia.' Holding on to me he directed us both to the sofa where we flopped onto it.

'Why are you back, Alex?' I reached out to get my mug of tea and release myself from his grip.

A smile swept over his face. 'I realised Georgina and New Zealand were not for me. There were people back in the UK that I missed and wanted to be around.'

I nodded, and once again he draped his arm over my shoulders. Wriggling free, I positioned myself sitting cross-legged away from him.

'The photos you sent of you and Daisy at Christmas made me smile. Especially the one where she was wearing toy reindeer antlers. I also thought you looked stunning in your tartan pyjamas. You both never left my mind.'

'Alex, you can cut the charmer act with me.' I chuckled, playfully swiping him.

He grinned. 'It's true. I would say ask Georgina, but I don't think I'm in her good books right now.'

'I thought it was love between you and Georgina.'

With a shrug he grabbed his tea mug. 'It was more lust than love. Let's not talk about her. How's your dad?'

Alex always remembered my dad, and never forgot to ask me how he was doing. It was one of the many reasons I loved him as a friend. His emails from New Zealand always started with a greeting, and then a question about dad.

'He's doing all right,' I explained. 'Still suffers with his speech, and limited mobility, but he's interacting with me a lot more when I visit him.'

Alex nodded. 'Let me know when you are going to visit him, and I'll come with you.'

'Where are you staying?'

I watched Alex's eyes droop and his bottom lip push itself out. It was the same face Alex used when he wanted Joe to go on holiday to Greece with him, the same face Alex used when he wanted Joe to work on his car or when he wanted me to play a new position in a football match.

'Well... that's what I need to talk to you about.'

'Alex?'

He let out a sigh. 'My house is being rented until the end of the month as you know, and I need a temporary place until then. They are moving out so there's no worries there. It will be temporary, and I thought as you had a spare room...'

'Alex, my box room is crammed full of old stuff. I have not been in there for months. It's got all of Daisy's baby stuff, and there's a lot of boxes containing Joe's things, which I have struggled to throw away.'

He raised his large hands. 'I will happily sleep anywhere. Show me now whilst Princess Daisy is asleep.'

On the landing, I leaned across him and pushed open the

box room door. 'As I said, there is a lot of junk.' We both stared at the array of baby clothes, a baby bath, boxes filled with things from Joe's past, toys, Joe's old rowing machine, which was coated in dust, a misshapen Christmas tree, and my old vinyl record player.

'Somewhere under all that is the bed.' I said, trying to block out the memory of Joe using his rowing machine in the lounge while I would be trying to watch Coronation Street.

A grin spread across Alex's face as he pointed at an old photo frame sticking out of a cardboard box. Smiling back was a younger version of us both holding a football trophy the Tigresses had won. 'Happy days,' Alex whispered. I looked back at him, and he held my gaze with his piercing blue eyes.

'Can I stay here?' he asked as we made our way downstairs.

'If you behave yourself,' I said, which made him chase me around the living room. It was too much, as he kept pulling me into a cuddle and I kept resisting him. I ended up shouting, 'Alex, please stop.' Daisy woke up with a start, and burst into tears.

Burrito kept watch from high up on my bookshelves in the living room. He wasn't a fan of newcomers.

Chapter 35

Mateo

When Stella arrived the following day, there was no sign of Lia or Kay. She signalled for me to get in the front. She cast me a puzzled look as I got in. 'No Lia today?'

I gave up on the smile, and greeted Stella with a grimace. She frowned at me. 'Why the look of misery? You've been a lot happier on a morning lately?' Grabbing her phone, Stella scrolled through her messages. 'That's strange. I've not had a text or a missed call from Lia.'

Sounds of laughter made us both look up. On the pavement in front of us was Lia, with Alex. My heart sank as I watched them joking about something. Stella was peering over her purple glasses perched on the end of her nose. 'Who is *that* with Lia?'

'Her new football friend,' I muttered.

She turned to me, and studied my face. 'I knew it!'

I stared back at her. 'Knew what, Stella?'

Folding her arms across her chest she glared at me. 'You must have thought I believed that nonsense you told me about Luke's TikTok. Since then, I have noticed more dreamy looks, the hand holding, and your lingering gaze.'

'Huh?'

She gestured towards Lia and Alex, still talking near her car. 'You're in love with Lia – aren't you? It's written all over your face.'

'No,' I snapped, flicking my eyes to the floor as my cheeks burned.

'You lied to me.'

'Stella, I don't need this right now.'

With a heavy sigh she tilted her head to one side, and arched one eyebrow. 'This car share of mine is supposed to be *calming*.'

I snapped. 'Stella, I wouldn't use the word *calming* to describe your car share.'

She sat back in her seat in shock. 'I beg your pardon?'

'Over recent weeks your unruly teenagers have been causing havoc, your driving skills are questionable, your kids and your mother are nightmares, and you're obsessed with that DJ Rick bloke.'

Lia stood by the passenger door. I could hear her saying to Alex, 'You're cooking tea tonight – really?'

Stella hissed, 'You don't get away that easy, Mateo. You're in love with her, and you're not happy because Mr Handsome over there has turned up on the scene.'

'Not now,' I snapped.

'Oh God,' Stella exclaimed, staring at my miserable face. 'Turn that frown upside down.'

I sent Stella a thunderous look. 'Hi, everyone. Stella, sorry I'm late. Blame my friend Alex.' She smiled as Alex pulled a silly face at her before walking off.

Lia tapped me on the shoulder. 'Hello, Mateo.'

I turned around and forced out a smile. 'Hey, Lia.'

'Where's Kay?' Lia asked.

Stella looked at Lia in the mirror. 'Oh, her car is fixed. I'm relieved as she was doing my head in with all that wedding planner stuff.' She turned on the radio.

'*Here's today's Breaking Commuter News. Fred's bike has a puncture, Gavin has twisted his ankle whilst running for his bus, Michelle would rather stick pins in her eyes than go into work today, and Helena is on the bus trying not to look at her boss who is waving to her from his car. Sandra's train is delayed, but she's happy anyway, as her girlfriend Suzie proposed last night. Congrats to Sandra and Suzie. Remember Steve, from last week, who had bought a new car and his child was sick in it on the school run?... Well, I can reveal his other child has thrown up today, in that same new car, on the school run. Let's all think of Steve while we listen to Duran Duran.*'

After fifteen minutes, Stella turned down the music. 'Lia, spill the tea on your new friend Alex.'

At the mention of his name, I sank down further into the car seat. *This was going to be torturous.* Lia laughed. 'He's not my new friend. I've known Alex for years. He was Joe's best mate, and he coached the Tigresses before he left for New Zealand.'

Stella sighed. 'Mmm... he looks like he works out. Does he have a partner?' She touched her gold hooped earrings, making them jangle.

To my dismay, Lia shook her head. 'He moved to New Zealand with a woman called Georgina, but he's come back to the UK as he missed it too much.'

Stella rearranged her purple glasses. 'Does he have any children?'

'No. He's amazing with Daisy, and I think one day he will make a great dad.'

'I thought that with Rob,' explained Stella. 'However, I have been very disappointed with his parenting skills for the past sixteen years. It's lucky my sons have me as a mother, because if Rob had raised them, they would have probably grown up living in tropical fish tanks. I feel sorry for Rob's new baby.' We all went silent as Stella accelerated onto the motorway. 'The thing I quickly noticed with Rob was that he was never there for me in the bad times.'

'What do you mean?' Lia asked.

Stella tapped her long aqua bluenails on the steering wheel. 'He would always have to work longer hours or have a tropical fish conference to attend if I was feeling down, in a low mood with the kids, exhausted or ill. He hated seeing me at my worst. However, demand in the local tropical fish market would always quieten down when I was in a good mood or life was going well. There would be a knock at the door, and he'd be stood there with a grin on his face, and he would beg me to go upstairs to the bedroom where he claimed he would...' She tilted her head to one side and exhaled. 'Show me a new species of fish. I was deluded for many years.'

I pressed my face against the car window. *The last thing we all needed to hear on a morning was the tropical fish expert's chat-up lines.* Stella dropped us both, and as she pulled away, I watched her wink at me.

Lia turned to me and beamed. 'Sorry about Sunday, and Alex.'

'I got to see you practise the game you love; that's the important thing,' I said, reassuringly.

She smiled. 'I missed seeing you over the weekend.'

My heart shook itself off the floor of my ribcage and did a few flips of joy.

'Alex has moved in with me for a few weeks so that's going to be interesting,' she explained, as my heart splintered. We walked to our offices, and she told me all about Alex moving into her box room. I zoned out for much of it, and tortured myself by imagining Lia confessing to me that she'd fallen in love with Alex.

Chapter 36

Lia

Daisy and I were on our way to visit Dad. I hadn't seen him for a few days. Alex was meeting us at Dad's nursing home, which I was relieved about, as Daisy was being hard work. She was tired, and had a tantrum on the bus when I wouldn't let her climb over the back seat. I knew she would brighten up at the sight of Alex.

As we crossed the road, Daisy began to grizzle in my ear. Exhaustion washed over me. I'd not gone to bed till late for the third night in a row, as Alex had insisted on talking to me about Joe, and the happy memories he had of his best mate. All the memories were so sweet, and nearly all of them ended up with me in tears on the sofa, and Alex hugging the life out of me. It then took me ages to get to sleep when I finally got to bed as my brain was wired and full of memories of Joe.

My phone buzzed as I got to the door of the nursing home. It was from Alex.

> Something has come up. I'll come next time to see your dad. See you at home.

Daisy screamed as I tried to put my phone back in my

handbag and keep hold of her. Once we got into the corridor, I could hear Mateo playing the piano. Daisy pulled on my arm.

As I stepped into the doorway of the back room Mateo, looked up and smiled. A combination of seeing him and hearing his wonderful music made my hunched shoulders relax, and my irritation subside. Daisy began to do one of her little dances and in a few seconds, everything was all right with my world again. Mateo kept his dark eyes on me whilst he played, and by the time he'd finished I felt relaxed and happy.

Dad waved at me as he was pushed out of the back room. 'See you in the other room,' he said with a smile. Daisy played amongst the empty chairs in the back room while I sat next to Mateo on the piano stool.

'Hello,' he said, laying his beautiful hands on top of the keys.

'Hello,' I whispered, with a smile.

We didn't say anything to each other as he played by my side. *It was like we'd found a little corner of heaven. The world fell away. All the stresses of the day disappeared, and I soon forgot about Alex not turning up to visit Dad with me. It was just, me, Daisy, Mateo, and a piano.*

'I better go see Dad,' I said, after he'd finished.

He nodded. 'I talked to your father for ages the other evening. He might mention it.'

I cast him a puzzled look. 'Really?'

Mateo smiled. 'I knew you were busy with Alex, and your dad looked like he needed a chat, so I went and sat with him.'

'You talked to Dad?' I watched Daisy dance around the chairs.

He stared at me. 'You sound surprised?'

'No one has ever done that for me. My sister is always promising to come down and see him. She always cancels. It's always just been me, Daisy and Dad here.'

Mateo gently brought the piano lid down. 'He told me all sorts.'

'Oh, no,' I groaned. 'Was it embarrassing?'

Mateo smiled. 'Your dad told me you were formidable on the football pitch.'

My cheeks began to heat up. 'Really?'

He nodded. 'He told me no one got in your way on the pitch, and you would shout at your team a lot.'

'That was the old Lia.'

'I think she's still inside you,' he said, softly. 'He also told me you changed your name to Lia after he and your mum named you *Julia*.'

I rolled my eyes, and smirked. 'I'm going to be having words with my father.'

Mateo shuffled his music sheets. 'He also told me your full name, Julia Claire Edwards, and that he still hasn't forgiven you for losing a gold bracelet he bought you which had your initials, J.C.E., on it.'

Letting out a groan I nodded. 'Joe lost it. I think it was around the time we adopted Burrito.'

'Your dad told me about how your mum died when you were five years old, leaving him to raise you and your sister Angel. I lost my mum as a child too.'

I remembered Dad holding my hand and Angel's, as we went to the hospital to say goodbye to mum. 'Yea, she'd fallen in our garden, hit her head. Dad told me she was very poorly after her fall, and the angels from heaven were going to come down and take her back to heaven, where they would let her sleep on a bed made of fluffy white clouds. I can still remember thinking how great it would be for her to sleep in a cloud bed. 'What about your mum?'

'I was a toddler. She was Spanish, and gave me the name Mateo. She and dad met when he was on holiday. One summer, she went back to see her sister, and died in a car crash.'

'Do you still see your Spanish family?'

He shook his head. 'Dad was so cut up over Mum, he made me promise to not go to Spain. Mum's sister Elena sends me a Christmas card each year, but I have never met her.'

'Don't you ever want to?'

I watched his fingers tap the tops of his knees. *He was anxious.* 'I want to,' he said, 'but I would feel guilty, like I was letting Dad down. I know Dad doesn't recognise me anymore, but...' His voice began to crack. I placed my hand over his tapping fingers.

'You love him, and even though he doesn't know who you are, you can't bear the thought of him being sad,' I whispered.

Mateo nodded. 'Lia, you're one of the few people who understands.' He pointed at Daisy, who was hiding behind a chair and giggling at him. 'We have an audience.'

'I better take her to see Dad,' I said, rising from the piano stool.

'Are you doing anything nice tonight?' he asked, standing up at the same time so we were facing each other. Once again, I found myself aching for him to kiss me. For a moment I thought he was going to lean towards me.

'Alex was supposed to meet me here, but he's been held up. So, I guess going home, eating my tea, and going down memory lane again with Alex.'

I noticed something flicker across his face. He nodded, collected his music sheets, and gestured for me to leave the room before him. 'Let's get out of here. After you both,' he said.

Our moment was gone. With a heavy heart I took Daisy to see Dad.

On the way home on the bus, Daisy fell asleep on me, and Dee messaged me.

> How's tricks? How's living with Alex?

Mateo was still on my mind.

> Yes, okay.

I decided to broach the subject of Mateo to Dee.

> We need to talk... I'm on the bus with Daisy asleep so we might have to talk on text.

Dee responded.

> About someone?

> Yes...

I started typing out a lengthy text about Mateo, how I met him, the connection we have and the recent events.
Dee was faster.

> There's something you need to know, Lia. Alex told someone he has feelings for you.

An uncomfortable feeling crept over me.
I tried to stay calm as I tapped out a reply.

> Alex is an old friend. That's it on my part. There's someone else...

Dee was quick to reply.

> Not that car share guy? Lia, think about this. You don't know anything about this guy who you travel to work with. Alex knows you; he knew Joe, he loves Daisy like she's his own, and he knows you love football. You've been through a lot. Lia, you're vulnerable. Alex will take care of you."

Frustration bubbled inside of me. I was not vulnerable, and everyone seemed to be making decisions for me. I recalled Bert talking about how people had decided the direction of his life for him.

Chapter 37

Mateo

'Lia's working from home. Daisy is not well,' Stella explained, after I climbed into the front of her car. My heart sunk. I prayed for Stella to announce that she wouldn't be talking to me for the entire journey.

'My three were always sick at Daisy's age,' explained Stella. 'At one point I asked the GP if he could place a *"reserved"* sign on a chair in his waiting room, as I was there every other day with the boys.'

I noticed her hair was no longer gelled back. It was standing so tall at the front the ends were touching her car roof. 'I see you're out of your slicked back hair era.' She ran her hand through her hair. 'Yea, I think I might grow it and start a whole new hair era.'

I nodded and slumped against the window. My head was like a train station at rush hour. It was mentally overwhelming. *The sooner Stella put on some music, and started the fifteen minutes of no talking, the better.*

She turned to me. 'I can see you're going to be fun on the journey to and from work.'

I grimaced and looked away. She put on her Guns N' Roses

CD, which surprised me. After ten minutes, I felt like a different man. The car was filled with pure guitar and drum chaos, amazing vocals, and delicious metal riffs. It also brought back funny memories of playing in the band with Harry and Claire on a Sunday afternoon in Dad's garage. I would be rocking out with my electric guitar, and Claire would be groaning at the way I moved across our makeshift stage. 'Mateo, you dance like my grandad,' she would say, 'please go play the keyboard.' Harry would be laughing, and I would then sulk for the rest of the band practice. I wrote a few rock songs for our little band, and once we'd stopped arguing, we would sing our hearts out in Dad's garage. The urge to go home, get out my old electric guitar and write something was powerful.

'That was what you needed,' she said, after turning down the music, 'to get you out of your head. Guns N' Roses never fails.'

'In my youth I did love a bit of rock.'

'I have been meaning to ask you – how's the piano playing at the hotel?'

'It's all right – why?'

She shrugged. 'Since I realised you have been lying to me about your strong feelings for Lia, I have been trying to find the hotel you said you played at – *The Traveller's Rest* – on Google Maps, but I couldn't find it.'

I groaned as she grinned at me. 'Do you want to tell me where you really know Lia from, and not feed me some more BS?'

'You should work as a spy.'

A cackle fell from her mouth. 'Not the first time I've been told that. It's the cynic in me.' She stopped cackling. 'Mateo, I know I lectured you on my car sharing rules, but I like you both. Lia is lovely, and so are you, Mateo... even though you have moaned about my driving – and my kids.'

'I questioned your use of the word "calming" to describe your car share.' She cast me a sugary smile. 'You're forgiven, and I'm willing to bend one of my own rules for you.'

'Why do you have the romance rule anyway?'

I watched her face darken, and her hands grip the wheel tighter. 'He was called Chris... an IT manager, late thirties, liked to work out in his spare time, and he wanted a car share as his ex-girlfriend had taken his car. After a few months we fell madly in love. I used to play a lot of Luther Vandross as we travelled to work.' She let out a heavy sigh. 'We started seeing each other outside of the car share. It ended badly after he confessed to sleeping with a woman from his office at a work conference. My car share became torturous. I got some bad reviews, as people picked up on the cold atmosphere, and a few mentioned the huge argument we had in the car where I asked him to get out on a roundabout.'

'Blimey.'

'Once Chris left, I vowed to ban all romance in my car.'

Stella gazed wistfully out of the windscreen. I stared at her chaotic red hair, her oversized purple glasses, and her ridiculously big earrings. Her car sharing arrangement was chaotic, but she had everyone's best interests at heart, and she was a good friend to me. Something inside me shifted. 'Look, I lied about the hotel because I was trying to avoid a subject that makes me sad.'

'Understandable.' Stella pulled into the fast lane on the motorway. 'You don't have to tell me. I sense oversharing is not something you enjoy. The last thing I want is to make you–'

The words burst out of my mouth before she could finish her sentence. 'My father has Alzheimer's, and he's in a nursing home. I play the piano for him and the other residents a few nights a week.' For a few seconds after the words had left my lips I froze in shock.

'I'm so sorry.'

More words rose to the surface from deep inside of me. 'Dad doesn't know who I am anymore. I'd give anything just to talk to him again. The last four years have been harder than I ever could have imagined.'

Stella listened and didn't say a word.

'When I play the piano, and I look across at him sometimes, I see something flicker across his face. I live for those moments.' My voice cracked, and my face felt hot. 'For years, Dad and I had this connection. We were so close even when I was a sulky teenager. He was my best friend.' I wiped a stray tear away from my cheek, and realised I was doing the very thing I swore I would never do – getting emotional in Stella's car.

She nodded. 'Cherish the memories you have of him, Mateo. It sounds like through your piano you are finding a different way to connect with him on a deeper level. That's real love.'

I sat back and thought about what she'd said. Music for me *was* about connecting with Dad.

'My ex-fiancée never understood why I spent so much time with Dad at his nursing home. Lia's father is in the same nursing home. Before we car shared, she was just a woman who used to stand and listen to me play, from the back of the room. Lia understands what I'm going through.'

'It's nice you've found someone like Lia.' She raised her manicured hand. 'Hold on. Did you follow my advice on rebuilding her? It was a bit of Ed's advice to be fair.'

I nodded. 'Yes... but.'

Clamping one hand across her forehead she let out a groan. 'Please tell me you didn't do a Rob style job of rebuilding her?'

'No I didn't, Stella,' I snapped. 'That's the issue. I haven't even kissed her yet because I respect her so much. I want her to take it slowly. Then there's all the crap I went through...'

'You haven't even kissed her yet?'

'No, I haven't, and it's becoming painful.'

I watched her swerve into the slow lane. During my time in her car, I don't think I'd ever witnessed her in the slow lane. 'So, what happened at that training ground?'

Plunging my face into my hands I let out a frustrated yelp. 'She went to kiss me, and I refused.'

Stella gasped. 'How did that work out for you?'

'Big mistake on my part,' I explained. 'She wasn't happy.'

Shaking her head Stella tapped the steering wheel.

'Thanks,' I snapped. 'Can I defend my decision? She was broken and emotional. The last thing she needed was for me to kiss her. She needed to play football.'

'This is warming my heart, Mateo.'

I nodded. 'The following week I borrowed some football boots, I bought a football, and I took her to the ground. She started kicking the ball again. Stella, it was amazing to watch her reconnect with her passion.'

After casting me a look of bewilderment Stella leant back in her car seat. 'That was such a great thing to do, Mateo. You went to all that trouble to get her back to properly kicking a ball?'

'We were doing great until Alex appeared.'

Stella nodded. 'I could see that from your face.'

'My ex-fiancée left me at the altar for someone like Alex. That was only a year ago. My heart has been broken for a long time. So many cracks.' I let out a nervous laugh.

Stella took a deep breath. 'Lia is the glue to your broken heart.'

'That's deep for half eight in the morning.'

She shrugged. 'You should be grateful to Lia.'

I sat and reflected on what she had said. 'Up until Lia came along, I was trying my best to hide my heart away. I even lied about Dad being unwell. Lia has made me see things differently. You're not just a crazy car share lady, are you?'

She smiled. 'I used to commute every day on my own. Every morning I'd stand and wait for the bus in the rain, hail, snow, and sunshine with the same people around me. We never spoke. A lot of people were still half asleep or busy cursing the early morning, which I can relate to, but I could tell some of them were burdened by worries, anxiety... the horrid stuff that keeps people awake at night. I wanted to reach out to those people and reassure them. One day I noticed a woman was quietly crying next to me. She wasn't saying anything, just staring out across the high street as tears streamed down her face. She'd been coming to the bus stop for over a year, and from our short time together I knew she loved her old brown leather handbag from the way she stroked it, her purple scarf, which she always wore on chilly days, her blue and yellow summer dress on warm days, and Take That was always blaring through her earbuds. On that day when she was crying, I reached out and tapped her arm. She turned to me, and I smiled. It was like a message to her that we shared the same forty-minute journey every day, and I was beside her. No matter what life threw at her I would always be there, beside her for those forty minutes, and I cared. A few weeks later she told me her husband had left her and said that my smile had been the most comforting thing anyone had done for her. That's why I now run my car share. I care about the people who travel with me.' After repositioning her purple glasses, she said, 'So, you're just going to lie down and let this Alex win Lia's heart?'

I shrugged and rested my head against her car window.

Stella continued. 'You've put in all these great foundations – you've respected her, you've not flung yourself at her, you've talked to her, encouraged her to return to the sport she loved, you've not asked her for nude photos like some of the men on my dating sites, and you've helped her come out of her shell. So, now it's time for you to give up and walk away?'

'I can't compete with him, Stella.'

She cast me a stern look. 'Stop the negativity, Mateo. By the sounds of it, you are way ahead of him. I took one look at Mr Handsome, and I thought, *player*. He loves the way he looks. I saw him in my rearview mirror as I pulled away, checking himself out in a shop window. I bet when he goes out on a night, he has a circle of women dancing around him, and he's the centre of attention. I'm sad to say, I've dated men like him.'

'I just keep thinking about what happened with Natalie.'

Stella playfully swiped my arm. 'Stop it. The past has gone, Mateo. You can't go back. Only forwards. Let Natalie go, and be appreciative of the fact you discovered her true colours before you got married and had a family.'

'What do I do now then?'

She smiled. 'Work on yourself.'

'Huh?'

She clicked her fingers. 'If money was no option – what would your dream career be?'

The words fell effortlessly off my tongue. 'Songwriter. I mainly play the piano, but I can also play the drums and guitar. Work with music artists and producers again. Build a platform for my music on social media.'

'Have you written any songs?'

Inside, I felt like something was waking from hibernation. I nodded. 'Loads. I studied music at university, played in various student bands, and I wrote loads of songs and melodies. One of my mates Pete from my course got into music publishing, and he put one of my tracks in front of the manager of a band. That song got to number eighteen in the charts.'

Stella's mouth was wide open in shock.

'It wasn't a big hit back then, but I was proud of it.'

'What was the song title?'

The lyrics and melody came rushing back to me. 'The Pieces of Us.'

'Tell me about it.'

'It started life on my piano. I wrote the chorus first. Anyway, it ended up being turned into a synth pop song. I can find it on my phone if you want to listen to it.'

She nodded, and I scrolled through my phone to find it. Seconds later, it blasted out from my phone, transporting me back to when I'd worked in the studio, writing down lyrics on the back of a beer mat, and the amazing moment when I heard my song on the radio for the first time.

'Sounds a bit like New Order and Human League,' Stella said, whilst bobbing her head to the beat. 'I like it. Gives me an eighties, nineties vibe.' Once it had finished, she smiled at me. 'So, what happened next?'

'The other songs I wrote after that never came close to that one. I lost my confidence, and then I met Natalie.'

Stella held up her hand. 'Let me guess, she wanted you to do something different?'

I nodded. 'I wasn't making regular money, and songwriting took up a lot of my time. I did loads of temp office jobs to keep me going, but there was nothing solid to build a life on. She got me a job working in this finance company as I've always loved maths.'

'But your passion has found you again?'

'Playing to Dad every week has helped, and seeing Lia listening to me on the piano.'

'When you get to work, put together a plan for how you can make this dream happen.'

'Will this really work with Lia?'

'Mateo, reconnect with what is inside of *you*. Oh, and you need to face your demons.'

Lucy Mitchell

'Demons?' I raised an eyebrow.

'If I were you, I'd make peace with the version of you who got jilted at that church across from where I had that flat tyre. The sight of it made you turn an odd colour.'

'You noticed me staring at that church?'

She nodded. 'So did Lia. It was obvious you still have issues. Go stand in that church, and face your demons.'

My response was instant. 'No way.'

Chapter 38

Lia

'How was your day, Lia?' Stella asked. We were on our way home. I reflected on my day. 'Mixed bag. I got a call from Sharon at Dad's nursing home this morning.'

'Is everything all right, Lia?' Mateo asked.

Stella tapped my arm. 'Also, don't worry, Mateo has told me all about his hotel lie. I know *everything*.'

'Has he?' I turned around to smile at him before continuing. 'Dad has got a bad cough. So, they called me to say they were organising for him to see the doctor.'

'He's okay though – yea?' Mateo sounded concerned. I nodded. 'At lunch I called Sharon, and she reckoned he was a lot brighter in himself, although his cough is bad.'

'Have you told your sister?' Stella asked.

'I've texted her to say he's unwell. She's read it. I'm not expecting her to show up.'

After the motorway, Stella pulled into a housing estate, onto a road with temporary traffic lights on it. She parked the car. 'Got a goody bag to collect. Will be two secs.'

I cast Mateo a puzzled look. He gestured towards the bus, which had pulled up beside Stella at the stop across the road.

We both watched Stella board the bus, and then two minutes later, appear with a supermarket bag.

'What the hell is she doing?' I exclaimed.

With a smile Mateo replied, 'That's her same day delivery service.'

Stella came running over to us clutching her shopping bag. She climbed in and passed me the bag to put on the back seat. 'Sorry about that. Tina, who car shared with me last year, was dumped last night by her boyfriend. I wanted to drop her off some stuff to cheer her up.'

I cast Stella a bewildered look. 'You get that stuff from a bus driver?'

Stella grinned. 'Only when I forget to go to a shop. That was my friend Josie's boyfriend Kenny. He loves to do a quick shop during his bus route. It's same day delivery if you can catch his bus, and Tina lives around the corner. Do you mind if I just go to the next street and drop off Tina's stuff?'

I shook my head as there was plenty of time before I needed to collect Daisy. 'Go for it,' said Mateo. 'I hope Tina is okay.' Stella smiled. 'She will be after she gets my goody bag.'

Stella opened her car door. 'Will be two secs.'

We both watched her sprint up a garden path with her bag of goodies. The front door opened, and a woman with a baby on her hip and a toddler clinging to her side stepped out and hugged Stella.

'How was your day, Mateo?' I asked, as Stella raced back to the car and yanked open the car door.

He nodded. 'Good day. I found Pete's email address; he's my friend who works in music publishing.'

I stared at Mateo. 'Wow, your music dream is taking shape.'

'I've just got to work up the courage to email him now.'

'Do it, make it happen.'

Stella climbed in and interrupted us. 'Thanks, both, for

letting me do that. Tina's got little ones, and the last thing she needed was her boyfriend dumping her and moving out.'

'Did she like her goody bag?' Mateo asked.

Stella nodded. 'I got her bath foam, chocolates, a little bag of chocolate sweets for her eldest, and her favourite shampoo.'

'Wow, you're so nice, Stella,' I said. Stella was a little wild and wacky in her ways, but it was clear she had a heart of gold.

Stella started her car engine. 'I love all my car sharers, and I never stop thinking about them. I have also been in dark times in my life. Sometimes you can get a lot of strength from seeing a friendly face on your doorstep and a bag full of goodies. What were you talking about when I got in the car?'

'Mateo's music dream.'

Stella turned to me. 'Lia, did you know Mateo once wrote a song which made it into the top twenty in the charts?'

'Wow, Mateo, you kept that quiet.' I turned round to face him in the back.

He shrugged. 'It was nothing.'

'Excuse me?' I screeched, which made Stella laugh. 'How is a top twenty hit... nothing?'

Stella raised her hand. 'Mateo, play Lia "The Pieces of Us".'

In seconds, an impressive catchy tune filled the car. I turned to him as the female singer's voice burst into song. 'Did you really write this?'

He grinned. 'I did, a long time ago.'

When it had finished, Stella and I cheered. 'Please tell me you're going to write again?'

I watched his face break into a huge smile. 'I don't want to work in finance for much longer. I want to get back to fulfilling my dream of writing songs professionally.'

'Mateo, follow your dreams,' urged Stella. 'I can't wait to hear your new stuff in my car. That's what life's about – doing what makes you happy.'

'That's really great, Mateo. What sort of stuff are you going to write?'

'I wrote down a few lyrics at work over lunch, and I already have a few possible melodies.' His eyes were shining with excitement.

'Oh,' Stella said, pulling onto the high street. 'I have a new car sharer starting tomorrow.'

'Oh,' I said, pulling myself away from Mateo's captivating eyes. 'Anyone we know?'

Stella smiled at Mateo in the rearview mirror. 'I think this car sharer will be nicer than Kay the wedding planner.'

Mateo nodded. 'Anyone will be better than Kay.'

Mateo was still on my mind during football training. As I practised my one-on-one training against Dee, the opposition defender, I thought about Mateo chasing his music dream. It made my heart go wild.

'What's up with you?' Dee asked, as we caught our breath. 'You seem away with the fairies tonight?'

'Just got stuff on my mind.'

She gestured behind us. Alex was watching me from the side of the training pitch. 'Is it to do with a very handsome football coach by any chance?'

'No. Alex really is just a friend.'

Dee shook her head. 'That's not what he's telling people. He told Gee it was a matter of time before you and he made a move on each other.'

'Really?'

She leaned in closer. 'You might want to avoid Mitzi as well. She's not happy.'

I glanced at Mitzi who was glaring at me. Before I had time

to get angry Alex began clapping his hands behind us. 'Nice work, Edwards,' he grinned.

I wanted to march over to him and demand why he felt the need to tell Gee stuff that wasn't even true, but he shocked me by saying, 'The second team has a match on Sunday, and I wanted to ask whether you wanted to be on the bench? We'll bring you on for the last fifteen minutes.' My heart broke into a gallop, and a warm fuzzy sensation coursed through my veins. 'Me – play in a match?'

Dee let out a deafening screech, and lifted me off the ground in celebration. 'The return of Lia Edwards.'

'You're not ready for a full game, but I would like to see you on the pitch.'

'Wow, Alex,' I gasped. 'I'd love to play.'

I noticed how he didn't break eye contact with me as he spoke. 'Edwards, seeing you playing a match again would make me so happy. It will be like the old times.'

Dee was jumping up and down with excitement, which made Hope and Jazzy come over. 'Lia's going to be on the bench in the friendly on Sunday.' Within a few seconds we were like a pack of excited children, all of us yelling and shrieking.

Once training had ended, I walked out of the changing rooms and bumped into Mitzi.

'You knew I liked Alex, Lia,' she growled. 'Who does that to a close friend?' She stormed off before I could say there was nothing between Alex and me.

With a heavy heart I walked over to where Hope, Ben, Alex, and the little ones were. Alex had Daisy in his arms, and was twirling her around. The sight of her ear-to-ear smile, and the way she hugged him, melted my heart. *He loved Daisy so much.* Dee tapped me on the shoulder. 'Have you seen how amazing he is with Daisy?'

'I know,' I murmured, watching Daisy playfully hit his head with her little fabric football.

Dee sighed. 'He's a natural. Joe would want Alex in Daisy's life, Lia.'

'He would,' I said, unable to pull my eyes away from Alex and Daisy. *She was right. Joe would want Alex in his daughter's life.* We all said goodbye, and Alex offered to carry Daisy all the way home, which she loved. I couldn't take my eyes off them both giggling and pulling silly faces. *Perhaps in time I could grow to love Alex?*

I suddenly felt weighed down with guilt. Mitzi was right. Seeing us together must have been so hard. *Mitzi didn't deserve to be betrayed by me.*

While I made us some soup, Alex read Daisy a bedtime story. Once I had kissed her goodnight, Alex and I sipped our mugs of soup on the sofa together.

'I am thinking of running a fun session for little ones.' He looked at me and smiled. 'Daisy would love the chance to run around carrying her ball. She has potential.'

I chuckled. 'Alex, she's not even two.'

He laughed and nudged me. 'You must start them young these days. Anyway, Joe would want me to get her into football.'

My "Joe wall" caught my eye. *He was right. Joe had adored football and he would have loved to have seen Daisy kicking a ball about.* My heart ached for Joe.

'Don't worry, Lia, I have Daisy's footballing career sorted.' Gently, he pulled me against his chest. 'You and I are going to make Joe proud.'

Wiping a stray tear, which had started its descent of my cheek, I nodded. *That was what we needed to do – make Joe proud.* After putting on my PJs, I walked onto the landing to put away the ironing board. As I slotted it back into the laundry cupboard, he opened the bathroom door, and came out with just a small towel around his waist. He grinned as he saw my eyes surveying his tanned muscular chest and his ripped abs. I turned back to the laundry cupboard and rested my head against the doorframe. There were no tingling sensations when I looked at Alex. There had been no electrical current like the ones I felt when I sat next to Mateo at the piano, or in the back of Stella's car. There was... nothing.

'Goodnight, Alex,' I said, watching the grin evaporate from his face. I went into my bedroom, closed the door, and sat on my bed listening to Alex go into his room. Once I was sure he was in bed, I lay back and wondered what Mateo was doing. Closing my eyes, I slipped into a dreamy world, where Mateo was playing the piano.

Chapter 39

Mateo

Lia arrived later than usual to our meeting point. She yawned, rubbed her puffy eyes, and cast me a tired smile. 'I'm knackered. Training was good, then I spent half the night awake.'

'Was Daisy up in the night?'

She shook her head. 'Just a lot on my mind. Did you play at the nursing home last night?'

'Yes, and I saw your dad.'

Her eyes brightened. 'How was he?'

'They wouldn't let him hear me play because of his cough and bad chest.'

A look of concern flashed across her face. 'I must get over to see him tonight.' She rubbed her temples. 'Alex has made plans for us to eat out at some restaurant, but all I want to do is see Dad.'

'I got to talk to your dad though.'

She smiled. 'Really? How is he in himself?'

'He was moaning about his cough, and how everyone keeps fussing over him.'

Lia chuckled. 'That's my dad. He hates all the attention. How's the songwriting going?'

I loved the way she looked at me when she asked about my music. There was something sexy about having another person actively interested in me. 'Going well. I'm enjoying writing lyrics again, and coming up with little melodies. Music makes me happy.'

She cast me a knowing nod. 'I can tell you love it.'

We stood for a few moments watching a gang of cyclists racing down the busy high street. 'Listen, Mateo, I...'

This was odd. She didn't usually struggle for words. I decided to jump in. 'How's life living with Alex?'

She nodded. 'Daisy thinks he's amazing, and he is really good with her.'

'That's nice.'

We both fell silent.

'Look, Mateo, ummm... Joe would have wanted him to be a part of her life. I need to... think about everything.' Her voice cracked. My chest began to ache.

She didn't have to spell it out. It was obvious. Alex had finally won her over. Inside my chest it felt like someone was scooping out my insides.

A horn heralded the arrival of Stella's car. 'Morning, Lia and Mateo,' shouted Stella after lowering the electric window. 'This is Grace. As she lives near me, it was easiest for me to pick her up first.

The lady cast us both a happy smile. I could see her complex braids, and hung from her ears were giant gold hoops, which were even bigger than Stella's. Instantly, I sensed Grace was a morning person. She looked vibrant, and her hazel eyes were almost glowing. *Why did Stella have to recruit a jolly morning person on the day Lia had told me she was going to make a go of her and Alex?* All I wanted to do was sink into my seat in the back of the car, and wallow in my misery.

Stella gestured towards Grace. 'Grace is joining us for a few days as her car is in the garage. Right, let's start the fifteen minutes of no talking.' She turned up the music and a lively Wham! track filled the car. Lia turned away to face the window. Once that had finished, we listened to DJ Rick Carter.

"Here's the Breaking Commuter News. Emily's grandpa sadly passed away last night. She's driving to work and wants to send Grandpa Harold a shout out. Apparently, he used to listen to the show from his shed in the garden. Grandpa Harold – you were a legend. Take it easy today, Emily. We have a commuter tanning update - Kylie had a spray tan disaster last night, and is on the bus giving out tangerine skin vibes. Kylie, we are all thinking of you. Mike has just bumped into his ex-girlfriend on the train to work, and realised how much he misses her. Do us a favour Mike, and go tell her. Keep smiling everyone."

'Has anyone got any good news?' Stella asked.

'I'm on the bench in my first match on Sunday,' Lia gushed. 'My fitness still needs working on, but Alex says I can see how I get on, and it's only a friendly. I can't believe he still believes in me.'

His name made me flinch.

'Alex the hero – huh?' Stella grinned at Lia.

'He's a good football coach, and he even thinks Daisy already has potential.' She laughed, and I pressed my face to the window.

Stella squealed at the wheel. 'Lia, I am so proud of you. Wow – that's exciting.'

She turned to Grace. 'Lia has returned to football after a three-year break, and as you can hear, she's already doing a fantastic job.'

Grace turned around in her seat to smile at Lia. 'You play for the Tigresses?'

'Second team,' beamed Lia. I noticed how proud Lia looked now when anyone asked her about football. 'Are you a fan?'

Grace nodded. 'Yes. I love watching Celia Jones, in the first team. She's phenomenal. There is a striker I also love in the second team called Hope.'

Lia squealed. 'Hope is one of my close friends. We still play together. You ever played, Grace?'

'I wanted to when I was younger, but I was always scared someone would tackle me. I'd get injured and my ice skating dream would be over.'

Stella gasped at Grace. 'Do you still skate?'

Grace pointed to a bag at her feet. 'My boots are coming with me today as I have skating tonight.'

'After all these years I still cannot stand up on the ice unaided,' explained Stella. 'I am always hugging the sides of the rink or falling on my backside.'

Grace laughed and all her braids jangled. 'For me it was an instant love. My brother took me when I was little, and I got the hang of it pretty much straight away.'

'So, have you been skating all your life?'

'I was good at skating, when I was younger. Even skated in some major competitions... and then I met someone who decided that he didn't want a skating girlfriend, so I stopped.' I watched Grace shake her head. 'I listened to everyone around me, who said ice skating was for younger people, and that this guy was the best thing to have happened to me.'

Stella let out a sigh. 'I'm sorry, Grace.'

I noticed Lia looking in my direction.

Grace continued. 'I listened to everyone else. Even my parents adored this guy. I listened to him when he laughed at the prospect of me going back to ice skating after our children had been born. I took all his jokes about me being not the right body shape to skate. He wasn't very nice to me in a lot of ways. No one could see what I was going through. It was like I no longer had a voice.'

Stella nodded. 'I've been there. I'm guessing you've found your voice again?'

Grace grinned. 'It was weird because I went to watch an ice skating competition with my daughter, who has always been a secret fan of my skating. I was days away from turning forty. She turned to me and said, "Mum, why don't you start skating again?" Well, I gave her a lengthy lecture on why women in their late thirties and forties shouldn't skate. I sounded like him.'

Lia was staring at Grace.

'My daughter took me for a surprise ice skating lesson. The guy didn't know as he was away at some conference. Later, I would find out he'd met someone else at work. Anyway, I loved skating again, and over a couple of months I found my voice again.'

Stella turned to smile at Grace. 'Daughters are lifesavers, aren't they?'

Grace nodded. 'Is your daughter a lifesaver, Stella?'

I stared out of the window and wondered how on earth Stella was going to explain to Grace how Lauren, her unruly and wayward teenage daughter, was a lifesaver.

'Lauren, my seventeen-year-old, has saved me numerous times,' explained Stella, making me sit bolt upright in shock. 'When she was fourteen, she persuaded me to leave my partner at the time, who was sleeping with multiple women behind my back. I'd taken to my bed, as my mental health had hit an all-time low. Lauren, bless her, sat by my bed for hours telling me to get up and fight back. She was a rock, and even found me and the kids a house to rent, as my partner owned the house at the time. Lauren also took up a paper round so that she could help me with the bills.'

I couldn't believe what I was hearing. Even Lia was wide eyed and open mouthed. Lauren, one of Stella's nightmare children, was actually an angel in disguise.

Grace grinned. 'My daughter's unwavering support gave me the strength to say to everyone – hold up, this is my life! I want to make my own decisions, one of which is to skate again.'

'What happened?' Lia asked.

'He didn't like me skating again at forty, but I didn't care. I ended up leaving him, which upset my parents, and was hard. My daughter and son came to live with me, and I've been ice skating ever since.'

These stories were starting to change my opinion of teenage children. Perhaps I had been too judgemental about Stella's kids. Lia's phone began to vibrate. Pressing it to her ear, Lia gasped. 'Oh no... Oh God... Okay... Yes... I'll be there.' Her face had gone chalky pale when the call ended. 'It's Dad, he's been rushed to hospital with breathing difficulties... I need to get to the hospital. Oh, Mateo, I don't want to lose him.'

I placed my hand over hers and turned to Stella. 'Can you drop us off on this road, Stella? I can hail a cab to the hospital. It will be easier from here.'

'You don't have to come with me,' Lia said, her voice small.

'I'm coming, and that's final. Come on, let's go.'

Stella pulled up on the side of the road, and Grace got out to let us out. 'Lia, you know where I am,' Stella called out, blowing a kiss.

At the hospital only Lia was allowed up to the ward to see her father. I camped out at the hospital café, and phoned work to say I wasn't going to be in. Two hours later, Lia came to the café. Her eyes were pink and puffy. Mascara had run down her cheeks. Without hesitation she fell into my arms. 'They've stabilised his breathing, and he's on medication for the infection. Mateo, he looks so poorly.'

I stroked the back of her head. 'It sounds like he's in the right place. Come and sit down; you look absolutely drained.'

She sat down, and I got her a vanilla latte with some cookies. 'I rang Alex, as Daisy might need picking up later, but something unexpected has come up, which he can't cancel.'

'Don't worry – we will get Daisy sorted,' I assured her.

I watched her take a sip of her latte, and nibble on a cookie. She took out her phone. 'I need to call Angel.'

She got up from the table, and walked to the far side of the café where it was quieter. After two minutes she returned. 'No answer. I left her a message. She's probably at some glittery celebrity filled event.

'Thank you for doing all this. You didn't have to, Mateo.'

Reaching over, I squeezed her hand. 'This is what friends are for Lia.' Pressing my ear to my phone I called Harry.

Chapter 40

Lia

It was Saturday evening, and I was on the bus home from visiting Dad. He was being kept in hospital until they were comfortable his chest was clear. My phone buzzed as the bus took me home. It was Angel. It had taken her twenty-four hours to call me back. 'How is he?' she asked. The background to her call sounded like she was busy socialising. I could hear music, chatter, and laughter.

'He's a little better.'

'I might come and visit,' Angel said, making my neck and shoulders stiffen. We both knew she wouldn't show up. The words, 'Angel, please stop doing this,' shot out of my mouth, which shocked me.

'What?' Her voice rose a few octaves.

'Stop making these ridiculous promises about coming to visit us,' I snapped. 'There's always a change of plan, a late work event or some other reason why you can't come. I know you struggle with seeing Dad, but... well... I have news for you. I also struggle with seeing Dad, hearing him speak, and watching him struggle to move. It doesn't stop me from loving and caring for him.' I was breathing fast, and people on the bus were looking at me. 'Now, if you don't mind, I am busy.' I hung up, took a deep breath, and gripped the bus rail with a trembling hand.

Alex had looked after Daisy for me, but I'd stayed longer than I'd envisaged, which he wasn't happy about. All afternoon, he'd bombarded me with texts about how he wanted to go out but couldn't as he had Daisy. I scrolled back through all the messages and felt my heart sink. *Surely, he knew how important my dad was to me.*

It was then I received a lengthy text from Mitzi about how let down she felt by my blossoming friendship with Alex.

My head felt like a fairground carousel ride of thoughts and worries. On one glittery horse was Dad's health, on another was my friendship with Alex, which had been a worry ever since he'd moved in. On a horse in front was the story about Grace finding her voice, which she'd shared with us in the car the previous day, on another was Alex's amazing relationship with Daisy, and how it could be difficult to replicate that with someone else, on a horse behind was my past life with Joe, and on a beautiful looking horse on its own was Mateo. I knew I'd hurt him It was like I'd turned the lights out behind his eyes. Yet he'd stayed at the hospital café that day when Dad got admitted, and in the afternoon when I needed to go and collect Daisy, he organised for his mate Harry to pick us both up from the hospital. I tried to speak to him in Harry's van, but he'd smiled and whispered, 'You have to do what's right.'

Alex met me at the door as I came in. He was wearing a fitted pink shirt and smart trousers. I looked around for Daisy. 'Hope has got Daisy. I said we'd collect her tomorrow morning. Bella and Daisy can have a sleepover.'

My heart began to thump, and I glared at him. 'Daisy's not even two, and she's never spent the night away from me.'

He raised his hands. 'I'm sorry. I wanted to take you out for a posh dinner at a fancy restaurant.'

'Alex, you can't just make that sort of decision without asking me.'

'Lia – you need a break from Daisy.'

A red mist slid over my eyes. 'I decide when I need a break from my child, not you, Alex.'

He tried to pull me into a hug, but I resisted. 'Lia, I'm sorry. Daisy kept grizzling and I had stuff to do, so I called Hope and took her over.'

I could smell beer on his breath. 'Have you been drinking?'

His face broke into a grin. 'Ben and I had a beer down the pub whilst Hope looked after the kids.'

Taking out my phone I called Hope. She picked up immediately, and I could hear Daisy crying in the background. 'Hey, Lia.'

'I'm going to come and collect Daisy.'

I heard what sounded like a sigh of relief. 'Alex turned up about three hours ago, Lia. I was supposed to be going out, and there he was on the doorstep with a screaming Daisy. I took her from him, and I left a message on your phone.'

'I'll be there in two minutes.'

Alex grabbed my elbow as I walked past him. 'Leave her, Lia. She'll be fine with Hope.'

'Get your hand off me. I think you'd better cancel the restaurant, Alex.'

He let me go, and went upstairs. With a thudding heart I jogged over to Hope's. Daisy rushed into my arms the second I got through the door. I hugged her like crazy, and dried her tears. 'It's all right. Mummy is here.'

Hope wrapped her arms around me and Daisy. 'I'm going to kick balls at Alex tomorrow, and I will be aiming for a certain part of his body,' she snarled. 'I rarely miss when I am angry.'

I smiled and she stroked my hair. 'Lia, this thing with Alex is now making me cross.'

'You're not the only one.'

Hope nodded. 'I love Dee to bits, but when she's got something into her head, she will not let it go. I know she means well with all this stuff about what Joe would have wanted, but I have to say that whatever you do with your life, Joe would be proud.'

'Do you think so?'

'Come on, Lia, you knew Joe better than all of us. He was very easygoing and never would have dreamed of forcing anyone to do anything.'

She was right. How had I become so wrapped up in everyone else's thoughts about Joe? He was a chilled guy. Even when his cousin came home from a holiday to Thailand and announced she'd got married to her boyfriend, whom her mother disliked, in a ring of flowers whilst naked, and was planning to emigrate, Joe was the only person in his family who hugged her and told her to go and be happy. He was supportive when Dee announced she was ditching her boyfriend and moving out of her flat so she could live with Shona after being in a relationship with her for three weeks.

Hope planted a kiss on my cheek. 'Remember, Lia, it's your life. Not Dee's, not Alex's, and not Mitzi's.'

I nestled my chin into Daisy's golden curls. 'Alex has always been so good with Daisy, and...'

Hope raised her hand. 'Alex makes out he's good with Daisy when you are near, but look at the mess he created today. I think he had her for an hour and then brought her over here.' Bella came running into the hallway, and started shouting at Daisy and waving goodbye.

Hope laughed. 'Bella likes to manage our guests. She loves a goodbye; you should see her manage Ben's mother. As soon as Gill sits down Bella starts shouting, "Bye."'

'Right, I better take this one home.'

'See you tomorrow at the match. Oh, and Lia – bring the old Lia Edwards with you.'

I cast her a puzzled expression.

'The formidable one. The Lia Edwards who took no shit from anyone.'

Alex put on his excited face at seeing Daisy when we got home. Over his shoulder I could see he'd laid the table.

He took her from me. 'I'm cooking us three some dinner to say sorry. Lia – I was wrong to behave like that.'

The dinner was nice, but uncomfortable. I tried to forget about how he had dumped Daisy with Hope, and gone for a beer with Ben, but it kept nibbling away at me. Once I'd put Daisy to bed Alex handed me a glass of wine. 'How's your dad?' He gestured for me to sit by him on the sofa. I told him about how Dad was brighter and had even cracked a few jokes during my visit.

'Lia, have you forgiven me for earlier?'

'I suppose so.'

Alex turned to face my "Joe wall". He raised his glass. 'Hey, Joe, she's forgiven me.' After he put down his glass, he pulled me into him. 'What you need is a cuddle, Lia.' Anger and irritation coursed through my veins. I wriggled away from him. 'Alex, please... I don't need a cuddle.'

'Look, Lia, I don't know how to say this, but I am in love with you. I can't go on hiding my feelings. I am making a mess of things.' He reached out and cupped the side of my face. 'Sweet Lia, I love you.' I tried to speak, but before I knew it, he'd pressed his lips hard against mine. I tried to push him away, but he was insistent. His hands ran over my hips, and I noticed he was breathing fast. 'Joe would want us to be together, Lia,' he moaned. 'Let me take you to bed.' The weight of him forced me back onto the sofa. 'I want to kiss you from head to toe, sweet Lia.'

Hot, fiery anger sped throughout my body. Somewhere deep inside me a door was unlocked, and out stepped the old Lia Edwards. Letting out an angry howl, I pushed hard against his chest, brought my knees up, and kicked. 'GET OFF ME!'

Alex shot up with a horrified look on his face. 'What the fuck?'

I leapt to my feet. 'GET OUT OF MY HOUSE!'

'Lia, calm down.'

He tried to touch my arm, but I stepped back. 'Alex, please go. Get out of my house.'

His eyes widened in shock, and his mouth fell open. I watched him grab his coat and leave.

Once he'd left, I ushered Burrito inside, put the chain on the door, and wrapped my trembling body in a blanket on the sofa. I stared up at my "Joe wall". The words tumbled out of my mouth. 'I will always love you, Joe, but there's something I need to do.'

Chapter 41

Mateo

Claire and two of her kids, Raff and Reg, had come over under the pretence of collecting her old football boots, but I knew she had an ulterior motive. Those football boots had been buried at the bottom of her wardrobe for years before I'd borrowed them. There was no mad rush for Claire to have them back straight away. I was trying to multitask by making sure the boys went nowhere near my piano and electric guitar with their grubby hands, while attempting to guess the reason for Claire's visit.

'Mateo, Harry was worried about you last night,' Claire said, before taking a mouthful of coffee, and stroking Ghost.

'He doesn't need to be.' Leaning back in my kitchen chair I craned my neck to see whether Raff had lifted my piano lid. 'I'm fine,' I lied, knowing full well I'd played my piano until four in the morning, pouring all my emotion and frustration onto the keys. This morning, when Claire had knocked on my front door at nine, my eyes felt like holes in the snow. I'd gone to bed still in my clothes from the day before, and Claire's initial reaction when I opened the door to her looking like a dishevelled wreck was, 'Ugh,' and Raff once again made the loser sign at me.

'Harry said Lia has relegated you to the friend zone.'

I sighed. 'She's doing what she feels is right for her and Daisy.'

Claire took another sip of her coffee, and studied my face. 'You look tired.'

'I didn't sleep well last night.'

She reached her hand across the table, and squeezed my arm. 'I'm here for you if you want to talk. You do know that – don't you?'

I sat up straighter and smoothed down my hair. 'Look, I'm happy for Lia. I'm trying to get started on my new music career.' She knew it was a lie, and so did I.

'What does that involve?' Claire asked. 'Have you emailed Pete yet?'

I recoiled inside. *It was all very well me coming up with all these great ideas in Stella's car, but putting them into practice was a different matter. My mind had created a long list of reasons why I couldn't follow through with my life dream.* 'Still working up my confidence to email him. I'm not cool anymore. I'm just a thirty-something guy who has been working in finance for years. Pete probably has other people–'

'Please phone or message him. If you don't, I will take over your phone again.' She put her hand inside her coat pocket. 'Oh, I have some news for you. We've decided to get rid of the old sofa.' She chuckled. 'Harry says it's time for you to stop using our house like a hotel.'

'What? You can't get rid of my second bed. I have stayed in quite a few hotels, and I have never slept below a load of shelves that cats hang off to dangle half chewed mice near my face when I am asleep.'

She laughed and brought out something from her pocket. 'Harry and I removed all the cushions last night, and we had to put them at the end of our drive, as someone Harry knows is going to get rid of it for us.' She opened her hand. 'As we were staggering out of the house Ronnie noticed this fall out of the sofa.' I looked in her hand to see a delicate gold bracelet chain. 'You are the only one who has slept on the sofa for years. Even before you met Natalie, you were still staying at our house after a night at the pub. Harry wants to know if it's yours.' She passed it to me. There were three tiny letters dangling from the chain, 'J', 'C' and 'E'. My heart broke into a gallop. 'This is Lia's.'

Claire's mouth fell open in shock. 'Please tell me you did not have a midnight rendezvous with Lia on our sofa whilst we were asleep. You wait till I tell Harry.'

'Calm down, it's not what you think. You know how I told you that Lia's cat is Dave? Well, I reckon her partner Joe must have taken the bracelet to be repaired and, on the way home after collecting it, he must have collected Burrito from you. He must have sat on your sofa whilst you sorted out the adoption paperwork, and it somehow fell out of his pocket.'

Claire nodded. 'Yes, that is possible. I did used to make new cat owers sit on that sofa. I wish I remembered the faces of the people who adopted my cats. Will you give it to Lia?'

'Yes, I will do on Monday. She'll be made up. Her father bought her this bracelet, and she lost it around the time they adopted Dave. Well, he's now called Burrito.'

Claire rested her chin on her palms. 'Right, the last thing I need to tell you is... Natalie is getting married today.'

I stared at her. 'Why do I need to know that information?'

'Someone on Facebook I know is friendly with her mate from the gym, and I was made aware of the wedding date. Anyway, it's at the same church as last year.'

'Claire, why are you bringing this up now?'

She took a deep breath. 'Harry told me last night that, after Lia left his van, you had a heart to heart.'

My shoulders and neck stiffened. 'We did not have a heart to heart.'

'You told him how that car sharing woman thinks it would be good for you...'

I raised my hands. 'No, I am not going anywhere near that church.'

Claire stared at me. 'Mateo, you must confront the demon. You must bring closure to the whole Natalie situation.'

'This is nuts!'

She placed her palms flat on the table. 'Mateo, listen to me. I have been told something about Natalie, which may or may not happen today. If it does happen today, you need to see it for your own eyes.'

I snorted with disgust. 'What – is she planning to run away from Zane?'

Claire held my gaze. 'I'm not going to say, but I need you to come with me.'

'Natalie had an affair because I wasn't good enough,' I snapped. 'I wasn't like her gym buddies. I wasn't–'

'MATEO,' Claire shouted. 'Stop. Just stop. For goodness' sake, I am trying to help you.'

It was time to confront my demons. *I had to do this. Stella and Claire were right.*

All the way to the church I felt like I was going to throw up. My stomach groaned and ached. Claire drove in silence whilst Raff and Reg sat in the back on their games consoles.

We parked near the church. From where we were, I could see a throng of wedding guests milling around the front of the church. The array of colourful hats, fancy dresses, smart grey suits and little children in posh frocks made me want to vomit into Claire's glove compartment. She pointed to the dashboard. 'The wedding was due to start twenty minutes ago.'

I turned back to the guests standing outside the church. Their faces were etched with concern and worry. A man in a smart morning suit marched out with his phone stuck to his ear.

Claire squeezed my hand. 'Natalie has commitment issues. Apparently, there was someone before you who she did the same thing to.'

I stared at her in horror.

'I only found out last night. Natalie has been seeing someone else at the gym behind Zane's back.'

Winding down my window I could hear exasperated voices. 'Where is the bride?'

The man in the smart grey suit turned to the guests. 'She's done a runner. The bloody bride has legged it.'

Claire leaned over to me. 'It was never about you, Mateo.'

I plunged my face into my hands and Claire pulled me into a hug. As I tried to not cry in Claire's arms, I could hear Raff say to his little brother, 'Uncle Mateo is such a loser.' A smile crept onto my face and then I began to laugh. The weight of my disastrous wedding had been lifted away from my shoulders.

Chapter 42

Lia

'Alex, bring Lia on,' shouted Jazzy from the side of the pitch. 'We're two goals down, and there's only eight minutes left.'

I watched Alex roll his eyes and look away. Frustration and anger swarmed around my body. *This was my punishment from Alex.* The second I'd arrived at the club house that morning I'd sensed a coldness from him. As I'd walked past him and a few of the first team women I overheard him asking for sympathy as he'd spent the night sleeping in his car. He saw me pass by, and scowled. On my way to the ground for the match I'd hoped he would have the decency and respect to apologise for making me feel frightened on the sofa. That was clearly delusional thinking on my part. Instead, he cornered me on my way to the changing room. 'I still need somewhere to live so you will have to let me stay at yours.'

'Where's my apology?' I hissed.

He took a step back, and raised his hands. 'No need to apologise. You overreacted, Lia.'

'WHAT?' I shouted, as everyone milling outside the

changing rooms stopped talking and stared at us. 'Alex, you took things too far, and you know it.'

Shaking his head, he glared at me. 'It was just a kiss.'

Blood started to thunder past my ears, and my body began to tremble with rage. 'It was *not* just a kiss. After all the years we've known each other, I can't believe you treated me like that.'

'It was just a kiss,' he muttered, flicking back his hair. 'You need to calm down.'

The words shot out of my mouth in an angry torrent. 'I never asked you to kiss me, Alex. You flung yourself at me. You pinned me down. You had zero respect for me. I don't want you in my house. Your stuff is in bin liners outside.' Tears bubbled up in my eyes. To my surprise, Mitzi came to my side and took hold of my hand. She gave it a gentle squeeze. Turning to Alex, she barked, 'I have heard enough. Alex – you need to apologise to Lia.'

He let out a nervous laugh. 'Ladies, please calm down, we have a match to win.'

This was his way of making me feel small and stupid. I knew he'd punish me on the football field. I just didn't realise he wouldn't bring me off the bench.

Jazzy was now joined by Mitzi. 'ALEX, bring Lia on,' she screamed at him. Once again, he looked away, and it was then that I snapped. 'Alex, don't be an idiot.'

His head snapped around to look at me. 'What?'

'You heard them – put me on that pitch.'

He sighed, folded his arms, and cast his eyes towards their goal. 'You're way behind with your fitness, Lia.'

I ignored his comment. 'Are you going to let what happened between us ruin the Tigresses' football game?'

He didn't answer.

'Be a sodding adult, Alex. Accept that you were in the wrong, and put me on.'

'Warm up,' he said quietly.

With five minutes left, and an extra two minutes of stoppage time, I came onto the pitch. Everyone on my team grinned, and adrenalin pulsed through my body. *I was back.*

Out of the corner of my eye I noticed Petra was watching the game.

Mitzi sent the ball up to the halfway line. I started running towards the opposition goal. Jazzy had the ball and was dodging defenders like they were cardboard cut-outs. She didn't have space to shoot. I sprinted as Jazzy sent a curving ball in my direction. As it came down, I had a split second to get myself ready. I saw a flash of white race across the goal mouth. Somehow, I managed to do a fake pass, get past a defender, and kick it to Hope who hammered it past the goalkeeper. The crowd erupted into a huge cheer. There was no time to get carried away. We were still one goal down, and there was time to score again. After the whistle, Dee was able to get the ball to Jazzy, who sent it in my direction. I began to race up the field, weaving past exhausted defenders. My path was blocked, but out of the corner of my eye I saw Flo charging up to the right of me. I sent the ball towards her, and she sent it past the goalie and into the net.

When the final whistle blew the Tigresses had drawn their friendly. We all hugged each other, cheered, and patted Hope on the back for her amazing header. 'We didn't win,' shouted Jazzy, 'but we didn't lose either. Good work, ladies.'

Dee tapped me on the shoulder. She'd been quiet all day. 'I didn't know Alex would go weird on you, Lia. I am so sorry for encouraging him.'

Hope, Mitzi, Jazzy, Flo, and Gee gathered around us on the pitch.

'You were trying to help,' I said, holding open my arms. 'You are also the truest Sagittarian woman I have ever known. You never give up!'

Dee burst into tears. 'I thought Joe would have wanted Alex in your life. I thought Alex would have looked after you.'

'I don't need looking after anymore, Dee,' I said. 'Joe's gone, and I've accepted that. I can't recreate the past.'

Jazzy put her arm around me. 'I'm so proud of you, Lia Edwards. You are radiating this new vibe. It's like a stronger version of the amazing woman you once were.'

Flo tapped Jazzy on the shoulder. 'She'll be after your captain armband soon.'

Everyone burst into laughter, and Jazzy raised her eyebrow at me. 'You can try, Lia Edwards.'

Mitzi was staring at me as Dee pulled away. She stepped in front of me. 'Babe, I'm sorry I shouted at you and sent you that text about how you'd let me down over Alex.'

Jazzy laughed. 'Lia has done you a favour. Alex is a scumbag. No more manifesting, Mitzi.'

I hugged Mitzi. 'I still love you, Mitzi.'

Jazzy gave Mitzi a playful swipe. 'I expect more from you at training now that your stalking Alex on the Gram era has ended.'

Gee barged her way into the middle of us. 'I let two goals in, ladies. I need some love too.'

As we all trooped off the pitch, I looked for Alex. He was nowhere to be seen. I hoped he'd gone back to the house to collect his stuff.

Petra grabbed my arm as I went into the changing room. 'You made us proud today, Lia.'

'Aww thanks, Petra.'

She nodded. 'The goals you set up were impressive.'

'Thanks.'

After she'd gone Dee rushed up behind me. 'Petra doesn't compliment anyone. Lia, you should feel very special.'

Hope drove me back to her house, and I collected Daisy. Hope's husband Ben had been looking after Bella and Daisy. Daisy and I walked home. Burrito met us at the top of the garden path. Once inside, I dumped all my football gear in the hallway, which I intended to sort out later. In the bath, Daisy and I listened to the music from Frozen on my phone, which made Daisy squeal, and I relived the memory of Petra telling me about how the goals I'd set up were impressive. I let Daisy have a go at washing my hair, which she thought was hilarious. She laughed as she tipped her little jug of water over my head. After our bath, we both put on clean clothes and went into the living room. Then I spotted the letter on the table. Letting Daisy go, I opened the envelope.

Inside was a card in Alex's handwriting. *"Good luck with your football. I'm going to find a new team to coach. Thanks for leaving my stuff outside. The key I had is on the matt. Sorry it didn't work out between us."* I tore up his envelope, and put the pieces in the bin. Irritation at his inability to apologise properly for what he did to me, and how he treated me on the pitch today, prickled inside of me.

Daisy brought me a tiny plastic frying pan containing a toy fried egg. I smiled and pretended to eat it. The bare wall in front of me caught my eye. It was adorned with tiny nail holes. Last night I had taken down my "Joe wall". All the photos were now in a box upstairs. The wall was ready for new memories.

A knock at the door made me jolt. My sister Angel was on my doorstep. 'Angel?'

She fiddled with a strand of her curled caramel hair. 'Hello, Lia. Look, I've been to see Dad in hospital, and I thought I would call in before I head back to Manchester.' Angel looked immaculate in her beige trench coat, her fitted black dress and leather boots. I stepped aside to let her into the house. She went over to Daisy, who was standing by her toy stove. 'Hello, Daisy.'

I watched Daisy smile and hand her a toy plastic broccoli floret. Angel smiled and turned back to me. 'I can't promise I'll be down here all the time from now on, but I will try to do more.'

'Oh... well it's nice to see you.'

Angel flicked her blue eyes to the floor. 'I thought about what you said on that call.' Silence descended. She nudged one of Daisy's princess dollies with the toe of her boot. 'Look... it's been difficult. I've been struggling mentally with Dad and his stroke.'

All I could think about was her Instagram feed: her extravagant lifestyle, her glamorous job, selfies of her in posh hotels, kissing her rich boyfriend, and grinning in swanky cars. I had to remind myself that issues with mental health were not always visible.

'Do you want a coffee or a tea, Angel?'

I expected her to politely decline and leave. Instead, to my surprise, she nodded. 'Tea would be nice.' After surveying the living room, she took a seat on the sofa. Daisy gave her a plastic loaf of bread to go with her broccoli.

'Thank you, Daisy, is this for me?' Angel asked, grinning at Daisy.

'Yes,' said Daisy, 'Do you want cake too?' She ran over to her toy stove and grabbed a plastic cake.

Angel laughed as Daisy thrust the cake at her. 'Yummy broccoli, bread and cake.'

Daisy gave her a little bow, which made me laugh.

'Lia, she's not a baby anymore, she's a little person,' cooed Angel.

'She's growing up fast.'

I handed her a cup of tea in the orange and black Tigresses

football tour mug. She smiled, and gestured towards my football gear in the hallway. 'You're playing football again?'

With a nod I sat in the armchair next to the sofa. 'Yes, a good friend of mine persuaded me to return. I played in my first match today.'

She gave me a warm smile. 'That's good, Lia. Football was always special to you.'

'How are you?'

I watched concern flicker across her face before she hung her head. 'Lia, you know I have never been good with family stuff.'

'Yes, I know.'

She took a sip of her tea. 'You must hate me for not being here for you when Joe died, when Daisy arrived. If I was you, I would hate me too. You've had Dad to sort out as well.'

'I know.'

'You must think I am a crap sister.' She looked in my direction, and I noticed her cheeks were damp. 'I couldn't cope after Dad had his stroke. Seeing him like that made me want to run away.' She hung her head, and her curls tumbled down around her face. 'It's his lopsided smile which makes me sad, and seeing him get helped out of his chair is upsetting. So, I ran away. It's been easier to ignore what happened to Dad when I've been miles away.'

The urge to rage was strong, but I heard Stella's voice in my head. Angel needed to know that I also struggled. 'Seeing Dad hurts me every time I see him.'

Angel's eyes widened. 'Really?'

I nodded. 'All I think about is how amazing he was before that stroke happened, all the hiking he used to do, those outdoor swimming events he did, and–'

'The wonderful holidays he used to go on,' Angel said, wistfully.

I took a deep breath. 'Angel, that version of Dad has gone. It's hard I know. At times it is bloody hard, especially when he's choking on his food, struggling to move in his chair, or getting frustrated. He's still our father, though.'

She shook her head, and began to cry. 'I've been having counselling, working up to coming down to see you all. I know you must think I am a selfish cow. When Joe died, I had no idea how to help you either. I am rubbish with this stuff.'

'Being here beside me would have been good,' I said, quietly. 'Even if you had come down and simply made me cups of tea, that would have been great.'

Lifting her tear-stained face she looked at me. 'I'm sorry, Lia. I let you down at the worst time. You've needed me during the past two years, and I've been living my best life in my PR job. You must hate me.'

'Angel, I don't hate you, I've spent the last two years getting angry at your Instagram feed and your broken promises, though.'

She wiped her face with the sleeve of her coat. 'That phone call we had where you shouted at me brought me to my senses.'

'Really?'

Rising from the sofa she came to perch on my arm rest. 'For the past few months, I have been thinking of quitting, and moving out of Manchester. It's time for a change.'

A little part of me wanted to believe her about leaving Manchester, but the cynic in me sensed it was going to take time for Angel to change. 'I appreciate you coming down Angel,' I said, giving her hand a squeeze. *It was time for me to me the bigger person and accept that Angel and I were different in so many ways. She dealt with problems by partying, and filling up her life with expensive things and people. That was who she was.*

'You are always welcome here, Angel.'

She nodded. 'Today is a new start, Lia. I've been to see Dad, and it wasn't as bad as I thought it would be.' Her face brightened. 'He actually made me laugh.'

I smiled. 'I think his jokes have improved.'

We both laughed. 'Lia, I would like to spend time with you and my niece. I need to shoot back. I promise I will be down soon.'

'Baby steps, Angel,' I said, and she smiled.

Chapter 43

Mateo

Lia was waiting for me when I arrived. To my amazement she was ten minutes early on a Monday morning. On the way up to the high street I'd hoped her father was better. I'd missed hearing his thoughts on my music last night.

'Hey, Lia, how's your dad?'

She nodded and grinned. 'He's coming out tomorrow, fingers crossed.'

'I'm so pleased for you both.'

'Mateo,' she smiled, 'are you doing anything after work tonight?'

'Huh?' This was not what I was expecting.

'Are you free after work?'

'Errr... yes. Why?'

A beautiful smile swept across her face. 'You'll see. Will you come with me after Stella drops us off later? Oh, and I will have to pick up Daisy on the way – okay?'

'Is Alex joining us as well?'

Lia's face darkened. 'No. Alex has moved out. For good.'

'Oh... I see.' I don't think the word "berserk" even came close to describing the celebratory state my heart went into.

Turning around we saw a pink Mini coming towards us. 'Morning, both,' Stella moaned as Grace got out of the car to let us in the back.

As Stella signalled the start of the fifteen minutes of no talking, I noticed Lia looking in my direction. Once the no talking ended, I caught Stella staring at me in the driver's mirror. 'Mateo, how's that music dream coming along, made any progress?'

'I still need to email with Pete.'

'That's taking a while...' Stella raised her eyebrows at me. 'Surely, it's a case of emailing, saying hello and suggesting meeting up?'

I blew the air out of my cheeks. 'I need to summon some confidence.'

'You could wait forever for that,' Grace said, turning around in her seat to stare at me. 'If I had waited for the confidence to ice skate again, I would still be pondering it well into my nineties.'

'She's right,' Lia whispered, giving my hand a squeeze.

'But what happens if none of my new songs are a success? What happens if I don't fulfil my dreams?'

Grace let out a sigh. 'Mateo, you will have tried, that's the important bit. Also, you will not have wasted a gift which was given to you when you were created. We're all given gifts, and I think too many people waste them. They don't do anything with them.' She dug out her mobile phone from her handbag.

Handing me her phone, she asked me to press play on the video. Lia leaned over my shoulder as we watched Grace skate out onto an ice rink. She waved at the person holding the camera, and then began to skate. Lia gasped as Grace began to twirl on the ice. Soon, she was gliding around the outer edge of the rink at speed, and then she did a jump into the air. She made it look so effortless. 'Wow, that's impressive,' I said, looking up to see Grace beaming at us.

'Mateo, if I had waited for the confidence to come to me,' Grace said, 'I really would still be sitting by the rink.'

Stella's car phone beeped. 'Excuse me a minute, folks, I have an emergency call from one of my children.'

Grace gasped. 'Oh, my goodness, Stella.' She placed a hand on Stella's arm. 'Keep calm, my new friend.'

I let out a silent groan. *Some things never changed.* Stella pulled into a side street and pressed accept.

'Mam.' Lauren's voice filled the car.

Stella fiddled with her purple glasses. 'Lauren, please remember I have people in the car, so no bad words.' Placing her glasses on the end of her nose she stared at her phone. 'Is this an emergency?'

Lauren giggled. 'Turn on the radio. I sent in a shout to DJ Rick Carter.'

Stella let out a wail of frustration, which made Grace jolt with shock in her seat.

'Lauren, is this an *emergency?*'

'MAM,' Lauren shouted, causing Grace to put her hands over her ears. 'Turn on the radio. I'm going to school. Just do what I say.'

Stella leaned over and turned on the radio.

DJ Rick Carter's voice filled the car.

'You've just been listening to Dollar with their hit, "O L'amour" from 1987. Now, here's the Breaking Commuter News. Scott is feeling hungover on his bus to work, Lou has taken back her ex-boyfriend who dumped her by text the other week and is on the train to work regretting her decision, and Lauren has contacted the show to ask whether I am single and whether I would be interested in dating her mum, Stella. She's even sent me a link to her mum's Instagram.'

Stella screeched, 'Oh God, she's hooked me up with DJ Rick Carter.'

'If Stella is listening then yes, I would be happy to go on a date with her.'

We all cheered and clapped. Grace turned to Stella. 'I take it you like this man?'

Stella squealed. 'He's a hot silver fox, Grace.'

Lia piped up. 'What happened to Wayne?'

Stella sighed. 'We ended after the motorbike date. I was upset, and Lauren said she would get my smile back.'

After I walked Lia to her office, I went into work and did something extraordinary. After watching Linda, opposite me, console an emotional colleague who had been dumped by her boyfriend, I went to the drinks machine and bought Linda a coffee. She stared at me as I placed it in front of her. 'Well... this is a surprise, Mateo. Thank you.'

'Linda, I think what you did there was amazing.'

She smiled and we started our first proper conversation, about the thriller she'd been watching on TV.

Later that day when I climbed into the back of Stella's car, I must have looked different as Stella gave me an odd look. Grace was out with friends, so she didn't need a lift back. Lia was sitting in the front.

'How was your day at work, Mateo?' Stella asked.

I smiled. 'It was alright. Linda, the woman who sits opposite me, and I talked to each other.'

Stella cast me a puzzled look via the rearview mirror. 'Hang on – didn't you and Linda used to talk?'

I shook my head. 'Don't judge me, but for a long time before finding this car share I did nothing but silently curse Linda.'

'What had Linda done to you?'

'She is happy all the time, and I was very grumpy for a long time–'

Stella interrupted me. 'You can say that again.'

Lia giggled as I continued. 'This car share has made me see that Linda is doing her best to get through the working day, and she does spread a bit of joy to others in the office. Like you, Stella, she's helping others survive the working day.'

Stella squealed. 'Exactly that, Mateo. Some might say my car share is crazy, but getting through the working week is tough. A little bit of craziness goes a long way.'

The rest of the journey home dragged due to sluggish rush-hour traffic and Stella's excitement over DJ Rick Carter. After my revelation about Linda, I made the mistake of asking Stella how her day had gone. She proceeded to tell us she'd shown a few of the ladies in her office DJ Rick Carter's photos on Instagram, the ones where he was lifting weights. According to Stella, the ladies in her office were impressed with DJ Rick Carter's physique at fifty-one, and after much deliberation in the canteen, Stella had messaged him. I was relieved to escape when we reached the high street. Lia and I waved goodbye to Stella who was keen to get home and see whether he had replied.

'Are you going to come with me to collect Daisy?' Lia asked.

We walked together down the road to Daisy's nursery. 'I can't believe what Lauren did this morning,' chuckled Lia.

'This is the start of a new Stella parenting era,' I said, making Lia laugh. 'Forget hair eras; we are now into parenting eras.'

After picking up an excited Daisy, Lia took me down to the training field. 'Are you copying me, Lia?' I asked, as she let Daisy out of her buggy once we were on the grass. She grinned. 'Might be.'

We sat next to each other at the far end, and watched Daisy run about.

'How are you, Lia?'

She rested her head against my shoulder. 'Emotionally drained, but I'm okay.'

'You been worried about your dad?'

She shook her head, and burst into floods of tears. Between sobs and gulps of air she told me about what had happened with Alex. I listened in horror. Biting down on my tongue, I battled against the side of myself that wanted to pay a visit to Alex. *That was not what Lia needed. How could he have done that to her?* 'I'm sorry for how he made you feel.'

She drew her knees in and hugged them to her chest. 'Thanks, Mateo... for listening. I know why you didn't want to kiss me all those weeks ago.' She swept back a curtain of red hair. 'I wasn't in the right frame of mind – was I? You saw through me.'

'I would do it all again,' I said, quietly. 'You mean so much to me.'

She rested her head against my shoulder. 'Stella once said, "It doesn't matter where you're going, it's who you have beside you." That's so true. You chose to learn all about me before any romance, and for me that's something special. You helped me return to football, and you've been a rock for me whilst Dad has been unwell. Throughout all this you've been so respectful.' To my surprise, she pressed her forehead against mine. 'I want you beside me, Mateo, but I'm worried you're not ready for a relationship after what happened with...'

I knew she was talking about Natalie. An idea sprang to mind. I placed my finger on her lips before she mentioned my disastrous wedding. 'Will you and Daisy come somewhere with me? Would Daisy mind going in her buggy? It's a few streets away from here.'

She strapped Daisy into her buggy, and gestured for me to lead the way.

Chapter 44

Lia

As we turned onto the street where I had changed Stella's tyre, I glanced at Mateo. The last time we'd been here, he'd looked gaunt and frightened.

He gestured for us to cross the road and stand outside the white church. 'I'm not suggesting we get married,' he joked, 'but I want to show you something.'

Once by the church door, I put the brake on Daisy's buggy. 'This was the church – wasn't it?' He nodded and stepped closer to me.

'A few weeks ago, I struggled to even look at this building.'

I gazed into his deep brown eyes. They were not filled with fear. Instead, they were radiating warmth and passion.

'This was where it all happened last year. But that's the past. I have confronted my demons.'

'Really?'

He nodded. 'Stella made me see sense in the car, and then something happened over the weekend, which put everything in a different light.' Reaching for my hand he smiled. 'Let's not talk about the past. It's gone. I want to stand here and create new memories with you.' Pulling me into his arms, he looked at me. I wanted him to kiss me so badly that my body ached. 'Kiss me, Mateo,' I whispered.

He smiled, but frustratingly began tickling my nose with his nose until I laughed. 'Please kiss me... please... please.'

Pressing his soft lips against mine I felt my body melt into his. It was a beautiful kiss. Filled with so much promise and excitement. It left me wanting more.

Daisy grizzled, which broke us apart. Mateo stepped back to pick up her dolly, which she'd dropped on the floor. She yawned and began to rub her eyes. Mateo offered her the dolly, and she grabbed it with both hands. She grinned at him, and the sight made me smile.

'I better get Daisy home,' I said, as he put his arm around my shoulders. 'Maybe we should get together in the week for a proper date?' I asked him. 'The trouble is I might have to bring Daisy.'

He smiled. 'Why don't you both come over to mine?'

'Really?'

He nodded. 'Wednesday evening after Stella's dropped us off?'

'Okay, it's a date.'

He ran his hand through his hair. 'There is one problem though.' His hand circled my waist. 'I won't be able to wait until Wednesday to kiss you again.'

The next two days went by in a blur. Every morning, before Stella's pink car arrived, Mateo and I kissed each other in the doorway of the betting shop. Once we reached the city, we waited until she'd zoomed off, before holding hands and giggling like lovesick teenagers. In the afternoon we would walk towards Daisy's nursery hand in hand.

Wednesday arrived. Beth was beside herself with excitement for my first proper date with Mateo. Instead of talking through our latest campaign she interrogated me on my approach to a first date. 'Try not to sleep with him tonight, Lia,' she advised. 'I slept with Jez on our first date, and you know how badly that turned out.'

'Mateo and I are not rushing things,' I assured her.

She raised an eyebrow at me. 'I saw you kissing each other goodbye earlier, and he's HOT. Let's just say I would *not* be restrained with him. The Spanish, apparently, make good lovers.'

'He's *half* Spanish, and I will have Daisy with me tonight.'

Beth studied her nails. 'I can't stop thinking of *you know who* in the post room.'

'Has he forgiven you yet?'

She grinned. 'Lia, he keeps sending me work emails with suggestive comments.'

'What about Jez?'

Beth's smile disappeared. 'I unblocked him and he sent me a message. We are finally going our separate ways. He says it's hard to forgive me after I sold his favourite jacket.'

I checked my phone. 'Right, let's crack on, because I want to leave on time.'

The journey home was one of the best so far. Stella played Madonna's early hits, and we sang our hearts out. I took Daisy home, changed her, placed her in the buggy and set off.

Mateo's house was lovely. Ghost his cat came to greet us, and Mateo invited us into an open planned living room and kitchen area. It was airy and bright with white walls and wooden flooring. Presiding over the living area was a giant black piano.

A wonderful aroma of cooked chicken and herbs was circulating. My stomach gurgled in anticipation.

'Have a seat, and I will season the casserole in my slow

cooker. I am praying it's okay,' he said, with a smile. 'Will Daisy have a little bit?'

Daisy was busy crawling all over his sofa, and squealing at the sight of Ghost.

'Yes, she will. It smells delicious.'

We ate around his table. I had a squirming Daisy on my lap who refused to sit still. Mateo just smiled at her, and took her off to have a go on his piano while I finished my dinner in peace. I watched them both as I ate. He was showing her how to tap the keys, and she was hitting them as hard as she could.

After we'd eaten, he took us to see his father's old sports car. I held Daisy on my hip, and marvelled at the gleaming white Triumph. Mateo promised me he'd one day summon the courage to take us out for a ride in it. It wasn't long before Daisy fell asleep on me. I gently lay her in her buggy, and Mateo covered her with a little blanket.

'Hopefully she will stay asleep when I walk home,' I said, crossing my fingers.

'When *we* walk home you mean,' he whispered.

Mateo and I sat beside each other on the sofa. 'Oh, I've got you something,' he said, delving into his shirt pocket. To my shock he brought out my gold bracelet, the one with my initials on it. 'What the hell?' I gasped as light bounced off the tiny letters.

He gestured for me to hold up my wrist. 'This fell out of my best mates' sofa. Burrito used to be called Dave, and Joe adopted him from Claire a few years ago.'

'Joe adopted Burrito from your friend?'

He nodded and fastened the bracelet. 'It must have escaped from Joe's pocket when he sat on the sofa whilst Claire was speaking to him about the adoption.'

We both admired my bracelet. 'This makes sense now. Joe collected it from the jewellers, and on his way home he must have gone to see your friend Claire about Burrito.' Mateo leant over and placed a delicate kiss on my wrist.

'Dad will be over the moon.' The room went blurry. 'I thought the bracelet was lost forever.' He pulled me into a hug, and kissed my forehead. 'Your dad will be made up to see it.'

I extended my arm and gazed at the bracelet. 'This is madness, Mateo.'

'Lia Edwards,' he said, 'you know I won't rush you or anything. We can take it slowly, and I want Daisy to get to know me, but I–'

Leaning over, I silenced him with a kiss. 'Can I be your girl-friend, Mateo?'

He looked surprised. 'You want to be my girlfriend?'

'Yes,' I laughed. 'Is that all right with you?'

He held up his hand as if he wanted me to wait for his answer. He waved at Ghost who was lying stretched out across the top of his piano. 'Is that okay with you, Ghost? Am I allowed to have a girlfriend?' Ghost lifted her head, scowled, and went back to sleep.

We fell back into each other's arms. I whispered, staring into his dark eyes. 'I want you beside me.' He pressed his lips against mine, and kissed me. My phone began to buzz on the coffee table. I sat up and looked at the screen. It was Petra. 'Hello, Petra, everything okay?'

'Lia, sorry to bother you,' Petra said. 'Listen, the Tigresses are in a bit of a crisis, and I need a favour.'

My heart started to thump. 'Sure, what?'

'Celia has torn her hamstring, and Emma has just called me to say she's in hospital with appendicitis. We have the final league game on Saturday, and I was hoping... well... praying you and Hope would play.'

A shot of excitement zoomed up my spine. 'What? Oh God, yes.'

Mateo was looked bewildered. Petra continued. 'I know you're still not ready for a full ninety mins, but I will bring you on at half time. Lia – I saw the hunger in your eyes the other day. That's what I am looking for.'

Once I put the phone down, I squealed. 'Guess who is playing for the first team on Saturday?'

He rose from the sofa, pulled me into a hug and twirled me around. 'Congratulations. Can I come and watch?'

I grinned. 'You don't like football?'

He kissed me. 'I will make an exception, if you kiss me some more.'

'That would be nice,' I said, kissing him again. Holding onto his hands I thought about Stella. 'I've been thinking too. What shall we tell Stella about us? By keeping it a secret, I feel like we're letting her down. She feels like a friend to me. When I started car sharing, I was lost in my grief, which had taken me over. Stella's car sharing made me start loving life again, and if it wasn't for Stella, I never would have got to know you.'

'We will tell her the truth,' he said, without hesitation. 'Even though I have spent the last few months moaning about her driving skills, her car, her rebellious children, her parenting skills and her oversharing, I see Stella as a friend. I have learnt some stuff about myself – and Stella, Ed and Grace have all helped me in some way.'

'She might kick us out of her car share.'

He gazed into my eyes. 'Whatever happens we will be together on the way to work. I promise. We will also stay in touch with Stella. Now, I better get you both home.'

'You're so lovely,' I whispered.

'You better score on Saturday,' he said, with a sexy wink. 'I'm making an exception with you, Lia Edwards. I don't turn up to any old football match.'

Chapter 45

Mateo

It was Thursday morning. Daisy had a runny nose and a cough, so Lia was working from home. Grace's car was fixed so she no longer needed to car share. It was just Stella and me in her pink Mini.

The night before with Lia had been magical. After walking Lia and Daisy home, we'd put Daisy to bed and stood in the hallway for ages hugging, kissing, and whispering about all the things we were excited about; her football game, my dream of getting back into song writing, and us finally getting together. I smiled so hard as I walked back to my house, my face ached when I got in. The second I had taken off my shoes I thought about what Grace had said in the car earlier. *It was time for me to chase my songwriting dream.* I got out my phone, and sent Pete an email.

'Are you going to watch the Tigresses play at the weekend?' Stella asked, after the fifteen minutes of no talking had ended and she'd turned down her Pet Shop Boys CD. 'In her text to me this morning she told me about Saturday.'

I nodded. 'Yes, but my outfit is not going to plan.'

'Outfit?' Stella cast me a puzzled look. 'What do you mean?'

'I wanted to do something special. It's a big match for her. So, I have been trying to get hold of a Tigresses football shirt. They're orange with black stripes.'

Stella's pencilled eyebrows rose up her forehead. 'Oooh, I love this idea.' I nodded and gripped my door handle. Stella's driving skills always worsened when she got excited.

'But I can't get hold of a shirt. The club is out of stock.'

Stella tapped her gold nails on the steering wheel. 'The Tigresses. Let me think of anyone I know who might have a shirt.' She turned on DJ Rick Carter's radio show.

"In Breaking Commuter News, Sam overslept and has missed her train. Milly has a new haircut, and the man she secretly likes on platform 13 has just smiled at her. Rich is feeling hopeful about his interview this morning, and Lou is single again, and happy."

I smiled at the radio, and Stella laughed. 'You've changed, Mateo. When you first started my car share you were so grumpy. I used to watch you rolling your eyes in the back when I turned on the radio.'

'Breaking Commuter News has taught me there are others out there having a bad day.

Stella nodded. 'Agreed, and smiling does help.'

I wondered whether getting a Tigresses shirt was a step too far. Lia might think it was weird seeing me turn up in one. 'I will just wear a normal shirt to the match.'

Stella grinned at me. 'I know someone.'

I gasped. 'What? Really?' I stared at her. 'Do they go watch the Tigresses?' *Maybe it wasn't such a bad idea.*

'No, but they'll be able to get their hands on a shirt.'

I noticed Stella's smile. She began to say, 'Useful K–'

With a groan I shook my head. 'No way,' I snapped. 'I am not asking that woman to get me a football shirt.'

Stella gasped. 'Mateo, you've never bought anything from Useful Kim.'

'Ed did, and look what happened. You also never told us about your motorcycle date, which I am assuming didn't go well because of your outfit.'

She cast me a suspicious look. 'How do you know about what happened with Ed's travel bag?'

'I guessed.'

Stella shook her head. 'It was a faulty bag, Mateo.'

I laughed. 'When did it fall apart on Ed?'

Stella screwed up her face. 'The bottom of the bag came undone at the airport. His things went everywhere.'

I knew it. My suspicions were right. 'Poor Ed.'

She shrugged. 'He was so nice about it, Mateo. He could have shouted at Useful Kim. Anyway, Wayne and I ended because the biker outfit Useful Kim got me was skintight, and even walking was an issue. He got frustrated with how long it was taking for me to walk from my front door to his bike on the street. I tripped over a plant pot and couldn't get myself up off the floor. I saw the angry look he gave me, and it was then I decided that no one looks at me like that. So, I ended it and hobbled back to my front door.'

'I am not getting a shirt from Useful Kim.'

Stella grinned and gripped the wheel. 'I will phone her when you get out of the car.'

I turned to look out of my passenger window. 'Not interested, Stella.'

'Have you texted that guy Pete yet?'

I nodded. 'When I got back from Lia's.'

We were not planning on telling Stella about us until after the weekend, but from the way she peered over her glasses at me, I got the impression she knew our secret. 'Oh, really?' she cooed.

'Stella... Lia and me are together.'

The screech that left Stella's mouth was deafening. 'I am so pleased! What happened to Mr Handsome?'

Anger at Alex's treatment of Lia had been burning away inside of me ever since she'd told me about what had happened between them. Lia will never know how much restraint it took for me to not to track him down and hit him. 'He's gone.'

'Gone?' Stella cast me a puzzled look.

I ran my hand through my hair. 'He hurt Lia, and she told him to get out of her life. When I think about what he did, it makes me so cross.'

Stella shook her head. 'Try to not focus on him, Mateo. You and Lia are together, and that's what matters.'

'We can leave your car share. I know this goes against your rules.'

'Rules are made to be broken,' she said with a grin. 'You two make the perfect couple. As I said before, I like you both, and you've barely complained about my children.'

I smiled at her. 'Thanks, Stella. We are very grateful to you. Personally, you have helped me to fulfil a dream of mine. You also got me out of my head at times with your good taste in music.'

She grinned. 'Make sure I have an invitation to your wedding. I come to life on the dance floor at weddings.'

I must have looked frightened, as she giggled. 'It will be fine. Just book a venue with a big dance floor. I like to have some room when I'm busting my moves.'

When she pulled up outside the drop off point, she smiled at me. 'I'm proud of you both.'

I leaned over and gave her a hug. 'Your car share brought us together. We'll never forget that.'

She sat back and sighed. 'Mateo, in life it doesn't matter where you're going, it's who you have beside you.'

I nodded. 'So true. I hope one day you also have someone sitting beside you.'

With a little grin she tapped her car radio. 'You never know what might happen with a certain local DJ.'

Lia texted me a photo of her dressed in the kit for the first team at lunch. She looked breathtakingly gorgeous with her red hair, her doe eyes, and those shorts that framed her shapely hips so well. I felt a surge of pride. In a moment of madness, I texted Stella about getting hold of a Tigresses football shirt.

> I can't believe I am saying this, but can you ask your friend to get hold of the football shirt?

The response was immediate.

> Already asked her. Useful Kim can get hold of one. It will cost you though, as she's had to work some of her magic.

Before I had time to worry about Useful Kim, Pete messaged me to say Sunday would be a great day for us to meet up. Excitement bubbled inside of me. *A chat with Pete might not come to anything, but it was a start.* I texted Lia a screenshot of his message. She replied with:

> This is the start of our new and amazing future together, Mateo xx.

Chapter 46

Lia

It was a beautiful day for football – an endless blue sky, no rain, and not too warm. Excitement was pulsating through me, which was surprising given how little sleep I'd had. Daisy had been up half the night coughing. When I wasn't trying to get her back to sleep, I was either thinking about football or Mateo. After the game we were going to go back to his house. He'd set up a little camp bed for Daisy, so it would be our first night together.

Hope had video called me before I'd gone to sleep to show me her match preparations of a spray tan, new eye lashes and a facial. She made me laugh, saying she was going to bring some style and glamour to the first team.

After Daisy's final coughing fit at four in the morning, I lay awake for ages thinking about Joe, and how pleased he would be to hear that I'd been asked to sit on the bench for the first team with the possibility of getting to play. A few months ago, the mere thought of football or Joe would have brought tears to my eyes.. I took a deep breath, and smiled into the darkness of my bedroom. 'It's all right, Joe. I'm okay now.' Mateo's face appeared in my mind, and I had closed my eyes.

Daisy was babbling away to her dolly in her buggy. Whilst I'd got us both dressed, I had put on my old Sound of Music album, and she'd gone wild with her dancing. Her cold was better, and she seemed brighter today. Mateo was meeting us there, as he was going to watch Daisy for me. My phone started vibrating. It was Angel phoning me. This was a surprise. 'Everything okay?' I asked.

'Yes, it's great.' She sounded bubbly. 'Lia, is the offer of staying with you for a few days still on if I promise not to cancel?'

My heart broke into a wild gallop. 'Oh God, Angel, you know it is.'

'Lia, I'm leaving Manchester,' she squealed down the phone.

'Really?'

'I've given my landlord notice.'

Pulling the buggy to a halt I wondered whether this was a turning point for us. Angel would move down here, get a job, and we could get to know each other again. She could come to watch me play football. We could visit Dad together. Daisy would love her. 'Oh, Angel, that's great,' I gushed. 'I can keep a look out for places to rent for you.'

'Lia, I won't be needing that. A few months ago, I applied to become an air hostess on long haul flights. I have been accepted.'

'What?' I gasped.

Angel laughed again. 'It's time for me to head for the skies. I'm desperate to travel. I'll stay for a few days max. I then need to prepare for my new life and career.'

My heart sank, and then I heard Stella's voice in my mind. 'Some people never change.' I couldn't control my sister, and I was wasting my time wishing she would be the sister I wanted her to be. It was time for me to move on, and stop torturing myself with Angel's lifestyle choices and her Instagram feed. Angel was living her life the way she wanted.

I got to the pitch feeling calmer than ever about the situation with Angel. For the first time in years, I didn't feel angry with her.

The Tigresses second team had come to watch the game. They all sat behind me on the sub bench. The first half was spent trying to watch the match, listening to my teammates giving their own running commentary on the game, and trying to calm my jangling nerves about playing in a proper match.

We watched the Tigresses take a corner. It sailed beautifully past the goal mouth and was met by the head of Zoe the Tigresses striker, who slotted it into the back of the net. In a second everyone was on their feet, shouting, clapping, and dancing. I looked around at everyone's grinning faces. *This was where I belonged.* I scanned the crowd for Mateo. He was looking for me too, and waved. I was so grateful to him for persuading me to return to football. The sight of him made my heart skip a few beats.

In a matter of minutes, the opposition responded with a goal, which had come from a careless pass from our midfielder. With fifteen minutes to go, Petra made a substitution, and I got my chance. My legs were like jelly, as I ran onto the pitch. All the members of the second team were chanting my name from the bench. Hope grinned and mouthed, 'Let's score some goals.'

It was a hard half to play in. My fitness was still lacking, and the girls who we were playing against were on top of their game. The defender marking me was brutal. She wouldn't give me any space. My legs ached, I was pink faced and wished I'd come on for the last five minutes.

I was starting to think we were not going to win. Hope had missed several chances, Zoe had been stretchered off with an injured knee, and Petra was not looking happy. Then Tash from our team curled a brilliant long pass down the inside right. The ball connected to my foot, and I broke into a charge. *It was time to forget about my aching muscles, and dig deep.* The defender tried to tackle me, but I somehow managed to flip the ball into the air, jump over her leg and keep the ball in play. The cheers from the crowd died away as I glanced at the goalie. Looking down at my boot I silently said, 'This is for me and Mateo,' before side-footing a shot from 12 yards. It flew into the net. It was a goal. I'd scored. With my arms out I ran towards Hope, screaming, 'I scored!' She lifted me up and I looked over at the stand. It wasn't Joe I was searching for; it was Mateo. He had Daisy in his arms, and they were both waving. Tears rushed to my eyes.

We won the match, and once the whistle blew, I raced across to Mateo and Daisy. After kissing Daisy on the cheek, I grinned at Mateo. His coat was unzipped, and I could see he was wearing the tightest Tigresses football shirt I had ever seen. One arm had split open, and there was a rip across the chest. Despite the state of it, the sight of his toned broad chest stirred something inside of me.

'Amazing work, Lia Edwards,' he said, in a sexy voice.

I touched his shirt. 'Mateo – you're wearing Tigresses merch. It's umm... a little small for you, but I like it.'

He rolled his eyes. 'Never ever ask Useful Kim for *anything*.' We both laughed. 'Mateo, you look so sexy,' I said, leaning in for a kiss. 'By the way, I scored that goal for us.'

He pressed his lips against mine. 'I still can't believe I fell in love with you in the back of Stella's pink car.' We kissed until I was mobbed by a cheering crowd of Tigresses teammates.

Epilogue

Six months later:
DJ Rick Carter

'That was Cher. In Breaking Commuter News, Lia and Mateo are leaving Stella's car share as they've moved in together and now have their own car. They want to say a huge thank you to the one and only Stella, and her crazy car share, which brought them together. As Stella always says, in life it doesn't matter where you're going, it's who you have beside you.'

THE END

Also by Lucy Mitchell

Instructions for Falling in Love Again

———

I'll Miss You This Christmas

Acknowledgements

Thank you for taking the time to read my book.

This book idea was inspired by my years of commuting to and from work, the regular family visits we used to make to take our children to visit their much loved great grandmothers, Nana Pat and Gramma Connie in their respective nursing homes, the Lionesses and their amazing footballing achievements, the ten-year old version of me who always wanted to play football but never had the guts, and the parent car sharing trips I used to participate in when my youngest daughter and her friends needed lifts back and forth from college.

A huge thank you to the Bloodhound team, especially Betsy, Shirley and Tara, who have brought my book to life. Shirley – your fabulous editing transformed this story.

Thanks to Mum and Verity for the encouragement, support, and love.

Thanks to Seren and Flick, who give me so much fodder for my novels when it comes to creating teenage characters. Ha ha!

Thanks to Catherine and Sue for being amazing and supportive friends who are always at the end of a WhatsApp message when I have a book question or need a good quote. Also, thanks for joining me in the Nags Head for a scampi and chips when I should be writing.

Thanks to Ali and Rach for sharing your commuter experiences and being the inspiration behind Breaking Commuter News.

Rach – thanks for the cups of tea, the cake, and the giggles when I should be writing.

Thanks to Tracey for taking me shopping when I should be writing.

Thanks to Bettina Hunt who is always at the end of an Instagram DM when I need a giggle about writing romance.

Thanks to Candice for being my favourite American writer friend.

Thanks to Claire Sheldon for your advice and support.

Thanks to Sarah, Lynda, Meg, Grace, and Flick for hours of car sharing fun, which included singing back and forth to Abergavenny, gossiping and laughing about my dodgy driving skills.

Thanks to my fabulous husband Huw – I couldn't do this without you.

Finally, thanks to all the 'Stellas' in my life – the strong, inspiring, and funny women who I know and have known. The women who have shown up in my darkest hours with their banter, their jokes, their words of wisdom and their encouragement.

A note from the publisher

Thank you for reading this book. If you enjoyed it please do consider leaving a review on Amazon to help others find it too.

We hate typos. All of our books have been rigorously edited and proofread, but sometimes mistakes do slip through. If you have spotted a typo, please do let us know and we can get it amended within hours.

info@bloodhoundbooks.com

Milton Keynes UK
Ingram Content Group UK Ltd.
UKHW020357050424
440577UK00004B/313

9 781916 978690